Secrets of the Heart

Book Two of the Wild Hearts Trilogy

Sabrina Wagner

Stay Connected!

**Want to be the first to learn book news, updates and more?
Sign up for my Newsletter.**

https://www.subscribepage.com/sabrinawagnernewsletter

**Want to know about my new releases and upcoming sales?
Stay connected on:**

Facebook~Instagram~Twitter~TikTok
Goodreads~BookBub~Amazon

**I'd love to hear from you.
Visit my website to connect with me.**

www.sabrinawagnerauthor.com

Books by Sabrina Wagner

Hearts Trilogy

Hearts on Fire
Shattered Hearts
Reviving my Heart

Wild Hearts Trilogy

Wild Hearts
Secrets of the Heart
Eternal Hearts

Forever Inked Novels

Tattooed Hearts: Tattooed Duet #1
Tattooed Souls: Tattooed Duet #2
Smoke and Mirrors
Regret and Redemption
Sin and Salvation

Vegas Love Series

What Happens in Vegas (Hot Vegas Nights)
Billionaire Bachelor in Vegas

Table of Contents

Prologue

Secrets of the Heart

Secrets.
Everyone has them.
We keep them locked up tight.
They're like skeletons in a closet.
They hide there and mock us.

The darkest secrets are the ones buried so deep,
That you pretend they don't exist.
You keep them close to your heart.
Never wanting them to escape.

But secrets rarely stay buried.
And when those secrets are finally revealed,
They have power.
The power to heal...
Or the power to destroy.

Chapter 1
Chris

I'd fallen asleep, only to wake after the sun went down. My head throbbed, my knuckles ached, and my mouth tasted like shit. I wished I could say I didn't remember what happened. But that would be a lie.

I remembered every nasty word that came out of my mouth.

Every accusation I threw her way.

The look on her face when she left.

The tears that streamed down her cheeks.

I destroyed the best thing in my life.

Maybe it was a bomb that had been waiting to go off and I just lit the fuse. She needed me too much. Depended on me. I didn't even know who I was anymore without her.

This was for the best. I couldn't spend the rest of my life, worrying about how she was going to react to any girl who showed interest in me. There was more to life than that. There was more out there waiting for me. I could still go to Michigan State, maybe not to play football, and it would take me far away from Tori.

I tried to reason with myself, what I had done was a long time in the coming. I didn't need her. She wasn't the reason my heart beat. She wasn't every breath I took. But as hard as I tried, I couldn't do it.

Regret sat in my chest.

The self-hate tore at my heart.

But what was done… was done.

I climbed out of bed and headed down to the kitchen to get something for my head. It was hard to believe that it had only been six hours since everything fell apart. Since I destroyed her. Since I slammed my hand, fist first, into the bathroom mirror. Since I let her walk out the door.

The house was dark and quiet. The calm after the storm. The only light came from above the sink. I filled a glass with water and grabbed some aspirin from the cupboard.

3

"Got a headache?" The voice in the dark startled me.

I spun around in the dim light to see my mom sitting at the table in her robe. A glass of wine in front of her.

"Just a little," I answered.

"That was quite the show you put on earlier. Tell me, did you plan that out or were you just playing it by ear?"

"How much did you hear?" I questioned without answering her.

"Pretty much all of it." She took a big drink of her wine, draining the glass, then picked up the bottle and refilled it.

I threw my hands up in the air. "What do you want me to say?"

"Oh, I don't know. That you acted like an ass. That you didn't mean it. That you're sorry. Or maybe that you're not. What was that all about?"

"She accused me of cheating on her," I spat out. "Our fighting is what caused the accident. I wasn't paying attention when I should have been. And now, I can't even play football. Do you know how much that sucks? It's all her fault!"

"Is it? Were you cheating on her?"

"No!" I didn't need this from my mom too. I turned to go back to my room, but she stopped me.

"So, that's it?"

"Yeah! That's it!" Even as I said it, my gut turned. I wondered if I had made the right decision.

I continued towards the stairs. "Don't you dare walk away from me, Christopher! You did this, now sit and face it like a man." I don't know that I'd ever heard my mom talk to me like that before. Her usually sweet disposition was gone. My dad was always the hard ass, not my mom.

I turned back and plopped into the chair. The last thing I wanted to talk about with my mom was the reason Tori thought I was cheating. The reason I ended things today. My own guilt weighed heavily on me, but Tori should have known better. She should have known I wouldn't do that to her. Her insecurities were killing me. "Why are you drinking?" I asked her, as I sat down, trying to take the attention off myself. "You never drink."

"I guess it's because a girl, who's like my daughter, left in tears today. Because my son," she tipped her glass at me, "decided it would be a good idea to get drunk and destroy her. I'm gonna ask you again. Did you cheat on her?"

"No!"

"Then why the fuck was Susie standing on my doorstep today?" My eyes widened, and I pulled back in shock. I had never heard my mom use that word before. "Because I'm trying to figure out why the girl who took your virginity, and half of the football team's, was at my house."

I leaned forward on my elbows and blew out a breath. "How do you know about that?"

My mom laughed. Yes, actually laughed at me. "Oh please, Chris. Just because I pretend to not know what's going on, doesn't mean I don't. People talk. I know all about Susie Deluca. Why was she here?"

"She likes me, okay? She's been trying to get back with me for a long time. I told her no. I can't control that she showed up here." Lord knew Susie had a mind of her own and a determination to match. Her timing today had been impeccable.

"And why would Tori think you were cheating on her?"

I sighed and dropped my head to the table. "Why are you asking me about this?"

My mom took another long drink of her wine and set it back on the table. "Because I'm your mother and I want to know. I think after what happened here today, I have a right to know."

I didn't want to get into this with my mom, but there was no way she was going to let it go. "Fine! On my birthday, Tori saw Susie kissing me at my locker. I didn't kiss her back though." That was my story, and I was sticking to it.

But truth be told, I should have known better. Tori would have never blinded my eyes. She would have spun me around and pushed me back into my locker. That was the fire Tori and I had. There was no pretending with us.

I should have told Tori right when it happened. I shouldn't have hidden it from her. I lost her trust when I didn't tell her the truth. If I had done that, Tori wouldn't have been upset with me. We wouldn't have ever fought in the truck. I would have seen that damn deer. We would have never gotten in the accident.

It all came back to that fucking kiss.

My mom pursed her lips and nodded her head. "Sooo, let me get this right. If you saw some guy, who Tori had a past relationship with, kissing her…and said guy randomly showed up at her house… you wouldn't think that she was cheating?" I stared at her like that goddamn deer stared at my headlights the other night. She tapped her fingers on the table in an annoying rhythm. "Well? What would you do? His lips pressed tight to hers?" I kept quiet. The picture she was creating in my mind was pissing me off. All I could see were Matt's arms wrapped around Tori and his lips on hers. "Come on, Chris. Some guy's hanging all over your girlfriend, kissing her." The rage inside me built. "What would you do? What would you think?" She kept prodding.

I pushed away from the table and stood up, knocking the chair to the floor. I pulled at my hair. "I'd knock the shit out of him! And yeah, I'd think she was cheating!" I yelled. My chest heaved, and a fire burned inside me.

My mom smirked at me, as if she had won. Had proved her point. She waved her hand at me. "And there you have it."

"What do you want me to do? Be mean to Susie?" I questioned. I wasn't going to let her win so easily.

My mom stood from the table, shaking her head, and started walking to her bedroom, taking her wine with her. I could tell that she was disgusted with me, with my behavior, with the whole situation. Then she stopped and turned to me. "Well, you certainly didn't have a problem being mean to Tori." She held up her finger. "Oh, and by the way, I took care of your little problem with Susie. She won't be coming here anymore. Maybe you should take a lesson."

It hit me like a ton of bricks. She was right. I couldn't be mean to Susie, but I had no problem destroying the girl I loved. That logic made no sense. It was totally fucked up.

I went back to my room and pulled out the album Tori made me for my birthday. I looked at each page. Really looked at them. Read every caption. I remembered every moment she'd captured. The pictures of us together, stared back at me. Our smiles lit up every page. There was no denying what we meant to each other.

Maybe she needed me too much, but I needed her just as much. I was nothing without her. My heart ached.

What had I done?

6

I picked up my phone and called her. It went right to voicemail. I texted her.

Chris: *I'm so sorry. Please forgive me.*

She didn't text back. After the way I'd treated her, I really didn't expect her to.

Ty picked me up for school the next morning. I gave him the short version of what happened.

"Why'd you do it?" he asked.

"I don't know. I was pissed and drunk."

"What are you so pissed about? I know it sucks that your truck is fucked, but insurance will cover most of it."

I blew out a breath. "I got my letter from State. They offered me a full scholarship to play football."

Ty got a huge smile on his face. "That's so cool. We're gonna play college ball together. Why didn't you tell me you applied?"

"I didn't want you to think I was a loser if I didn't get it," I admitted. "And it would have been cool, except the doc said college sports are out for me. I can't play. Our accident assured that." I huffed out my frustration and pulled at my hair. "It fucking sucks!"

Ty stared at me and shook his head. "Number one... I wouldn't think you were a loser. You're awesome at what you do and fucking fast as hell. The championship game, that was all you. You're the only reason we won. Number two... I'm sorry about your knee and you're right it does fucking suck. But how long have you and Tori been together?"

"A year and a half," I answered.

"And that's worth throwing away because of a stupid scholarship to play a game? I thought you guys were tighter than that."

"We are. We were. Fuck! I don't even know anymore. I was awful to her. She'll never take me back after the things I said."

Ty tapped me on the shoulder. "You've been walking a fine line with Susie. I've seen it. Tori has seen it too. And up until now, she's been patient because she loves you. And I think you love her just as much. You need to set things straight with Susie and admit to Tori that you were an asshole. That's nothing new. She might surprise you."

"Gee, thanks," I grumbled. "I'm gonna try. But if I know Tori, she's not going to make it easy on me."

"Yeah. You're right about that. I don't envy you."

I limped through the hall, hoping to catch Tori by her locker, but she wasn't there. She wasn't in any of our classes either.

But I did see Susie. She tried to avoid me, keeping her eyes pinned to the floor in the hallway, but I stepped in front of her. "We need to talk," I demanded.

"About what?" she asked meekly.

"You know what. This thing between you and me. It's not happening. Ever! I'm with Tori. End of story."

She narrowed her eyes and pursed her lips, "Really? Sure didn't seem that way yesterday. I heard you through the door." She acted as if she knew a secret and had caught me in a lie.

There was no way I would let her think she won. I crossed my arms over my chest, "We had a fight. Couples fight. It doesn't mean we're over," I defended even if I wasn't sure it was the truth.

Susie crossed her arms in a challenge. "Then, where is she? Where is the queen bitch?"

That was it! I was done with this shit. My temper flared, and I tried to reel it in. I had never hit a girl, but she was damn tempting. I stepped towards her and she backed up. I kept at her until she was up against the lockers and a sense of fear crossed her face. I refused to back down. "Don't fucking call her that! You're nothing but a jealous little bitch who's tried to sabotage our relationship since the beginning. I can't believe I ever wanted anything to do with you. You're nothing compared to Tori. And you never will be." I clenched my teeth. "Hear my message and hear it clearly. Stay the fuck away from me and stay away from Tori. This is the last time I'm telling you!"

A tear ran down the side of Susie's face and I should have felt bad, but I didn't. She reached out to grab my arm. "But Chris…"

I quickly pulled my arm back. "But nothing," I interrupted her. "The next time it'll be Tori telling you. And trust me, she's been looking forward to it for a long, long time. She won't be nearly as nice as me!"

I picked up my backpack from the floor and headed down the hallway. As I turned the corner I came face to face with Kyla. This, I didn't need.

I waited for her to lay into me, but she didn't. Instead, she clapped her hands together dramatically. "It's about fucking time."

I looked down at my feet. "It was overdue."

"Yeah, it was, but better late than never. I hope you have some more surprises up your sleeve, because you really fucked it up this time."

"I know. But I'm going to get her back. This can't be the end of us."

Kyla pursed her lips to the side and pointed at me, "I shouldn't be on your side, but I am. Make it right, Chris." Then she turned on her heel and walked away.

Well, that was unexpected. Maybe there was hope.

The next day was the same. Tori was AWOL. I'd texted. I'd called. I'd left her a thousand messages. I even sent her flowers. I hadn't sent her flowers in forever and it was a reminder that I should have.

Everything went unanswered.

I missed her. God, how I missed her.

I couldn't remember a time when we'd gone this long without talking. Pain and regret filled my chest. I deserved all of it. I'd blamed her for everything wrong in my life.

She didn't deserve any of it. She was the only thing right in my life.

Chapter 2
Tori

It'd been two days. Two days of torture. Two days of trying to get my heart to agree with my brain. Two days of misery.

Yeah, he'd texted. He'd called. He'd sent me flowers. A beautiful bouquet of purple roses.

I'd ignored all of it!

How could he think it was that simple? A text? A phone call? Flowers? None of that was going to fix my broken heart. I couldn't get his words out of my head.

I just followed you around like a goddamn puppy. It's pathetic really.

I'm not sure you're fucking worth it!

Don't let the door hit you in your fat ass!

He'd made it blatantly clear how he felt about me; I was the cause of everything wrong in his life. That I wasn't worth it.

Fuck him!

Fuck his texts! Fuck his phone calls! Fuck the flowers!

Walls. That was what I needed. I needed time and distance to erect them around my heart. I wouldn't let him destroy me again. Once was enough!

Fool me once, shame on you. Fool me twice... That wasn't going to happen.

But there was a bigger problem at play. I still loved him.

No matter how much I tried to tell myself I didn't, it was all a lie. I had planned a future with him. I was totally invested in Chris being my husband someday. It was so silly. Who finds their husband at sixteen? It was childish and immature.

I needed to disconnect. Taking this time away from school was the best decision I could have made. By the time Christmas break was over, I was sure I could erase him from my mind. From my heart.

10

He was just another guy. I'd see him at school, but it wasn't like we were connected at the hip. We'd been friends before with nothing else. Surely, we could go back to seeing each other every day. We just wouldn't be friends anymore. Couples broke up. It was totally normal for high school kids.

But… we weren't normal. What we had together was something so much more. Or so I had thought.

That was the kind of thinking I needed to avoid. We weren't something more. We were nothing. We were over. Plain and simple.

I wrapped my robe around myself and crawled back between the sheets of my bed. It had become my sanctuary. The place where nothing could hurt me. I was safe here between the soft cotton sheets. He couldn't hurt me here. I couldn't hear his empty promises. I couldn't see his adorable smile. I couldn't feel his lips on mine. I couldn't be sucked back in.

But when I closed my eyes, it wouldn't go away. I heard his promises. I saw his smile. I felt his touch.

Fuck you, world! Fuck his promises! Fuck his smile! Fuck you, Chris!

Chapter 3
Chris

I was done playing around. Obviously, the texts, phone calls, and flowers weren't working. It was on to Plan B.

Saturday, I borrowed my mom's car and drove to Tori's house. I wanted to see her. That wasn't true. I *needed* to see her.

It was her eighteenth birthday. I grabbed her present I'd wrapped days before and headed toward the door. I was so nervous. What if she refused to see me? What if it really was over?

I rang the bell and waited. And waited. And waited. The seconds felt like hours as I stood on the doorstep shuffling side to side.

Finally, the knob began to rattle, and the door creaked open. Mike stood there staring at me. "Chris," he said in a cold greeting.

"Hi, Mike. I need to see Tori." I held up her gift as a peace offering.

Mike disappeared for a moment, then came back with his coat on. He stepped outside onto the porch and motioned for me to sit in one of the chairs. "That's not going to happen. Not today. She's hardly been out of bed in three days."

"Is she sick?" I asked stupidly.

"She's heartbroken, Chris. I don't know exactly what happened between you two, but she's barely functioning."

Guilt. It ripped through me and tore at my heart. "I said some really mean things to her. I don't know why I did it, but I was drinking. Not thinking clearly." I said it as if it was an acceptable excuse. It wasn't. "I was an asshole," I conceded.

"Well...I guess that, on top of the rest of her week, did her in. A girl can only take so much."

"What do you mean?" We had a fight. Couples fought, right? Only, it wasn't really a fight. I had attacked her for no reason. Annihilated her. I was ashamed of what I did, and I was glad Mike didn't know the details.

12

"First the pregnancy scare, the accident, her doctor's appointment, and then the fight. It was all too much."

His words rattled around in my head. I sat there and let them process. "She thought she was pregnant?"

"She didn't tell you?" he said with surprise.

"No. When?" Tori and I had talked about what would happen if she got pregnant. We were supposed to handle it together. Why would she hide a pregnancy scare from me?

Mike sighed and ran a hand over his face. "I don't even know if I'm supposed to be telling you all this. It was on your birthday. She realized she was ten days late. She didn't want to call you because... well, it was your birthday. I guess I figured she would have told you by now."

No wonder she didn't tell me. That was the day she saw Susie kiss me. She didn't trust me. And now I felt even worse, if that was possible. I let her go through that alone. I was supposed to be there for her. "But she's not pregnant?" I questioned.

Mike shook his head. "No. The test was negative, so her mom took her to the doctor on Wednesday. Turns out she has Polycystic Ovary Syndrome."

All this time I'd been drowning in my own self-pity over football, a fucking game, when Tori had real problems. Problems she hadn't told me about because I never gave her the chance. And then I hurt her. I was such a fucking shit. I should have been there for her. "What is poly... poly... poly-whatever-you-said syndrome?"

"Polycystic Ovary Syndrome. It means she has cysts on her ovaries. She'll need to have the cysts removed surgically. It was a lot for her to take in."

Tears filled my eyes, and I pounded a fist on my knee. I hadn't even given her a chance to tell me before I had laid into her on Wednesday. "I should have been there for her! I'm such a fucking selfish bastard! Instead, I destroyed her. I made everything worse. I love her, and I destroyed her!" The tears fell down my face like I was a child and not an eighteen-year-old guy. "Please," I begged Mike. "Please let me see her."

Mike looked at me with pity. "You know I like you, Chris. Always have. But she's not ready. She's my daughter. It's my job to protect her, and right now I think it's best if you don't see her. I'm not saying never, but not

13

now. I don't know what you said to her, but she's been locked in her room ever since."

I nodded my head. I didn't like what he said, but I understood. "When is she having her surgery?" I hoped she was talking to me by then, because I needed to be with her for that.

"The day after Christmas. They're going to keep her overnight."

"Shit. That's the same day I'm having my ACL surgery."

Mike laughed. "Aren't you two a pair? Maybe you could share a room," he joked.

"If I wrote her a note, would you give it to her for me? Please?"

Mike nodded. "That, I can do."

I hobbled to my mom's car and dug around in the glovebox, finally finding a piece of paper and a pen. I quickly scribbled her a note.

Tori~

I love you! I'm so sorry I hurt you. Please forgive me.

Please talk to me. I can't live without my heart.

I'll always love you! ~Chris

I folded it up and limped back to the porch. Mike took the note from me. "Thanks. Tell her I'm not giving up. I don't care how long she makes me wait. I'm not going anywhere. I'll wait forever if I have to." I handed Mike Tori's birthday gift and stepped off the porch.

I heard the door open behind me.

"What are you doing here?" Tori's voice was pissed. "I don't want to see you. Haven't you gotten the message yet?"

I spun around to see her in the doorway. Her hair was piled on top of her head, sticking out in all directions. Her eyes were red and puffy, and she was wrapped in her favorite bathrobe. She was a mess, but she had never looked more beautiful to me.

Mike pushed past her and thrust the gift and note into her hands. Tori looked down at them in confusion. "It's your birthday," I stated.

"And? Why do you even fucking care?" She threw the gift back at me and I caught it against my chest. "I don't want a goddamn thing from you!" She ripped up the note without reading it, dropping the pieces on the porch, and turned to go back in the house.

"I need you, Tori!" She froze, so I kept going. "I don't know how to be without you," I confessed.

14

She stepped out onto the porch in her fluffy, gray elephant slippers, shutting the door behind her. She crossed her arms and her eyes narrowed in anger. "Well, I guess you better fucking learn how to live without my *fat ass*. It's kind of *pathetic*, don't you think? Always following me around like a *goddamn puppy?*" She threw my words back at me like venom. And they stung. Like a thousand bees invading my heart.

I dropped my head in shame and shoved my hands in my pockets. "I'm sorry. I'm an asshole."

"Yeah, you are," she confirmed.

I took a tentative step forward.

Then another.

And another.

Every step forward, bridged the gap between us. She put her arm out. "Stop! I can't do this! You don't deserve my forgiveness."

I kept moving forward. "You're right. I don't."

"Then what are you doing?" She took a step back.

"I don't care about any of it. My truck. Football. The scholarship." I took the final step that closed the space between us and ran my fingers down the side of her face. "Do you know why?" Her eyes locked on mine as she shook her head. "Because none of it means anything without you."

A single tear ran down her cheek. I wiped it away with my thumb. "No more of these," I said softly. "I'm done making you cry."

I wrapped my arms around her. "I shouldn't take you back," she said.

I tucked her head to my chest. "You're right. You shouldn't."

"I don't need you," she lied.

"Maybe not, but I need you." I lifted her chin and softly kissed her lips. Then I pulled out my phone and clicked on the song I saved there. It worked once before, and I was hoping it would work again. Her eyes widened in recognition when she heard the song I played for her the first time I fucked up. I held her in my arms and swayed with her to Buckcherry's "**Sorry**". When it got to the chorus, I started singing to her. I'd do anything to get her back. *"I'm sorry I'm bad, I'm sorry you're blue. I'm sorry 'bout all the things I said to you. And I know, I can't take it back."*

Tori giggled. "Oh, my god! You're singing to me? How fucking desperate are you?"

I put a finger to her lips and continued to butcher the song. "Shhh! Very desperate. *I love how you kiss. I love all your sounds. And baby, the way you make my world go 'round."*

She put her hands over my mouth. "Stop. You're a total cheeseball, you know that?"

I pulled her hands away. "Yeah, but I'm your cheeseball."

She pursed her lips. "I haven't decided if I'm going to claim you yet."

I dropped to one knee and held her hands. "Tori, I don't deserve you, but I can't live without you. I'm so sorry I hurt you and if you give me the chance, I promise to make it up to you. I'm so in love with you. Please tell me you still love me too."

She released my hands and cupped my face. "How could I not love you?" Tori brushed her lips against mine in a featherlike kiss. "You're kind of cute when you pout, you know that?"

I stood, loosely wrapping my arms around her waist and did an exaggerated pout. She pulled on my bottom lip. "That's too much," she laughed. The sound was like music to my ears.

I buried my head in her neck. "I love you, Tor. I can't promise you that we'll never fight, but I want every fight to end in kisses," I paused for dramatic effect, "and phenomenal make-up sex."

She smiled up at me. "Me too."

"Can we go inside now?" I asked. "Because I'm pretty sure my balls are going to freeze and fall off, and then I'll be no good to you."

Tori laughed again and grabbed my hand, pulling me behind her. "As long as your dick doesn't fall off, I'll be fine." We stepped into the foyer. I took off my coat and hung it on the hook behind the door. "Let me go clean up a little bit," she said.

"You look beautiful, just as you are."

"Okay, smooth talker. I don't believe you for a second. I'll just be a minute." She bounced up the stairs and disappeared.

I knew I didn't just have to win Tori over, but her mom and Mike as well. They needed to understand that my love for Tori was real. This wasn't just some game we were playing. I hesitantly walked into the kitchen to face the fire.

"Chris," Mrs. Russo acknowledged me.

"Hi," I said. "Tori said I could come in." I struggled to find the words that would make her mom forgive me. I took a deep breath and confessed my sins. "I'm sorry I made Tori so sad. I'm not proud of what I did, but I'm sorry. So sorry I hurt her. I just want you to know that it'll never happen again. Ever."

Mrs. Russo's face softened. "She's been a wreck. I love my daughter fiercely and I don't like to see her hurt. Where is she?"

I pointed toward the hall. "She went upstairs to clean up."

Mrs. Russo rested her head on her hand. "Thank God. I'm so sick of seeing that stupid robe and those elephant slippers."

"It's kind of cute," I said, shrugging my shoulders.

She shook her head. "Not after three days, it isn't." Then, she pointed her finger at me. "I'm warning you right now. Don't fuck this up!"

I chuckled. "I don't intend to. She means everything to me."

"I know. That's why I'm giving you a get-out-of-jail-free pass. After this, you're on your own."

I held my hands up in surrender. "Point taken." I went over and placed a kiss on her cheek. "Thanks for giving me a second chance."

"Back off, Capizzio," Mike joked. "That one's mine!"

I laughed. "No offense, because she's totally hot for her age, but I'm not into the cougar thing." I winked at Mrs. Russo. "If you were twenty years younger, I'd be all over you." I gave her my killer smile.

"Out!" Mike roared. "Family room! And stay away from my woman." Everyone was laughing now, and it felt good. It felt like home.

17

Chapter 4
Tori

I looked at myself in the mirror. *Damn him!*

I'd been doing so good until he showed up today. I'd been rebuilding that wall around my heart. It was only half constructed, and then he had to reach in and wiggle the bricks. Start shaking the foundation.

But half a wall was better than no wall at all.

Chris hurt me. I wasn't over it. I still felt the pain his words caused.

But I also felt the love in the words he just said to me. I ran my hands through my hair and let out a frustrated groan. If I didn't take this chance with him, I would always wonder what could have been.

I promised myself to enter this cautiously. I wasn't going to tell him about my pregnancy scare or the cysts. Not yet. It was too personal. But then again, maybe I should. Maybe he wouldn't even want me after he knew the details of my diagnosis. It would be good to know upfront how he felt about all of it. Why waste my time if this was a deal breaker?

Everything I decided over that last few days was shaken. I had to set him straight though. I wouldn't be treated this way. He couldn't be this careless with my heart. I wouldn't go through this again.

It was why I was leaving that wall half up.

I went back downstairs—face washed, hair combed, clothes changed. I sat in the spot next to Chris on the couch, tucking my leg underneath me. "We need to talk," I said.

"You're right, we do," he answered. Chris held my hands in his. "You go first."

"Number one, I'm sorry about your truck and I'm sorry I accused you of cheating," I started.

"Stop. I should have put a stop to the Susie situation a long time ago. I should have shut her down. If the situation were reversed, I'd never

18

have been as patient as you have been. My mom… put things in perspective for me. So, I'm the one who's sorry."

"Your mom is my hero." I giggled. "You should have seen her deal with Susie. It was great."

Chris lifted an eyebrow. "I'm not sure I want to know." He rubbed his thumbs along the tops of my knuckles. "I don't know why I went off on you like I did. You didn't deserve it. It just felt like everything was falling apart and you were an easy target."

"You hurt me. And I'm not going to lie, I'm not over it. I don't think I'll ever forget what you did to me or the things you said."

"I know you won't, but I'm hoping you know how sorry I am, and we can move past it. It won't happen again," he assured me.

It felt like an empty promise. I never thought it would have happened the first time, but it did. "I won't be your punching bag, Chris. I mean it. If you're upset with me, then tell me before it gets out of hand. If you're pissed off, go to the gym or something, because I won't go through that again."

"You won't ever have to."

"You better be damn sure. I know it was a rough week for you, but this wasn't an easy week for me either," I admitted and left it at that.

He pulled me between his legs, so my back was against his chest, and rested his hand on my stomach. "Why didn't you tell me you thought you were pregnant?" he asked, rubbing along my belly. "I've always told you I'd be there for you. Those weren't just words."

My head snapped up and I swallowed down the lump in my throat. "You know?" How in the hell did he know? I wasn't ready to tell him yet.

Chris rested his head on my shoulder. "Mike kind of let it slip."

Damn it! "It doesn't matter anymore," I said.

"It matters. Why didn't you call me? I would have been here," he asked softly.

"With what I'd seen at school, I couldn't. I couldn't put that on you."

Chris let out a sigh. "Stupid Susie and that stupid kiss. I've handled that situation. I should have done it a long time ago. I told her if she didn't heed my warning, that I'd let you at her next time. She doesn't want that. She shouldn't be a problem anymore." He ran his hand through my hair again, letting it fall through his fingers. "Baby, I love you. I never want you to feel like you can't tell me something. I'll always be here for you."

"It's over. It was a false alarm," I said without elaborating. I'd already told him more than I initially planned.

"And your doctor appointment?" he prodded.

I pulled back in surprise. "Mike?"

Chris nodded. "He mentioned it."

I huffed out a breath. "My mom took me to the doctor on Wednesday and they did an ultrasound. I have cysts on my ovaries, and I need surgery to remove them. Apparently, my hormones are out of whack. I have Polycystic Ovary Syndrome." It was the truth, just not the whole truth. I hadn't come to terms with everything yet, and I wasn't ready to share the rest.

"What happens after the surgery?" Chris pushed my hair over my shoulder.

"Nothing is for sure," I admitted. "They'll put me on birth control for one, to regulate my hormones, and probably some other meds. Chris," I paused and took a deep breath, "it could make it hard for me to get pregnant. I might not be able to have kids. Ever. You need to think about that. I don't want you to regret being with me. It would be easier if you just walked away now."

I laid out the irrefutable facts and gave him an out.

Chapter 5
Chris

I turned Tori so she could look at me. I needed her to know that my words were the truth. "I don't care. I want you. I always have. I just need you to be healthy. Need you to be with me. Forever and always. We'll deal with the rest later. Being with you is something I could never regret and I'm not walking away." I placed her hand on my chest. "You're my heart."

"Are you sure? Don't you want to think about it?" she asked.

"I'm sure. I don't need to think about it." I picked up her birthday gift and placed it in her hands. "Happy Birthday, Tori," I whispered.

She looked at the gift and then her honey-colored eyes locked with mine. Slowly, her fingers undid the wrapping, revealing the black box underneath. She opened the box and gasped. In it sat a gold necklace with the heart-shaped pendant, encrusted with ruby stones. "Chris, it's gorgeous. Thank you!" She wrapped her arms around my neck and hugged me tight.

"It's my heart, Tor. You own it," I said into her hair. "You own my balls too, but I thought they might look weird hanging around your neck," I joked.

She laughed. "Yeah, this is way better. Help me put it on?" She took the necklace out of the box and held it out to me. She turned, lifted her dark hair and I fastened it around her neck. Her hand ran over the heart. "I love it." Then she got serious. "Tell me about your knee. I know it was messed up before the accident and you let it go." She pierced me with her eyes. "Obviously, it's worse now."

I did. I told her about everything. I told her how I'd been worried about it during the season. I told her why I didn't tell her about my application to Michigan State. Told her I didn't want her to think I was a loser if I didn't make it. Told her I felt like I was competing with Tyler. I told her all my insecurities.

"Chris, I'm sorry I didn't think about what you wanted. I was so wrapped up in the idea of us going to school together that I never considered that you might want more. I think if you want to go to State, you should go.

Maybe after your recovery, you'll be able to play. Even if you can't play football, you should go. I'm not going to be the reason for you not going."

"No," I said definitively. "If I've learned anything this week, it's that I can't be without you. I won't be without you. These last few days have been hell. It's not like I was ever going to go pro. You're my future, and I won't risk it just to go to State. Instead, I want to take you to dinner and be wrapped in your arms tonight. Fuck State."

"Are you sure?"

"I'm sure. I already made reservations."

Tori rolled her eyes. "I'm not talking about dinner. I'm talking about college."

"I know what you're talking about, Tor. All you need to decide is if you want to go to a hotel tonight or hang at home."

Tori buried her head in my neck and whispered, "I wanna do hotel. You promised me phenomenal make-up sex. Plus, we're both having surgery in six days. It could be a while 'til we're recovered."

I showered, shaved, and put on a nice shirt. I stuck my head into Jim's room. He was home for break and crashed out on his bed. "Hey, that thing we talked about. It's still on."

He popped up to a sitting position and rubbed at his eyes. "She took you back, huh?"

"Yeah. You didn't cancel the reservation, did you?" I asked tentatively.

"Nah. But I should have. Sounds like you were a total dick, bro."

"I was," I admitted. "But I practically lost my man card begging for her to take me back."

"She took you back way too fast, in my opinion. She shoulda made you work harder for it."

I pulled on my shirt collar. "What can I say? I'm irresistible. She couldn't say no to all this."

He laughed. "Apparently, humble too. Want some advice?"

Jim had been with so many girls, it was sickening. I couldn't wait to hear his words of wisdom. "From Mr. One-Night Stand? Sure, since you're so great at relationships."

Jim pulled back looking offended. "Hey, I've had relationships with all those girls. Up close and personal relationships. And some of them were two nights, not one."

"Oh, pardon me." I rolled my eyes at him. "What's your advice?"

He got real serious and pointed at me. "Don't be a fucking dick."

I held my hands up. "I'm not! What's your advice? I seriously want to know."

He laughed at me. "That IS my advice, you idiot! Don't be a fucking dick. Tori is one of a kind. You're lucky she even wants to look at your sorry ass."

Now I was laughing, too. "You're right about that."

Jim reached over to his nightstand and grabbed his wallet. He pulled out his credit card and threw it at me. "Reservation is under my name. You're a big boy now, you can check yourself in. Just don't drink anything from the mini bar. That shit's expensive and I'm not paying for it."

"Thanks, man. What if they question me?" I asked.

Jim pulled out his driver's license and threw that at me too. "Take this. I'm staying in tonight anyway. We look so much alike, no one will question it."

"Cool!" I left his room and made it about two steps. Then I popped my head back in his room. "Can I borrow your car too?" I gave him a big, exaggerated smile.

He threw the keys at my head. "You're a fucking pain in the ass, you know that?"

I caught the keys in one hand. "Thanks, bro. Love ya!"

I took Tori to P.F. Chang's for dinner and then we were off to the hotel. I had Tori wait in the car while I checked us in. The guy at the desk gave me a weird look, but once I handed him the credit card, he passed over the key without any questions. I went out to the car and got Tori, then we headed to the room.

I closed the door behind us and wrapped my arms around her waist. "I have to be honest, Tor. I can't put much weight on my knee."

She threw her arms around my neck and stared into my eyes. "Then we'll have to be creative."

"Yeah?"

"Yeah. I've got some ideas," she said as she started to unbutton my shirt.

I took her hands in mine and backed her towards the bed. I grabbed the comforter and threw it to the floor. I would never make that mistake again. I internally cringed at the thought of what was on that comforter.

Tori finished unbuttoning my shirt and pushed it down my shoulders. Then she got to work on my pants. "Slow down, baby. We've got time. I don't want to rush anything with you tonight." I tugged at the bottom hem of her shirt and slowly lifted it over her head. Her tits spilled out the top of her bra and I ran my fingers over the swell of her breasts. "I want to savor you tonight. No rushing. No fucking. I want to make love to you. Let me take care of you."

I pressed my mouth to hers and ran my tongue along her bottom lip, nipping it gently with my teeth. Tori let out a little moan and my dick hardened. Her tongue eased into my mouth, and we became consumed by the kiss. Her hands pulled at my hair as I gripped her ass tightly and pulled her into me. "I've missed you, Tor. I never want to have that empty feeling again. If we're apart, it won't be because we're fighting. I couldn't take it."

"Me neither. I was barely hanging on," she admitted. Tori undid her jeans, shimmied them down her hips and kicked them to the side. She stood before me in her silky black boy shorts and matching bra.

I ran my hands over her breasts and down to her tiny waist, then over her voluptuous hips. "Tori, you're beautiful. All curvy, like my favorite fantasy. I don't think I could ever tire of looking at you."

She grabbed me by the waist of my pants and took two steps back, 'til her knees touched the bed. She sat on the edge of the bed and worked the zipper of my pants, then slowly pushed them down my legs, leaving me in my boxer briefs standing before her. I was so hard for her and the wet spot on my briefs showed her how much I wanted to be inside her. But that would have to wait. I needed to worship her first. I wanted to smell her. Taste her. Feel her from the inside out.

I flicked the clasp on the front of her bra and pushed the cups to the side, sliding it off her shoulders. I palmed her round, full tits and ran my thumbs over her diamond hard nipples. "I need your mouth on me, Chris." She covered my hands with hers, so that she was rubbing her own breasts. "Here." Then she spread her legs wide and dragged my hands down between them. "And here. I want to feel you everywhere." She pressed my hand into her heat, and I could feel how wet she was through her panties.

Tori put one foot up on the bed and scooted herself back. She beckoned me with her finger, and I crawled up on top of her. She palmed her tits and offered them to me. And like the selfish bastard I was, I took. My mouth clamped down on one nipple, while I massaged the other. I sucked and nipped and licked. And when I was finished with one, I started on the other.

Tori threw her head back and moaned. "Chris… that feels so good. I love when you suck my tits." Her dirty mouth turned me on. I feasted on her and slid my hand down the front of her panties. She bent her knees and let her legs fall open. I slid my fingers into her pussy and stroked her.

"Baby, you're so wet. You're fucking drenched." Her wetness covered my fingers, and I moved them up to rub agonizingly slow circles on her clit. Tori turned on her side and I moved with her, taking the pressure off my knee. Her hand slid into my boxer briefs and wrapped around my cock. She moved her hand down my shaft and cupped my balls, then ran her nails over the delicate skin behind them. I closed my eyes and enjoyed the sensation of her nails on my balls as she gently rubbed them in her hand. "Fuck, baby. That feels amazing."

I rolled on my back, taking Tori with me. She laid on top of me, with her hands on my shoulders. "I love you, Chris." Her voice was soft and raspy. I took her hands and laced them with mine, raising them above our heads and pulling us face to face. Our lips met and moved with all the passion in our hearts. Tongues tangled, and the kiss deepened. "Tell me what you want, Chris. Talk dirty to me."

She loved when I talked dirty to her, and I wouldn't disappoint. "Baby, I want all of you. I want to lick your pussy and suck your clit until you're screaming my name. I wanna eat you out, Tor. I'm starving for you. I want to feel you up under my tongue and taste how sweet you are." I felt her shudder at my words. If she reacted that way to my words, my actions were going to drive her insane. "Crawl up here, right in my face. And lose the panties."

Tori slipped off her panties and crawled up my chest. Her knees were next to my shoulders. "A little closer, baby." She walked her knees forward 'til they were next to my head. I pushed my fingers deep inside her, pumping her in and out, curling them inside her. She dropped her head back and whimpered. "You like that, baby?" Her response was the sound of pleasure that erupted from throat, encouraging me to take all of her. "Now, spread your legs, so I can lick you." She spread her legs and lowered herself toward my mouth. "Lower, baby. Wider. Spread your legs wider. And hold on to the headboard. You're gonna need it."

Tori did as I said and braced herself for the assault I was about to subject her to. I covered her in soft kisses, then spread her with my fingers and licked her from back to front. I felt her quiver above me. She tasted so good, that I stuck my tongue up inside her and ate her out relentlessly. She leaned forward and I moved to her clit, flicking it with the tip of my tongue. I alternated between licking, flicking, and sucking.

Lick.

Flick.

Suck.

Lick.

Flick.

Suck.

I was taking her to the edge over and over again, without giving her what she truly wanted. Tori looked down at me from between her arms on the headboard. "Baby, don't tease me. Make me come...please...please. I want it," she begged.

"Now?" I asked.

"Now," she gasped out.

I pushed my fingers up inside her, curling them the way she liked it. Then, I wrapped my lips around her clit and began to suck. And suck. And suck. She contracted around my fingers and then came long and hard. Her body quaked, and she threw her head back. "Oh, my god... fuck... oh...god." She pulsed around my fingers as I continued sucking her clit. When I finally released her, she sat back on my chest with a ridiculously content look on her face. "Sooo good. Best. Birthday. Ever."

"Oh...we're not finished yet," I told her. "Not by a long shot."

She lay down beside me. "Give me a minute to get my bearings."

"Thirty seconds. And then I'm inside you. I can't wait much longer," I insisted. I reached over, grabbed my wallet from the nightstand and pulled out a condom. I slid my boxer briefs down and rolled the condom into place. "Roll on your side, baby." I gently nudged her, so that her back was to me. This was the first time I'd seen the two-inch cut on her back. In my selfish rant and pity party over my knee, I'd lost sight of the fact that she'd had a huge piece of glass embedded in her back less than a week ago. I remembered what the doctor had said about it being close to her spinal cord. Everything could have been so much worse. Had her spinal cord been severed... I didn't even want to go there. She was here with me now, and she was okay. That was all that mattered. I rubbed my fingers over the stitches. "Does it hurt?"

"A little, but the endorphins are helping." She smirked at me. "Keep 'em coming, baby."

"Whatever you want. It's your birthday." I pressed my chest to her back and lifted her leg over mine. "Open for me."

Tori arched her back and pushed her hips back, putting her just where I needed her. I pushed between her legs and entered her in a slow, deep push. We both moaned out in pleasure. She was so tight like this. I slowly slid my dick out and pushed back in. Her hips started to move with mine and we found our rhythm. I wrapped her in my arms, as we continued to make love. It was slow and intimate. Fucking perfect.

I rolled to my back, without pulling out, taking her with me. She laid with her back on my chest and hung her head over my shoulder. I kissed the side of her face, as I pushed up into her. Tori bent her knees and put her feet on the bed. She moved with me. I slid in and out of her, slow and deep. So deep.

We'd never done this position before and I loved it. Loved the intimacy it provided. The closeness we shared. And to think, just a few days ago, I had almost ruined it all. I still couldn't believe the things that had come out of my mouth. The nasty things I had said to her. Just thinking about it, I felt ashamed. If the situation had been reversed, I don't know that I could have been so forgiving. It was a testament to how Tori felt about me. How we felt about each other. Never again, would I take her granted.

Chapter 6
Tori

And just like that, we were back together. I knew what Chris had done and said to me were awful. Hurtful. Nasty. Unforgivable. Three days of crying had nearly broken me. But I also knew it wasn't him. That wasn't *my* Chris. He'd been hurt and frustrated. The pressure and disappointment had gotten to him, and he'd cracked. Didn't just crack, he broke. What I witnessed and had been the target of, was a major breakdown. I understood it. I didn't like it, but I understood it. Under all that anger, was a lot of hurt.

I also knew he loved me. Honestly, truly, loved me with all his heart. The silence I gave him after his breakdown, hurt him almost as much as his rant hurt me. He was desperate to have me back. So desperate, he actually sang to me. The words he sang melted the ice from my heart and in that moment, he had me. I couldn't not forgive him.

Maybe I should have made him sweat it out longer. Maybe I shouldn't have taken him back at all. But the truth was…I was as desperate for him, as he was for me. I didn't know what my life looked like without him. I couldn't see a future without him. He was woven into every fiber of my being. He was my other half, and I couldn't live with half of myself missing. And neither could he.

Since both of our birthdays were so close to Christmas, we decided last year to forgo the Christmas presents and just do birthdays. That way we could put more thought into one really nice gift, instead of struggling to figure out two gifts. Our Christmas gift to each other was being able to spend time together.

This year, our time together was overshadowed by the fact that we were both going into the hospital the day after Christmas. Chris's surgery was outpatient. I, however, had to stay the night. And I was really scared. There was something I hadn't told Chris. Not only was my doctor going to remove the cysts, but he was doing a biopsy to check for cancer. He said the chances were low, and it was just a precaution... but what if?

I didn't want Chris to worry about that. I was worried enough for both of us. It was bad enough the Polycystic Ovary Syndrome put into question whether we would be able to have kids... but cancer, that was a whole different situation. It would mean possible removal of my ovaries and chemotherapy.

Only my mom and Mike knew. I didn't even tell Kyla. Truth be told, I would have told Chris before I told Kyla. But I didn't tell either of them.

I wasn't a religious person. Hell, our family hadn't gone to church in years. But in the days leading up to my surgery, I'd made a deal with God. I didn't have much to offer, except myself. I promised that if I came out of this cancer free, that I would be the best daughter, friend, and girlfriend anyone could ask for. I'd be kind, thoughtful, understanding, and supportive. I'd be the best me I could possibly be.

It was Christmas Eve. We had just left Chris's grandma's house and were heading back home. We were really making the rounds in these two days. Since neither one of us could stand to be away from the other, we attended all the family parties together. I wouldn't trade it for anything. I wouldn't give up one moment with him.

Chris drove us in his new truck. The old one had been totaled out and the insurance money was enough to pay off the old truck and put a decent-sized down payment on a new one. I looked out the window, watching the world pass us by. Chris held my hand across the seat, and he gave it a little squeeze. "Are you feeling okay, Tor?" he asked.

I turned to him and gave him a forced smile. "Just thinking."

"Are you scared about your surgery?" He squeezed my hand again.

I shrugged my shoulders, trying to keep the tears out of my eyes. "A little," I lied. I was scared to death about what I might find out.

"It's okay to be scared, you know. What you're going through is a big deal. Did they tell you how big of an incision they're going to do?" he asked.

I held my thumb and forefinger open. "About five inches. Just above my pubic bone. I'm going to have an ugly scar." I looked back out the window.

"You think I give a fuck about that?" I shrugged again. Chris brought my hand to his lips and kissed it. "Tor, I could give two shits as long as you're healthy. You'll always be beautiful to me."

I unbuckled my seatbelt and slid over next to him. I wrapped myself around his bicep and held on tight. I swallowed down the lump in my throat. "I don't want to do this, Chris. I know I put up a good front, but I'm really not that tough."

Chris kissed the top of my head. "Put your seatbelt on, baby." I reluctantly fastened the center seatbelt over me and leaned back into him. "Tor, you're one of the strongest people I know. You don't really have a choice about the surgery. You can do this. And I'm going to be there with you."

"How?" I asked. "You're having your ACL done on the same day."

We pulled up in my driveway and he unfastened both our seatbelts. He pulled me onto his lap and cradled me. I willingly went and snuggled into him. My safe place. "I've got it all worked out. I'll be there when they take you in, go for my surgery, and I'll come back to your room after. I'm not going to be doing much but sitting around. I can rest my leg in your room as well as I can at home. I'm not leaving you. I'll stay the night with you."

Tears ran down my face. "You'd do that for me?"

Chris wiped my tears. "Baby, there isn't anything I wouldn't do for you."

"What do your parents think about this plan?" I asked.

He smiled down on me. "Who do you think helped make all the arrangements? My mom and your mom have been conspiring. They have it all figured out."

This man never failed to amaze me, and I knew taking him back was the right decision. I cupped his face with my hand. "You're the best, you know that?" I placed a gentle kiss on his lips. I pulled back and blew out a breath. It was truth time. I owed him that much. "Don't be mad," I started, "but I haven't been completely honest with you. I just... I didn't want you to worry until I knew for sure." I dropped my head, and the tears ran down my face again.

Chris lifted my chin and brought my eyes back to his. "What is it, Tor?" He brushed away my tears, but it was useless.

I closed my eyes and let the tears fall. "They're doing a biopsy of the cysts. It could be cancer." My body shook as I sobbed. "The doctor said it was unlikely, but they want to be sure." I leaned into him and let out everything I'd been holding in.

Chris wrapped his arms around me and held me tight to his warm body, tucking my head under his chin. I felt his chest heave and his voice hitched. "It's not. I know it's not." He sniffed back his own tears. "And if it is, we'll get through that too. I'm not losing you. That's not an option."

"I'm really scared," I admitted. "I'm sorry I didn't tell you sooner." I snuffed up all my tears and I knew the sound was less than attractive.

He squeezed me tighter. "Don't worry about it. I didn't exactly make this any easier on you. I know now. If I hadn't been such an ass..."

I put my fingers to his lips. "Don't go there. You're more than making up for everything. I love you, Chris. I wouldn't trade you for anything."

We sat there in silence, holding each other, knowing the next few days could change everything.

The day after Christmas, I had to be at the hospital by eight in the morning. My nerves were out of control. Not only was I going to be cut open, but I would find out about the dreaded C word.

Chris and his parents showed up at our house around seven-fifteen. Chris jumped into the backseat with me, and his parents followed in their car as we all headed to the hospital. Chris and I sat in silence, holding onto each other like there was no tomorrow. He absentmindedly ran his fingers through my hair in a calming manner. I didn't know if it was more for me or for him. I just knew that having him with me right now, was everything I needed.

Mr. and Mrs. Capizzio went to the cafeteria while I got checked in and prepped. My mom, Mike, and Chris all stayed with me until the last possible moment.

"It's going to be okay, sweetheart." My mom kissed my forehead.

I just nodded because I was too afraid to say anything.

"You're tough, baby girl. This is going to be a walk in the park. You got this," Mike offered. He was so sweet. I knew he was worried too, but he was putting on a brave face for me.

Chris was still holding my hand. He wouldn't let go. I didn't want him to. The nurse came in and injected something into my IV. The last thing I remembered was his soft lips on mine. "I love you, Tori."

Chapter 7
Chris

Watching Tori get rolled away, was the hardest thing I've ever done. That fucking sucked. There was nothing I could do except wait, like everyone else, to get the results of her biopsy. There was no way I could lose her. Everything had to be okay. It was the only choice.

Mike slung his arm over my shoulder as we walked out of the surgical prepping area. "Tori's tough and stubborn. She's going be fine. Don't worry, son," he said. "I'm so glad you two patched things up. She really needed you today."

"I wish I wasn't getting my knee done today. I should be there in the waiting room with you guys. What if something happens?" I worried.

"Nothing's going to happen," Mike assured me. "Get your knee taken care of. You'll be out of surgery around the same time. When they get her in a room, we'll bring you right up."

The three of us walked down to the cafeteria to find my parents. I spotted them at a table by the window. We walked over and sat down.

"How'd our girl do?" my mom asked.

"She was a trooper," Mrs. Russo answered. "Now we wait." She looked to my mom for support. "It has to be benign, right, Trina?"

My mom wrapped Tori's mom in a tight hug. "She's going to be fine, Elena. Sal and I will meet you in the waiting room once we get Chris all set."

I gave Tori's mom a hug. "I'll be there as soon as I can. If Tori wakes up before I get there, tell her I'm on my way."

She looked up at me and cupped my face in one hand. "You're the best thing that ever happened to my daughter. We'll see you soon. Good luck, honey."

We went our separate ways and all I could think about was my girl. I needed to get back to her. I wanted to be there when she found out the results of the biopsy.

When I woke from the anesthesia, my knee was sore, but I didn't give a shit. It was the last thing on my mind. I opened my eyes, and my dad came into focus. "How's Tori?" I asked.

"She's doing fine. She was coming out of surgery the same time as you." He rubbed my arm up and down, "How does your knee feel?"

"It's sore, but it's fine. Not life threatening." I looked down at the IV in my arm. "How long 'til I can get out of here?"

"Relax. She's not going anywhere. You need to take care of you, or you won't be any good to her."

"I know," I huffed. "This is just so hard."

My dad looked at me skeptically. "You almost lost her ten days ago. You were ready to give her up. What changed?"

"Someone put things into perspective for me. Between you and mom, I saw things more clearly. And then to find out she was sick… all I could think was that if I didn't fix things between us, I would never forgive myself. You were right. She is the best thing that ever happened to me. Do you think that she'll ever forgive me for the things I said to her?" I asked. We were back on the right track, but what I did couldn't be erased.

"She already has," my dad said without hesitation.

"How do you know?" I asked.

"I see how she looks at you. How she goes to you for strength when she doesn't have any of her own. How she would do anything for you. Like I said before, you're her whole world."

"She's mine, too."

An hour later, I was being wheeled into Tori's room. She was sleeping peacefully, and I felt some relief seeing her. But I wouldn't feel fully relieved until we knew the results of the biopsy.

I looked at Tori's mom. "Has the doctor been by yet?"

She bit her lip and shook her head. Seeing her like that, I realized how much Tori looked like her mom. "Not yet," she answered.

My mom spoke up. "That's a good thing. If it were bad news, they would have already told you."

She might have been right, but I wouldn't believe it until I heard it with my own ears. I was sitting next to Tori's bed, holding her hand. My fingers lightly brushed over her knuckles, and I touched her purple nails. Tori wouldn't ever paint her nails pink, she always used dark colors. It fit her. She wasn't girly in the sense that she didn't fuss over her makeup and hair. She wasn't into frou-frou and frilly clothes. Her tastes were simpler and more classic. It was one of the many things I loved about her. She always looked put together and beautiful, but she was far from high maintenance.

Her eyes fluttered and tried to focus. I squeezed her hand. "Hey, baby. Welcome back."

She licked her lips, and her voice came out raspy. "How did your surgery go? Does it hurt?"

I smiled at her. This girl was amazing. Everything she'd gone through, and her first concern was me. "I'm fine, Tor. It's a little sore, but manageable. How are you feeling?"

"Tired." Her mom brought her a cup of water. Tori took a couple of sips and handed the cup back. "Thanks, mom. Did the doctor come by yet?"

"Not yet, Sweetie."

Tori turned to me. "How long have you been here?"

"Not very long. But I'm here until you go home. I'm not leaving you," I assured her.

There was a knock on the door and Tori's doctor walked in. "How are you feeling, Tori?"

"Hi, Dr. Sommers. I'm tired and I'm sore. What did you find? Is it cancer?" Tori's eyes watered up when she asked.

"Do you want us to leave?" my dad interrupted. "We can wait in the hall."

"No," Tori said definitively. "You're my family too. I want you to stay."

"Okay, sweetie," my mom said, as she clasped my dad's hand.

I held Tori's hand tighter as we waited for the Dr. Sommers' answer. "We removed multiple cysts from both ovaries. We biopsied all of them. There was no sign of cancer." Everyone let out the breaths they were holding, and a sigh of relief filled the room. "You're going to be fine. With hormone therapy, I think we can prevent them from coming back and you can live a normal, healthy life."

I raised Tori's hand to my lips and kissed it, then rested my head on her chest. Thank God. My girl was going to be fine. I realized how scared I had been, even though I was trying to be strong for Tor.

"Thank you," Tori croaked out. A tear slipped from her eye, and she quickly wiped it away.

"You're very welcome. I'll be in to check on you in the morning and we'll see about getting you home." The doc smiled at Tori and patted her leg.

Tori's mom was locked in Mike's arms and tears were running down her face. "It's not cancer," she cried.

Mike rubbed her back. "I heard," he smiled.

My dad spoke up, "Well this is reason for celebration. When you two kids are feeling better, we're going to have a celebratory dinner. Trina will cook up something delicious for us. She's the best cook in the county." He winked at my mom.

"You're sweet, Sal." She hugged my dad around the waist. "It'll be Tori's choice. Whatever you want, sweetie. You just let me know."

My head was still on Tori's chest. It was soft, because well… she had big boobs. I felt her fingers run through my hair and I lifted my head to face her. "You okay?" she asked.

My eyes were watery, and I really didn't give a fuck. "I'm perfect, because you're perfect." I leaned as close to her as I could with my leg propped up on the chair, and Tori met me halfway to place a kiss on her lips. "I love you. Forever."

"Forever," she repeated.

I'd been sitting in this chair for what seemed like hours. My body was stiff, and my knee throbbed, but there was nowhere I'd rather be. Tori had been sleeping on and off all day. Visiting hours ended two hours ago, and now it was just the two of us and the TV. Right now, she was sleeping peacefully. I needed to get some rest myself, but nature called and if I didn't get up, I was sure my bladder was going to burst.

I reached for the crutches behind my chair and pulled them to the sides. This was going to be tricky. I was in no way an expert with these things yet. I eased my leg off the chair in front of me and cringed as the pain shot through my knee. "Son of a bitch," I hissed out.

I turned toward Tori to make sure I didn't wake her. She moved her head to the side but was still sound asleep. I carefully stood and made my way to the bathroom as the crutches clinked on the floor.

When I came back from the bathroom, Tori was sitting up in bed. "I was afraid you changed your mind."

I gave her the *Really?* look. "Baby, I promised you I'd stay. And I always keep my promises. I wouldn't walk out on you." I hobbled back to the chair next to her bed, put my leg up on the other chair and held her hand.

"I know," she said. She met my eyes with concern. "I need to talk to you about something. And I know you're going to get upset with me, but I want you to hear me out. And then you can say whatever you need to say. But I need the truth. The whole truth. Because I can't keep these thoughts out of my head, and I need to put them to rest."

She was scaring the shit out of me. I didn't know what was coming, but I would listen to her. "Okay. What is it?"

She took a deep breath. "When you came to my house on my birthday, you got more than you bargained for."

"Tor…" She held up her hand to silence me.

"Let me get this out. You didn't plan on hearing that I'd had a pregnancy scare or that I was sick. That was a lot to take in. But I'm okay. I'm not pregnant and this isn't cancer. The doctor said I'm going to be fine." I was dying to interrupt, but I bit my tongue and held it back.

Tori took another deep breath and continued. "You said some pretty harsh things to me, and I know you weren't yourself. You were drunk and hurt and frustrated. And I get it. I really do. But I also think you wouldn't have said those things if you hadn't been thinking them for a while. And maybe it was a dose of truth that I needed. I love you. I can't imagine my life without you, but I won't have you be in this relationship because of some kind of misplaced guilt about me being sick. The fact remains that I might not be able to have kids. That's not going to change."

"I want you to be happy, Chris. There's nothing I want more for you. And if you have any reservations about this relationship, I need to know. I never want you to regret being with me or resent me for holding you back. So, I need to know... why did you come back? If it was because you felt bad about the things you said to me, that's not a good reason. An *I'm sorry* would have sufficed. And I don't want you to stay because I've got this thing going on and you feel guilty leaving me. I only want you to stay if I have all of you. Heart, mind, and soul. I won't take anything less."

She stopped talking and I took that as my cue to respond. "Are you done?" I asked. She nodded weakly. "First of all, I came back because I realized what a total jackass I was. I didn't think I deserved you. I thought you deserved better, and I tried to push you away. But I was too selfish to let you go, even though I *know* you deserve better. I was empty inside. I stayed because I need you. Whether or not you're sick, I'll always need you. I love you more than anything. I'd give up everything to be with you. I'm a selfish bastard and I can't live without you. The only thing I would ever regret is not doing everything I could to get you back. So, do you have all of me? Yes. I'm in this...heart, mind, and soul. I won't give you anything less."

She scooted over to one side of the bed and patted the space beside her. "Come up here with me?"

I crinkled my eyes at her. "I don't think that's allowed."

"I don't care. I need my man up here with me. I need his heart, mind, soul, and most definitely his body."

I fiddled with the rail of the bed and finally got it to slide down. I sat on the edge of the mattress and maneuvered my leg up on the bed. "This is no easy task, woman," I teased her. It was a tight fit, but we managed. I wrapped my arm around her shoulder, and she rested her head on my chest. This was way better than that fucking chair.

"I love you, Chris. Thank you for staying with me," she said drowsily.

"I love you too, baby. This is my favorite place in the world." I held her tight and let her snuggle into me. "I'm not ever letting you go," I said as I closed my eyes and let myself drift off to sleep.

Chapter 8
Tori

It was early when I woke, warm and happy, tucked into Chris's side. I tried to turn a little bit, but his arm held me tight. I winced at the pain in my abdomen. Must have been time for another pain pill.

Right on schedule, a nurse walked into the room. She looked at the two of us in the bed and scowled. "He's not supposed to be up there," she grumped.

I cringed at her tone and held a finger to my lips to silence her. "Shhh! I know," I whispered. "Just give us ten more minutes." I gave her a look somewhere between *please* and *don't fuck with me.*

She must have gotten the message loud and clear because she pursed her lips and whispered, "Ten minutes. I need to check your incision and bring you a pain pill."

"Thank you," I mouthed.

She gave me a slight smile, turned, and left. I ran my hand through Chris's hair. "Time to wake up, baby." I placed a soft kiss on his lips. My breath was probably awful, but he wouldn't care. His lips started to move, and his tongue poked out to twist with mine.

I pulled away. "Nothing says true love more than sharing bad breath."

"I don't care." He kissed me again. "When we're both healed, I seriously want to have some dirty, freaky sex with you."

I ran my hand along his morning wood. He was thick and hard under his sweatpants. "I can't think of anything better, but right now you have to move back to the chair. Nurse Ratched is going to come back in a few to check my incision."

He gently ran his hand over my stomach. "Are you in pain?"

"A little. She's bringing me a pain pill, too."

Chris eased himself off the bed and over to the chair. He reached in his bag and pulled out his own pills. "Sounds like a good idea." He popped the pill in his mouth and grabbed my water from the side table to

39

wash it down. "I was thinking, when we get you home, we should alternate between your house and mine. We can watch movies and just cuddle up together. What do you think?"

"Sounds perfect."

The nurse returned with my pain meds, and I eagerly swallowed them down. "Let's take a look at your belly," she said. She pulled the blanket down and my gown up, so she could inspect the incision. Chris busied himself watching television, giving me a semblance of privacy.

She carefully pulled the gauze back and my eyes about popped out of my head. I don't know what I was expecting, but this wasn't it. "What the hell?" Tears welled in my eyes.

Chris's head snapped to me. "What's wrong, Tori?"

"What's wrong? I look like Frankenstein. That's what the problem is. I didn't know they were going to staple me closed. I assumed I would have stitches."

Chris stood to get a better look and leaned over the bed. "Tor, don't worry about it. It's temporary."

The nurse gave me a sympathetic smile. "He's right. The staples will come out in less than a week. The incision itself looks good, no signs of infection. I know it looks awful now, but trust me, it'll fade over time. It'll just be a fine line."

"Ugh!" I laid back on the pillow and closed my eyes. "It's so ugly."

"Nothing on you could ever be ugly, baby. You're beautiful inside and out." Chris leaned down and kissed me.

"Now I know why he was in your bed this morning," the nurse smiled. "He's a keeper for sure." She rebandaged me and pulled my gown back down.

"Yeah, he is," I agreed.

The next week and a half passed in lazy days resting and watching movies together. Netflix was our new best friend. Our moms were awesome, waiting on us hand and foot. We tried not to be too much of an inconvenience, but I think they secretly liked having us dependent upon them for a change.

We were getting antsy though, and honestly, I was getting horny. This was the longest we hadn't had sex in what seemed like forever. I knew we couldn't actually have sex, but we could do other things. The problem was, we had zero privacy. All the doting meant that someone was always around. I was ready to explode from sexual frustration. I didn't know how Kyla and Tyler did it. This not having sex thing was brutal.

I was nestled between Chris's legs on the couch. His bad knee sat along the back of the cushions, and I laid back into him. My head was resting on his chest and his arms were wrapped tightly around me. I must have drifted off to sleep. I could feel his hot breath on my ear, his soft whispers sending shivers over my skin. "Wake up, Tor."

"Mmmmm," I moaned.

Soft breath was at my ear again. "Wake up, baby. We're all alone. I wanna see if you're as wet for me, as I'm hard for you. I need to touch you, Tor."

My eyes were still closed, because if this was a dream, I didn't want to wake up. I felt his hand snake down the front of my leggings. It glided carefully past my incision, over my clit and down between my legs. "Fuck. You're so wet, baby. Spread your legs for me."

He was all dominant alpha when it came to sex and I was more than happy to submit. I spread my legs open and let him in. He slid two fingers into me and gently pumped them in and out.

"Mmmm…aaaah!" I was still in a sleepy haze. The feeling was so good. God, I missed him between my legs. I arched into Chris's hand, as he slowly finger fucked me. "More…please, Chris."

He increased his speed, curling his fingers inside me to hit that spot that made me go crazy. "You want to come, baby? You want me to hit that clit and make you come? Tell me you want it."

"Yessss. Make me come," I hissed out.

He spread my wetness over my clit and rubbed me in small circles, occasionally pinching me between his fingers. I arched more, trying to increase the pressure. My muscles clenched and the orgasm began to build. Chris knew my body so well. He slipped his fingers back

41

in me but kept the pressure on my clit with his thumb. The feeling was so intense I gasped for air. "I'm right there, baby."

"Come for me, Tori," he ordered. And as if on command, I shattered. The waves of pleasure surged through me, sending tingles up and down my spine. I rode out the blissful high and sank back into him. His fingers continued to work their magic until the high was over. He slowly pulled his fingers out and raised them to his lips, sucking them clean. "I missed the way you taste. Next time I make you come it's going to be on my face."

I turned and kissed him, tasting myself on his lips. Then I pulled his fingers to my mouth, slowly sucking each one of them. His eyes hooded with lust. "Fuck me with your mouth, Tor. I want my dick deep in your throat."

"Are you sure no one's coming home?" I asked. I had no aversions to giving him a killer blow job, but I didn't want to get caught with his dick in my mouth either.

"No one's coming home for at least an hour. Mom's out running errands." Chris pushed my hair behind my ear and kissed me gently, twisting his tongue with mine. "Blow me, Tor."

"I love giving you blow jobs." I started to pull his sweats down and Chris helped to push them over his hips. I slowly dropped to my knees in front of him and wrapped my hand around his dick. "I can't wait to have you inside me again." I licked the head of his cock, then wrapped my lips around the soft skin and sank down deep.

I was just getting into a rhythm when I heard the front door open and close. I froze with Chris's dick in my mouth. He quickly threw the blanket from the back of the couch over me. "Mom?" I heard Jim yell out. Fucking great! Jim was home and I had his brother's dick down my throat. What the hell? I might as well finish. I started to bob up and down and I felt Chris's hand on my head to still me.

"What are you doing here?" Chris asked.

"I live here, asshole." Jim answered. I could hear footsteps, which meant he was moving into the family room. I couldn't help but mess with him. I cupped his balls, rubbing them in a way I knew would make him lose his shit.

"Actually, you live in the dorms. What do you want? Mom's not here." I could hear the agitation in Chris's voice. His hand was on my back, trying to get me to stop. But I didn't.

"When's she gonna be…" His voice came closer with every word. "Oh Fuck! Are you getting a blow job? Jesus Christ!"

"Yeah, I am. And you're fucking ruining it. So, unless you want to watch me blow my load, you should probably wait upstairs." Chris's voice was harsh, but I couldn't help the giggle that escaped me. I felt his hips buck and then his hand was back on top of my head.

"Hey, Tori. Glad to see you're feeling better," Jim said. I raised my hand from under the blanket and gave him a little wave. Jim laughed. "I really got to get a better girlfriend. Carry on. I'll wait in my room." I heard him going up the stairs and then his door shutting. Music started to blare from upstairs.

Chris pulled the blanket from over me and smoothed back my hair. "Sorry about that."

I released him with a pop of my lips. I shrugged my shoulders, "You want me to finish or not?"

"Fuck, yeah, I want you to finish," he said with a wicked smile.

"Hold on. I'm gonna make this fast and hard so we don't get interrupted again." I sank down until he hit the back of my throat, swirling my tongue along his dick. I opened my throat and swallowed him down, taking him deeper with every swallow. One hand was holding the base of his shaft, while the other massaged his balls and the sensitive skin behind them. He lifted his hips, fucking my mouth with every thrust.

"Fuck, baby. I'm gonna come. Fuck!" His hands pushed on the back of my head, not letting me escape. Two more pulses of my throat and his cum filled my mouth. I took it all and slid my lips up his dick. "Shit, Tor. Your mouth is a deadly weapon. I think I died and went to heaven." I crawled back up his body and kissed him. He pulled his sweats back up and I curled into his chest.

"I can't wait until we can have sex again." I smiled. "And…the best part is now I'm on birth control. In a month or so, no more condoms. Just you and me and nothing in between.

"I can't wait to feel my dick in your pussy. It's gonna be sooo good. My cum dripping out of you."

I put my hand over his mouth, "Stop or you're gonna have to get me off again."

He smirked down at me. "That would be my pleasure."

Kyla picked me up for school after the break. I hadn't seen her much since she started dating Tyler. Those two became inseparable. I was happy that she finally fell in love. Tyler seemed to be good for her. She smiled more and was starting to come out of her shell.

"How's the V card?" I asked.

She huffed. "Still intact."

I crinkled my eyebrows at her. "Seriously?"

"Yeah. I'm just not ready yet. I love him, but..." She shrugged her shoulders.

"You're scared, aren't you?"

"Honestly? Yes. What if I'm wrong? What if it doesn't last?"

I patted her leg. "There are no guarantees. You need go with your gut. If you're not ready, you're not ready. What about other stuff?"

"Like what?" she asked innocently.

Come on, she wasn't that clueless. We'd been reading the same damn smutty books for years. "Blow job?"

"Nope."

"Suck on your tits."

"Nuh-uh."

I couldn't believe this. They'd been dating almost three months. "What the fuck do you do? Tell me you've at least felt his dick. Stuck your hand down his pants?"

She peeled her eyes from the road and nodded like a bobblehead. "Yes. Yes, that I've done. And let me tell you... he's big. Like really big. I don't even think that will fit inside me."

I rolled my eyes. "Trust me. It will. Has he fingered you yet?"

Kyla narrowed her eyebrows at me. "Why do you have to ask such embarrassing questions?"

"Kyla, it's not embarrassing. It's foreplay to sex and eventually you're going to have it. So, has he?"

"Yes," she said with hesitation.

"And?"

Her head snapped to me. "And what?"

"Oh my, God! You act like I'm interrogating you about a major crime. You wanna know all the things Chris has done to me? Will that make you feel better?"

She threw her hands up over her ears. "Definitely not!"

I pried her hands from her head. "And did he make you come?"

She let out a breath of frustration. "He tried, but I stopped him."

"What?" I was seriously in shock. The way Chris made me feel, I couldn't imagine passing that up. "Why?"

She shrugged her shoulders. "I don't know. It started to feel really intense, and I freaked out."

"Jeez, Kyla. It's supposed to feel intense. That's how you know it's gonna be good. The more intense the build-up, the better the orgasm." I shook my head at her and then it dawned on me. My eyes got wide. "You've never had an orgasm before, have you?"

She shook her head.

"No wonder it freaked you out. Okay, I'm giving you homework. I know you're an overachiever, so if I call it homework, maybe you'll actually do it. Go home and read a bunch of smutty sex scenes or think about Tyler touching you…whatever gets you wet…and when you've got yourself good and horny…touch yourself. And when you feel like the pressure is so intense that you think you can't take anymore… keep going. We've read enough smut that you know the mechanics of how and where to touch. Once you've fallen over the edge, you'll get over the fear of the unknown. Then maybe you can let Tyler have a crack at it."

Embarrassment crept up her neck. "You think?"

"Sweetie, you gotta try. You can't be afraid of sex. If you're afraid of an orgasm, how will you ever take it to the next level?"

Kyla's eyes began to tear up. "I know. He's been so patient with me. I don't want him to move on to someone who's willing to do stuff. You know? I mean… what if Susie sets her sights on him?"

I reached for her hand over the seat. "Kyla, listen to me. That boy is totally in love with you. He'll wait. I'm just saying, maybe give him a little something to look forward to while he's waiting. As for

Susie… that bitch better stay far away from our men, or I'll sic Chris's mom on her again."

Kyla started laughing. "I wish I could have been there for that. Sounds classic."

I laughed at the memory. "It was. The funniest part was seeing her face after Chris's sweet mom called her a whore. Fucking fantabulous! And now, Chris has laid down the law with her too. It was way overdue, but she shouldn't be an issue anymore."

After our laughfest, my mind moved back to the issue at hand. "Girl, blow jobs can do wonders too. The poor boy is probably getting himself off every day in the shower. He's got a sweet piece of ass— you—that's sexy as hell, and he's not getting any. Throw the dog a bone and blow the boy. At the very least, give him a hand job."

Kyla nodded. "You're right. I can do this. I want to do this. I need to do this." Her enthusiasm and confidence built with every word. "I'm not going to let him get away from me. And I'm certainly not going to let someone steal him from me," she said with determination.

"Damn right, girl!"

Later that day, I was helping Chris at his locker. Using the crutches was tricky, but he was quickly becoming a pro. He still had another two weeks to go. He'd be done with the crutches about the same time I would be completely healed. We were on our own countdown.

I switched out the books for his next class and shoved them into his backpack. "Thanks, baby. You don't know how much this helps."

I raised up on my tiptoes and gave him a peck on the lips, "We take care of each other. That's how this thing works."

"I know. We're lucky we have each other."

My conversation with Kyla from the morning flashed in my mind. "Speaking of perfect couples. This thing with Kyla and Tyler is really moving forward."

"Seems like it," he replied nonchalantly. "I'm kind of surprised, to be honest."

"Why?" I asked.

"I don't see her giving it up. The guy has got to be frustrated as hell. I mean she's pretty and sweet, but guys have needs."

"So… you're saying if I didn't give it up, we wouldn't still be together?" I quirked my eyebrow at him.

"That wouldn't happen," he said confidently.

"Oh yeah? Why is that?" His cocky attitude was coming through loud and clear.

He laughed at me. "Have you met my dick? You'd never be able to resist it. Who wouldn't want all of this," he cupped his package, "up in their vajayjay?"

I couldn't help laughing at his cockiness—pun intended. "Yeah, well I'm the only one getting that in the vajayjay, so everyone else can fuck off. But Kyla said Tyler's packing some serious equipment too. You don't think he'd cheat on her, do you?"

Chris scowled at me. "First of all, why are you talking about Tyler's *equipment*?"

I put a hand on his chest. "Don't worry she knows you've got a big dick too. We're best friends. We talk about shit. I don't tell her all the nasty details because I want to keep that just between us. My point is… do you think he's a virgin too? I mean she hasn't even given him a blow job yet." I lowered my voice. "She hasn't even had an orgasm yet. That's crazy, right?"

"Crazy to us," he conceded. "But it must work for them." Chris balanced his crutches under his arms and cupped my face. "All I know is that I wouldn't trade what we have for anything."

Months passed by and prom was right around the corner, which to me meant only one thing. An epic night of sex with my man. This needed preparation…aka a trip to Naughty Novelties.

I picked Kyla up for lunch but didn't tell her about our little side trip. I kept that tidbit of information to myself, but when Kyla found out where we were going, her reaction was going to be priceless. "So…" I started. "You and Tyler are finally gonna bump uglies, huh?"

She swatted me on the arm and scrunched up her nose. "Don't say it like that! That makes it sound cheap, and dang we've waited long enough. I want it to be perfect, but I have to be honest...I'm getting nervous."

"I was just trying to lighten the mood. It won't be cheap. A hotel room at the Hilton is just the opposite. And if I know Ty, he's going to try to make it perfect for you. Not like my debacle in the back of a truck. You're doing this right. You want some advice?"

Kyla looked at me nervously. "I'm afraid to ask."

I hated to give her advice because she was totally afraid of everything. But there was one thing I could tell her that wouldn't lead her wrong no matter what. "Shave everything."

Kyla eyes got super wide. "What?"

"You heard me. Shave it all. It will be a total turn on to him. No guy wants to go down on you and have that in their mouth."

"Really?"

"Really. If he wants to go down on you, let him. I promise, you won't regret it. Have you given him a blow job yet?" We had arrived at our destination, and I parked the car. Kyla's mind was so distracted that she hadn't even noticed where we were.

Redness started to creep up Kyla's neck. "No."

Seriously? She *still* hadn't given him a blow job yet? Poor guy. That was just sad.

Kyla had always been the smart one in our friendship. For once, I knew something she didn't, and I was happy to impart all my wisdom on her. "When you go down on him... and you are doing that...watch your teeth. Lips and tongue are good. Teeth are bad." I paused for dramatic effect, "Last thing... when he does something that makes you feel good, let him know. Don't hold back. Nothing is sexier than a sweet woman with a dirty mouth. Trust me. He'll love it!"

Kyla shook her head. "This is so overwhelming. Sex shouldn't be this hard."

"Sweetie, it's not hard. You make him happy, and he'll make you happy. Trust me. The only thing sure to be hard, will be Tyler."

She giggled. Her giggle became a full out belly laugh. "We better eat. I think I'm becoming delirious. All I can think about right now is his hard dick and how much I want to fuck him." She covered her

48

mouth with her hand to try to smother her laughter, but it was a lost cause. "Do you think he'll want to… you know… go down on me?"

"Are you kidding me? Trust me. The guy has been thinking about it for months. By holding back on him, all you've done is build the mystery and anticipation. He's going to be all over you. You're going to unleash something you've only dreamed about."

Kyla's laughter rolled out and filled the small space inside my beetle. She threw her hands up to cover her face and let out a muffled scream. "I can't believe I'm finally going to have sex with Ty! He's so fucking sexy!"

I stared at her like she'd sprouted horns out of her head. This was not normal behavior for my best friend. Maybe she really was becoming delirious.

She threw her head back and screamed. "I can't wait for him to fuck me!"

I grabbed her by the shoulders and pulled her towards me. "Who are you? And what have you done with my best friend?" I demanded.

Her giggle was out of control, "I don't know," she confessed. Taking deep breaths, she finally got herself under control. "I think that was sexual frustration that finally broke free." After a few more controlled breaths, her brain went back to the girl I knew. Her practical and logical side kicked in. "It's going to hurt, isn't it? Oh, my god! What if it hurts so much that I hate it?" She kept rambling. The words came out in steady stream. "Then what? And there's going to be blood too. Of course, there's going to be blood! I'm so stupid! I can't have sex with Tyler. It'll be too embarrassing! What if he gets grossed out and never wants to touch me again? I'm going to die a virgin! I don't want to die a virgin!"

Definitely delirious! Desperate times called for desperate measures. I shook her shoulders. "Pull it together, woman! You're acting crazy! Don't make me slap you!"

She narrowed her eyes at me. "You wouldn't!"

"I would if I thought it would help. But fortunately for you, I don't think it would. Just breathe." Kyla calmed down enough to be coherent. "It'll just be a pinch and yes, there will be a small amount of blood. Tyler already knows this. Don't worry about it. He's not going to be turned off. He loves you. He's waited this long and he's not going to care. Once the initial pain recedes, the pleasure will be so overwhelming that you'll forget all about it."

Her face contorted. "Are you sure?"

I pulled her into a hug. "I love you, girl. I'm sure." She hugged me back, our sisterhood firmly in place. I was so thankful for the relationship we had, and I almost felt guilty about what I was going to do to her next. I pulled back from the hug. "Now let's go shopping!"

As if just realizing we were already parked, she looked around. I could tell the exact moment she recognized where we were. I saw the panic set in. "Oh, shit!"

An hour later, with an embarrassed Kyla in tow, I left the store with a bag full of things that were sure to make prom night with Chris very memorable.

Chapter 9
Chris

My girl had been super secretive about everything regarding prom. All she would tell me about her dress was that it was black. She figured I needed to know that much to get my tux. Tor was so predictable though, that I'd already planned on black before she told me.

Now that we'd both been eighteen for over six months, we were a little more open with our parents about our intentions. They knew we planned on staying at the hotel for the night. They obviously knew we were having sex. They knew we were leaving for college together in the fall and would have lots of time alone. They knew there was no chance of keeping us apart.

To my surprise, Ty and Kyla were staying the night at the hotel too. I reserved us the rooms and Jim had supplied us with alcohol. This was supposed to be Kyla and Tyler's big night. They were finally going to have sex. I couldn't have been more stoked for Ty, because honestly, I couldn't believe they had waited this long.

Ty and I went to the hotel early to drop off our bags, and anything we needed for the night, while the girls were off getting pampered. I peeked in Tori's bag to see what she had up her sleeve. Inside the bag was a wrapped box with a note on top. I opened the note and read it. *Quit trying to be sneaky. You need to be a good boy and wait until tonight. If you do, I promise to be a very naughty girl. I'm looking forward to my punishment.* Fuck! If that didn't make my dick hard, nothing would. I was inclined to carefully pull the tape back and slip the box out of the wrapping. But I knew Tor. She would know in a heartbeat. I put the box back in her bag and tried to stop thinking about it. Mission impossible, for sure. Now, I was really curious about her plans for the night.

One thing I hoped was on the plan… no condoms. She'd been on birth control for a few months now, but I still suited up. I think we were both nervous about taking that step, especially after her pregnancy

51

scare. Even though missing her period had nothing to do with being pregnant, we were cautious. But I couldn't lie. I was anxious to stick my cock into her warm, wet pussy with nothing between us.

Thinking about not using a condom and the box Tor had left in her bag, I was hard as a rock. At this point, I was willing to say *fuck the dance* and go right to the after-party. I thought about the night and decided Tori and I would come up to the room before the dance for some drinks and a preparty. Yeah, that was an awesome plan.

I locked our room and headed over to Ty's room. He was standing there with his hands on his hips, scanning everything. He looked nervous as fuck.

"You alright, man? You're looking a little green. Cold feet?" I asked.

"Yeah, I'm good. Just don't want to fuck this up for her," he answered.

I totally understood. After the debacle Tori and I had the first time, I wished we had done it this way and not in the back of a truck. "Tori and me, our first time was in the back of my dad's pickup. Not exactly romantic, but memorable. I got an elbow in the eye. That girl's a wild cat when it comes to sex." I tried to laugh it off, even though it was one of my biggest regrets with my girl.

"I feel like a pussy, admitting this…but tonight's gonna be a first for me.

"I kinda figured that out already. Ain't no way a guy who's already had sex, is gonna wait as long as you did for Kyla. I get it though. She's as innocent as they come. Trust me you'll be fine. You're doing this up right," I encouraged. "Just do your thing, man. It ain't that hard. Word of advice?"

"Sure, shoot. I guess it couldn't hurt," Ty answered honestly.

"Don't go for the gold right off the bat. Girls want to feel special, like they're not being used. Pay attention to the details, make her come first. You make her happy, and she'll sure as shit make you happy." I wished I had done that with Tori, but we had more than made up for it since then. I pushed the thoughts aside and decided to bust Ty's balls. "Oh, and Tyler…don't forget to wrap your junk!"

Ty rolled his eyes at me as we headed out toward his Challenger.

I was dressed in my tux, and damn I looked good. I'd gone with a vest, instead of the cummerbund and I knew Tori would approve. I grabbed Tori's corsage of purple roses from the fridge and checked my wallet for the tickets. I was set.

"Are you guys ready?" I asked my mom and dad. They were following me to Tori's house so that they could get pictures.

My mom grabbed a bottle of wine from the fridge, while my dad put his shoes on. "What's that for?" I asked.

My mom smiled sweetly. "Elena and I decided we might as well have some drinks and get to know each other better. I think we're going to be related someday."

I looked at her pointedly. "If I had my way, that would happen sooner than later. However, I know you two," I pointed to my mom and dad, "would probably have a heart attack if we got married before we finished college."

"It's not personal, Chris," my dad explained. "We love Tori, but we don't want you to rush into anything either. Get that degree, and then you two can live happily ever after."

I rolled my eyes at him. "We'll wait, but not too long. As soon as we graduate, we're getting married. It's already been two years. I know what I want and that's not going to change."

We arrived at Tori's, and I couldn't wait to see my girl. I kissed Mrs. Russo on the cheek and shook Mike's hand. This would probably be the last time we'd be super dressed up until our wedding. My mom and dad followed behind me, and Tori's mom wasted no time getting out the wine glasses.

My girl was making me wait, as usual. Every time we went to one of these dances, Tori got all weird about wearing a dress and heels. When she finally made her appearance, my jaw dropped.

"Close your mouth, son." My dad jabbed me in the ribs.

Tori looked exquisite. All the time she had spent worrying about her curves was for nothing. She had matured into those curves and had become a woman right before my eyes. She was beautiful and voluptuous.

She had on a black strapless dress that nearly touched the floor. The entire top of the dress was covered in sequins and there was a split up one side of the skirt that almost reached her hip. Her legs looked a mile long with her strappy heels. Her hair was pulled up in some kind of knot on top of her head, exposing her slender neck, which was adorned with a choker that looked like diamonds. Tori's lips were painted a deep burgundy and her eyes were dark and smoky. She took my breath away.

My mom was the first to speak. "You look beautiful, sweetheart!"

Tori blushed. "Thank you."

I stepped to Tori and wrapped one arm around her waist. I whispered in her ear, "You look sexy as fuck!"

She stared at me from under her eyelashes. "Wait until later," she whispered. "This is just a preview."

My dick stood at attention, and I pulled my coat down to hide the evidence, as Tori and I posed for all the pictures our moms wanted to take. Finally, I had to cut them off. "I think you have enough. We don't want to be late." We were going to be late no matter what because we were making a stop at our room first. That was non-negotiable.

Tori and I made our way out to my truck. I opened the door for her and then looked at what she was wearing. "How are we going to do this?" I asked.

Tori pulled up her dress. "Just give me a little boost," she said. I did and planted her firmly on the seat of my truck.

I ran around to the other side and hopped up in the driver's seat. "I'm sorry," I apologized. "I should have driven my mom's car. It would have been easier for you to get in and out of."

She waved me off. "I love this truck. Some of my favorite memories of you and me, are in your truck. I wouldn't change a thing."

"Come here." I beckoned her with my finger. She scooted along the bench seat until she was next to me. "I love you, Tor. You look beautiful tonight. I want to make a quick pit stop at our room before we head to the dance. Are you okay with that?"

"I am," she answered. "But you're not getting the goods until after the dance. We only get one senior prom. I want to remember all of it. Did you peek in my bag?"

I took a deep breath. "You know I did."

"And is it still wrapped?" she questioned.

"It is."

"Good boy." She patted my leg. "Trust me. It's worth the wait."

When Tori and I arrived at the Hilton, we quickly went to our room. I pulled out the bottle of Absolute. "You want a shot?" I asked.

"Make it a double," she answered.

I poured the vodka into two glasses, and we clinked them together. "This is to the most beautiful girl I have ever seen. One day I'm going to marry you. It might be a while, but never doubt my intentions. I love you more than words can say."

"I love you too, Chris."

I stepped to her and ran my hand up her leg, along the slit of her dress. My hand crept underneath and cupped her ass. "You are so fucking sexy, babe."

She whispered in my ear, "Keep exploring. I think you'll find something sexier."

I didn't know what she meant, but that didn't keep my hand from squeezing her ass. I pushed between her legs and there was nothing but slick skin. The lacey panties, I'd assumed would be there, were missing. But then again, they weren't. I felt them on her ass cheeks, but between her legs, the fabric was missing. "You naughty, naughty girl," I scolded. "Are these crotchless?"

Tori nodded her head. "I bought them especially for you."

"Fuck me," the words came out in an exasperated breath.

"Oh, I plan on it." Tori ran her finger along my bottom lip. "But later. I have plans for us."

All I could think about was that wrapped box in Tori's bag and her pussy being on full display for me. What the hell was in that box?

We headed down to the dance and found our table. Tyler and Kyla were already seated, along with Trevor and Crystal. "Where have you two been? They're about to serve dinner," Kyla scolded.

I let Tori answer. I wasn't sure how much she wanted to tell. "We stopped off in our room first. Did a little pre-partying." Tori winked across the table at Kyla. I guessed we weren't hiding much.

Kyla pursed her lips to contain the smirk behind it. "I should have known." Kyla had really been coming out of her shell lately, but I wondered if she was ready for the night ahead of her.

"You got a room here tonight? So, does that mean the after-party is in your room?" Trevor asked.

"I'd love to invite you," I said. "But tonight, we're having a party for two, if you know what I mean." I raised one eyebrow to send home my message.

"Yeah, I get it," Trevor said with disappointment. "Don't you two ever get enough of each other? Don't you get sick of each other?"

Tori shook her head. "Never."

Tori and I were so addicted to each other, that we had become codependent. Some people would say that was a bad thing. But not for us. We were best friends, lovers, and soulmates. Sure, we fought some, but we couldn't stay away from each other. We were equals in every way, except in the bedroom. That was the only time Tori was submissive. She liked when I took control, made her submit to my wants and desires. I could make her do anything I wanted, but only because she wanted it too.

Honestly, the truth was, that she held all the power. She could bring me to my knees with a single word. It was a give and take. We enjoyed our roles and played them well. I could be rough and dominant with Tori, but at the end of the night, I cherished and worshipped her in every way she deserved. I would always take care of her. Nothing was more important to me.

There were still two empty chairs at our table, and I nearly choked on my water when I saw who was headed for our table. I knew Trevor had reserved our table and that Jason would be sitting with us. What I didn't know, was that Susie was his date. He dragged her behind him as he made his way to their seats.

Next to me, I heard Tori hiss out, "You've got to be fucking kidding me."

I wrapped my arm around her shoulder and leaned into her ear. "Just ignore her."

Tori started to unroll her napkin and silverware. "Seriously, they couldn't give us a sharp knife with our dinner?" She pressed her fingers to the tip of the fork, testing it out. "This should do," she whispered.

I grabbed all her silverware and moved it away from her. Tori scowled at me as I placed a soft kiss on her forehead. I got really close to her and said softly, "I won't be able to fuck you tonight if you go to jail for stabbing her. I'm yours. You're mine. Nothing else matters."

Tori leaned into the crook of my arm. "Make sure she knows that."

Jason and Susie took their seats at our table. "Hey guys," Jason greeted us. Susie gave a little wave but stayed unusually quiet. The reaction at the table was almost comical, as Tori, Kyla, and Crystal all instinctively wrapped their arms around their men. I guess Tori wasn't the only one who felt threatened by Susie.

Kyla was the first one to break the silence. "I didn't know you two were back together."

Susie perked up. "Oh, were not. But we both needed dates and thought, why not?"

Crystal leaned into Trevor. "But you're together for the night, right?"

Susie waved her off. "Oh, it's not serious. We're just here to have a good time, wherever that takes us. We're up for anything."

Tori straightened up and folded her hands in front of her, steepling her fingers. "I shouldn't have to say this, but I think it might be necessary. Your night is not going to take you anywhere near any of our guys. They are off limits. Understood?"

Jason tried to interrupt. "Relax Tori. Susie and I are together. You need to…"

But Tori wasn't finished. I almost stepped in to stop her, but I valued my balls. She held a hand up to silence Jason. "I appreciate your ignorance, but everyone at this table knows her games. I think I speak for all of us, when I say that we will not put up with any shameless flirting, accidental rubbing, or any other shit she likes to pull. We're done. If you don't like those conditions, then you can find somewhere else to sit."

I felt bad for Susie and the ass-ripping she was getting, but I wouldn't say a fucking word. I wasn't stupid. I looked at the other guys, and we were all on the same page. None of us said a word.

"I got it," Susie said. "No worries."

Tori broke out into an obviously fake smile. "Good. Now that we've got that straight, let's have a great night."

I wasn't the only one to let out a sigh of relief. Tyler and Trevor had been holding their breath as well. Jason finally got smart and kept his mouth shut too.

After dinner, the dancing began. Tori was a little restricted in her dress for the type of dancing we usually did, but we made do. I spun her around and dipped her low. The tops of her breasts pushed up in her strapless dress and I kissed the soft skin of her chest. I pulled her back up to me as "Tangled Up in You" by Staind started and I held her close. "I love this song. Think we can dance to this at our wedding?" she asked softly.

"I think it would be perfect," I whispered in her ear. Tori wrapped her arms around my neck. I snaked one arm around her waist and the other went to the slit in her dress. I pushed my hand through the fabric and grasped the back of her thigh, giving it a little squeeze. "Tor... I'm so in love with you. Promise we'll always be this way with each other. I want you to always want me, as much as I want you."

"I'll always want you. You're it for me, Chris," she answered.

I pressed my lips to hers and pushed my tongue inside. I wanted her so bad. I couldn't stop thinking about the box in our room. It taunted me. I needed to know what was inside. I pulled back from her and looked at my watch. It was almost 10:30. "Are you ready to get out of here?" I asked. "I wanna have plenty of time with you."

Tori bit her lip and looked at me from under her long lashes. "Let's go."

I laced my fingers with hers and pulled her out of the ballroom, over to the bank of elevators. We hadn't said good-bye to anyone. All we could think about was each other. The elevator dinged, and the doors opened. I led her in, and we waited for the doors to shut. As soon as they clicked closed, I pushed Tori against the wall, holding her arms above her head with one hand, my eyes locked on hers. I pressed my dick into her stomach, and she moaned. My other hand went to the slit in her dress and pushed it aside. My hand cupped her ass from behind. My fingers moved between her ass cheeks and quickly found her slick, wet pussy that was left uncovered. She was dripping for me, and I pushed two fingers deep inside her. Her eyes rolled back. "Oh, god," she rasped out.

The elevator dinged again signaling our floor. I quickly removed my hand and released her wrists. Tori's face was flushed as I pulled her out and toward our room. My little wild cat was going to get a workout tonight. If we didn't both wake up sore and exhausted, then something was wrong.

I unlocked our room and secured the door behind us as we entered. The dead bolt and "Do Not Disturb" sign were firmly in place. Tori pulled the comforter off the bed as I stalked toward her. I wrapped my arms around her waist from behind and nuzzled into her neck. "You've been a very naughty girl tonight. You've been teasing me. I'm trying to decide how I'm going to handle that."

She wrapped her hands back around my neck and turned her face into mine. "Everything I've done, I've done for you. What do you think my punishment should be?"

I'd been hard all night, but I was rock solid now. How I convinced this woman to be mine, I'd never know. "Will it even be a punishment, if you enjoy it?" I asked. "I've got a million nasty, dirty thoughts running through my mind."

"The dirtier the better. Do you want to know what's in my box?"

"I already know everything I need to know about your box," I assured her.

She turned in my arms and started to laugh. "Not that box, you goofball. The box in my bag."

"You know I do. Is it more naughty stuff?" I asked hopefully.

Tori unwrapped herself from me and walked over to her bag on top of the dresser. She unzipped it and pulled out the box neatly wrapped in black and silver paper. "I wasn't sure what to get, so I was creative," she said walking toward me. "I think you'll find something in here to your liking." Tori placed the box in my waiting hands as I sat on the bed.

"Something tells me that whatever is in this box, will definitely be to my liking." I carefully pulled the paper off and opened it. I pulled back the tissue paper and stared at the contents. "Are you serious?"

Tori simply nodded her head.

I removed the items one by one. A blindfold. Handcuffs wrapped in black velvet. A bottle of lube. A vibrator. A butt plug. And a riding crop? With leather tassels? What. The. Fuck? I was a little overwhelmed. "I… I'm not even sure what to do with some of this stuff," I confessed.

Tori moved the box to the side and sat on my lap. "That's the fun of it. We figure it out together."

I knew I had dirty thoughts, but obviously, my girl was way dirtier. I wasn't opposed to figuring it out. As a matter of fact, I looked forward to it. "Are you okay with this stuff?" I asked. I had pushed her limits before, but the box in front of me provided endless possibilities.

Tori put her hand under my chin and lifted it. She gazed into my eyes. "I trust you completely. You would never hurt me. I trust you to know when it's gone too far. I want to explore this with you. There is no one I trust more. I know I'm safe with you."

And just like that, she handed every bit of her trust over to me. I was going to push her past her limits, but I wouldn't abuse it. The things she had bought… we were going to need more than one night to completely explore them. And a few shots. "Let's have a drink first," I suggested. She nodded. I set her aside and poured us each another double-shot of Absolute. I sat back down, and she sat on my lap.

"To new experiences." She held up her glass.

I clinked my glass with hers and we both downed the alcohol. It burned, but I needed it to do this with her. Because pushing her limits, meant pushing my own too. I took her glass and set it on the nightstand next to mine.

Tori stood from my lap and started to undo my tie, and then the buttons of my vest and shirt, as I stared up at her. "Shall we begin?" she asked, pushing my shirt off my shoulders.

I shrugged out of my shirt and vest. "Yes." I was so fucking turned on by her. I grabbed Tori's hand and turned her around. I grasped her wrists in one hand behind her back and pulled the clip from her hair. It spilled down over her shoulders and back as she shook it out. I wrapped my hand in her hair and pulled gently. Her head tilted back, and I whispered in her ear, "If it becomes too much, all you have to say is 'stop'. Do you understand?" Tori nodded. "Say the words," I insisted.

She quickly slipped into her role of submissive. "I understand," she rasped out.

I let go of her hair. "Good." I ran my hand through her silky locks and kissed the side of her neck. "Do you have any idea how much I want to fuck you? I don't want to just fuck you. I want to own you. You're mine."

"I'm yours," she repeated.

"Always. There will never be anyone else." I kissed her neck, still holding her wrists.

"Never." Her words came out breathless.

"I love this dress on you," I said. "However, I think I'm going to like it more sitting on the floor. But, for now, it stays." I released her and went to the items spread across the bed. "What shall I try first?" I picked up the blindfold and snapped the elastic. "Come here," I ordered.

Tori didn't hesitate as she stepped toward me. "Good girl." She closed her eyes. I stretched the elastic out and slipped it over her head, blinding her. "Get on your knees."

Tori pulled her dress up and kneeled on the floor. She looked like an angel before me. Her hair draped over her shoulders in loose waves. She licked her lips in anticipation. I stepped in front of her and undid the button and zipper on my pants. "First, I want to fuck that dirty mouth of yours. Do you want my cock in your mouth?" I asked.

"Yes. I want your cock deep in my throat," she answered.

I pushed my pants down enough for my dick to spring free, it was aching and needed her mouth. "Put your hands behind your back and open your mouth." She did exactly as she was told. I ran my fingers along her jaw and stepped forward, gripping my dick in my own hand, and jacking it as I anticipated her sweet mouth. One more step and I was in her mouth. I groaned as she wrapped her lips around me. Her tongue tasted me, teased me, worked its magic along my shaft. I put my hand on the back of her head and gently pushed her forward to take me deeper. "Fuck, that's good," I groaned. My hips started to thrust in and out of her mouth. She may have trusted me, but I trusted her too.

I hit the back of her throat and I held her head there. "Deeper, Tori." Her throat opened and took me deeper. She swallowed me down and she strangled my dick with every pulse of her throat. "I'm gonna come in your mouth, Tor. Take me. Take it all!"

And, God, she did. She gave everything she had and took it all from me. I threw my head back and the muscles in my neck strained.

"Fuuuuuuck!" I roared, pouring everything into her and she swallowed it all like the good girl she was.

I slowly pulled out and kneeled before her. I pulled the blindfold up and kissed her lips. "Are you okay, baby?" Although I wanted to dominate her during sex, I never wanted to hurt her.

She nodded. "My knees..."

"I'm sorry," I apologized, pullin her to her feet. "You don't know what you do to me. I'm going to take care of you. It's your turn."

"I'm throbbing for you," she admitted. And even though I had just come, the blood rushed back to my dick, and I was hard again.

"Tori, you are so beautiful. I'm going to worship you, like you deserve. It's going to get dirty. But you knew that. This isn't just for me. I promise you'll get what you need."

She kissed me. I could taste my cum on her tongue. I didn't care. We were one. I would give my life for her. In a heartbeat. No questions asked.

I backed her to the bed. "I'm not ready for you to take that dress off yet, but I'm ready for what's underneath it." I gripped the fabric in my hands and gathered it towards her waist. Her lace panties covered everything, except the slick skin between her legs.

"You like?" she asked.

"Fuck, baby. I love it. I can't believe that's been waiting for me all night. Tell me what you want," I insisted, as I pushed her back on the bed.

She let out a little giggle as she fell back onto the sheets. "We didn't have desert at the dance. I would think you'd be starving by now."

"I am." I grabbed her thighs and brought her to my face as I kneeled at the edge of the bed. Her panties were so fucking sexy. It was like a forbidden pleasure. I buried my face in her pussy and ate. My tongue ran over every inch of her wetness. She was so soaked that it smeared all over my chin. I couldn't have given two shits. I stuck my tongue deep inside her, lapping her up as she squirmed beneath me. Her legs were over my shoulders, and they wrapped around my head. Her heels pressed into the back of my head, pulling me in tighter. I reached over on the bed and grabbed the vibrator. "Have you tried this?"

"Only once," she moaned out. "I had to make sure it was worth the money."

"Was it?" I questioned.

"Every penny," she exclaimed.

I turned it on to the highest setting. The device vibrated in my hand. I slowly pushed the head of it into her pussy, while my mouth clamped down on her clit. I pushed it in further, burying it deep inside her. I ran my tongue over her clit and then sucked it deep into my mouth. She writhed on the bed and grabbed the sheets, trying to find something to ground her. "I'm gonna come, Chris. Fuck! It's so good. Don't stop!"

I didn't. I sucked her clit long and hard. I wanted her to fall apart. I moved the vibrator around inside her, hoping to hit every hot spot.

I pulled back and gazed at her laying on the bed in front of me. Her head was thrown back and her eyes were closed, as her back arched off the mattress. I moved the vibrator in and out of her, then slid it through her folds and over her clit. "Oh my... Chris...mmmm. Pleeeease," she begged.

"Please what? Tell me what you want, baby." I loved when she begged. I loved seeing her like this. So needy and wanting everything I could give her.

"Please... make me come. I'm so close. I want your mouth on me. I need it." Her words were breathless and raspy.

"I'm gonna make you come so hard, Tor. Over and over again, before this night is over." I fucked her with the vibrator and sucked hard on her clit. Her hips bucked off the bed, as she threw her arm over her mouth and screamed into it. Her body stilled except for her chest that rose and fell with her panting.

"That was intense," she gasped.

I crawled up next to her and pushed her hair out of her face. "You're so beautiful when you come." I kissed her swollen lips and our tongues tangled together. I hovered over her and caged her in with my arms. Her arms wrapped around my neck. "I should take this dress off you, so it doesn't get all wrinkled."

"That would be a good idea," she agreed. I pulled her up off the bed. She turned her back to me and lifted her hair. "Unzip me?"

I ran my fingers along the soft skin of her shoulders and down her exposed back. I slowly slid the zipper down her back and over her ass. The dress fell to the floor, and she turned to face me. She wore a lace corset, held together by a red ribbon that wove up the front and tied just below her breasts and those fucking sexy lace panties. The lace was sheer, and I could see her nipples through the fabric. "Do you like it?"

She was perfection from the sparkling choker around her neck to the strappy heels that adorned her feet. She wore more makeup than usual, but it wasn't overdone. The loose waves of her dark hair covered her shoulders and grazed the tops of her tits. I don't think she had ever looked more beautiful. I was speechless as I stared at her. "Chris?"

I snapped myself out of it. "You're gorgeous, Tori."

She stepped out of the dress pooled at her feet and put her hand on my chest. Her honey eyes peered up at me. "You're still wearing pants." Her hands pushed them over my hips. I slipped off my shoes and finished removing them, then picked her dress up off the floor and hung it over a chair.

My dick strained against my boxer briefs, as my eyes traveled up and down her body. "Go lay on the bed, baby." She narrowed her eyes at me. "I need to remember this." I reached in the pocket of my pants that were on the floor and pulled out my phone.

She started laughing. "Seriously?"

"I've never been more serious." She went to the bed and laughed as she struck pose after pose. She was perfect. I took a ton of pictures, then crawled up on top of her and clicked a few of her tits and one between her legs. I kneeled back and scanned through the pictures. *Fuck me!*

"If those end up on the internet, you're dead," she joked.

That was not funny! Not one little bit. "No one is ever seeing these. Ever!" I laid next to her and held my phone up, so she could see the screen. "Look how fucking sexy you are. I don't know whether to strip you down or leave you as you are." I stared at the screen.

"We have the whole night. You can strip me down later. All the important stuff is accessible."

Our heads were on the pillow, eyes locked to one another. I ran my fingers down her face. "Did you like the vibrator?"

She nodded slightly. "Yes. It was different, but good."

"I'm afraid of hurting you," I confessed. Yeah, I wanted to have kinky, dirty sex with her, but I never wanted to hurt her. Not in any way that didn't lead to pleasure. "We don't need to use any of that other stuff."

"You won't hurt me. I trust you. I want to try this with you. If we decide we hate it, then we dump it all in the trash. But we'll never know if we don't try."

I pushed her hair back. "I love you, Tori. You'll tell me if it's too much, right?"

"I'll tell you," she promised. "I love you, Chris. No condoms tonight. I've been on birth control for months now. I wanna feel you and only you. I want your cum inside me. I want all of you."

"You already have all of me," I assured her. "I can't wait to feel your pussy on my cock. I want my cum dripping between your legs."

"You're making me horny. Give me your phone." I grabbed it off the bed and handed it to her. She started scanning through my music until she found what she was looking for. "Closer" by Nine Inch Nails started playing and I groaned. This song made me want to fuck her. Bad. She knew it too. It was one of my weaknesses.

I hovered above her and started kissing her plump lips. She bit my bottom lip and then ran her tongue along it. "Touch me," she whispered. "Don't be gentle. I wanna feel you." I kissed down her neck and ran my tongue over the swells over her breasts. Her hard nipples poked through the lace, and I took one between my teeth, gently biting and nipping it. Tori's back arched as a moan escaped her lips. "Yesss," she hissed. I nipped at her other nipple, biting the hard tip.

I crawled down her body to her ankles and pulled her to the edge of the bed. I flipped her over quickly, so she was face down into the mattress. Tori went to push herself up with her arms, but the handcuffs caught my eye. "I don't think so," I growled. I grabbed her one arm roughly and pulled it behind her back. I reached for the handcuffs and clicked one over her wrist, then pulled her other arm to join it. She lifted her head from the bed and eyed me over her shoulder. I gathered her hair in my hand and pulled her head back, as I spoke in her ear. "You asked for this. You made me lose control."

"I'm not complaining," she sassed. "Fuck me."

"So impatient," I tsked. I was going to get creative with her. Why had she bought the plug if she didn't want me to use it on her? It was something we had never considered before. Or maybe she had? It turned me on. Another forbidden pleasure.

I pushed it aside for now and grabbed the vibrator. I slid one arm under her hips and rubbed it along the front of her panties over her clit. "Oh god...." After working her over good, I pulled it away and pushed her chest to the mattress.

"Lift your hips," I ordered. She pushed her hips back and up, putting her drenched pussy on display. I ran my finger through her wetness and brought it to my lips. "You are perfection." I slowly pushed the vibrator inside her, letting it pulse as she squirmed on the bed. "You like that?" Her breathing increased, making her pant. "Answer me, Tori."

"Yes. I like it!"

"More than my dick?" I asked, pulling it from inside her.

"Never!"

"Good girl." I tapped her ass. Pushing my boxer briefs down, I kicked them to the side and palmed my dick. Her eyes were glued to me. There was something erotic and sexy about her watching me jack myself. "You want this?" I asked.

"You know I do," she rasped. "I need to feel you, Chris."

I stepped forward and pushed the head into her dripping pussy. Oh, my god. She felt like heaven. I'd been inside her dozens of times, but nothing compared to feeling just her, with nothing between us. I pushed a little further and groaned. She was going to kill me. I finally pushed all the way in, burying myself balls deep. I pulled back and ran my hand from her hips up her back as I pushed back in. "You feel like heaven, baby." I grabbed her shoulder and used it as leverage as I leaned over her and pushed into her pussy over and over again. I'd never felt anything like this. There was no way we were ever going back to using condoms.

I wondered what it would feel like to fuck her with the plug in. Would it just be good for her, or would it be better for me too? There was only one way to find out. I pulled my dick out and ripped her panties down her legs. Her sweet ass stuck up in the air, waiting for me. I reached for the lube and uncapped it, then let it drip down between her ass cheeks. I ran my thumb through it and grazed over her sweet pucker. "I've never touched you here before. Are you sure you can handle it?"

"I wanna try," she breathed out.

"Let me know if I hurt you."

Tori nodded her head. "I'm ready."

I rubbed my thumb through the lube and circled her. Then slowly pushed it inside. Her body tensed, and she was so tight. "I think you need to relax a little if this is going to work," I told her. I rubbed my other hand along her lower back, and I felt her body ease. "I'm gonna push a little further baby." I pushed in more and then slowly slid out and back in. "Are you alright?"

"Yes. It feels good. But…can you undo the cuffs? My shoulders are starting to hurt."

Fuck! "I'm sorry baby," I apologized. I removed my thumb and carelessly wiped it on the sheets. I quickly found the keys and undid the cuffs around her wrists, throwing them to the side. I ran my fingers over her wrists gently as she pulled her hands apart. I rubbed her shoulders. "Better?"

"Yes. Thank you." She stretched her arms out in front of her like a cat. My wild cat. "Better." Tori turned her head and gazed over her shoulder at me. "Continue."

"Are you sure?" I questioned.

"Yes," she smiled at me. Thank God, because my dick was all kinds of hard and having my thumb in her ass just turned me on more.

I grabbed the lube again and dripped more down between her cheeks. I picked up the plug and stared at it. It wasn't that big, but bigger than my finger. I ran it through the lube and held the tip to her, then pushed slowly. She clenched again, and I ran my other hand along her back. "Relax. It'll be easier." Tor let out a deep breath and her body sagged. I pushed in further, pulled it out a little, then pushed it in the all the way. "How does that feel?"

"Good, but full," she gasped. "Now fuck me. I want to feel your cock inside me. Please, Chris… don't make me wait."

I loved when she fucking begged me for my cock. I would give her exactly what she wanted. I stepped behind her and eased in, "Shit, Tor. You feel super tight on my cock." I started slow, the feeling indescribable. Her pussy was so tight on my dick, but she was so wet, that I slid right in. I held it there, letting both of us adjust to this new feeling. Between not using a condom and the plug, I was never going to be the same. "You feel so perfect. It's fucking amazing, babe."

"I know. I can feel everything. Please, baby…"

I started moving slowly, but that didn't last long. She felt so good. I picked up the pace and thrust into her again and again, pushing as deep as I could go. Sex was always phenomenal with Tori, but this just kicked it up another notch. I grabbed for the vibrator and slipped it between her and the bed, holding it on her clit. I held her hip with my other hand and continued to pound into her from behind. "Oh fuck, Chris… I'm gonna come so hard!" Her breathing became erratic, and I could feel her pussy start to squeeze my dick.

"Come Tori! Come for me, now!" I ordered.

Tori buried her head into the mattress and let out a scream. Her pussy was like a vice, strangling me. I thrust in harder and harder. I wasn't going to last much longer. My balls pulled tight, and my muscles tensed as my orgasm built. "Fuuuck!" I roared. Electric currents zinged through my body and left me drained as I poured everything into her. She was so slippery, with my cum inside her. And it felt good, like I was marking her as mine. Forever. And she *would* be mine forever. There was no doubt.

I slowly pulled out of her and draped myself over her back. "Wow!

Chapter 10
Tori

Chris went to the bathroom and brought back a warm washcloth. "Plug in or out?" he asked.

"Leave it in," I said.

He nodded and wiped me down, cleaning off all the lube. "Better?"

"Yes. Thanks, baby."

He threw the washcloth to the side and flipped me on my back. "Come up and lay by me," he said. He crawled up and laid on the pillows. I snuggled up next to him and rested my head on his chest, listening to his heartbeat. Chris ran his fingers through my hair. "So, what's the verdict?"

I leaned up and kissed him, "The verdict is that you never disappoint. I loved every minute with you and there is no one I would rather try and share this with."

"Tori, you felt so tight with that in your ass. It turned me on. I like being filthy, dirty with you, but I just want to be us too. You know what I mean?"

"Yes. I would never change what we do or how we are together. But it was fun to mix it up a little, don't you think?" I asked. I hoped I didn't push him too far tonight with my box of naughty toys, but I wouldn't change it. I loved exploring things with him. The plug in my ass reminded me of how good it was and how amazing we were together.

He kissed my lips. "You are so fucking sexy. I love everything we do. I wouldn't change a thing."

I rubbed my hand along his hard chest. "Chris?"

"Yeah, baby?"

"I love you. Thank you for loving me. For being everything I never knew I wanted. I can't imagine my life without you. I just want you to know that you're my whole world." I rested my head back on his chest and closed my eyes. When we started dating, I didn't know that it would turn into this. This feeling of complete love and trust. This feeling of never wanting to be anywhere else than in his arms. When I wasn't with him, I ached.

Chris kissed the top of my head, "I always knew you were made for me. Realistically, how soon do think we can get married? I don't know if I can wait four more years, Tor. I can't imagine loving you more than I love you right now."

I breathed out a sigh of frustration. "You know our parents would have a fit, right? I'm not going anywhere. I'll always be yours. I don't need a ring to be completely committed to you."

"I know, baby. But I need you to know, that our parents are the only thing holding me back. You're all I'll ever want. I can't wait to make you my wife." His arm pulled me in tighter.

"I want to be your wife more than anything, but I don't even know what I'm going to do with my life. I need to have a job, Chris. I can't have you support me. It wouldn't be right," I insisted.

"Baby, we're a team. I would support you. We'll figure it out. I'll wait. But just know… it's not what I want. I want you with me, every minute of every day for the rest of my life." His fingers ran through my hair and caressed the side of my face.

"I want that too," I whispered.

He pulled me up and started kissing me. It was soft and seductive. He rolled me to my back. I still had on the corset and my heels. Chris decided to finally rid me of the corset. He pulled on the bow that sat beneath my breasts. Once it was untied, he pulled his fingers through the laces from my breasts to my stomach. Once they were finally undone, he pushed the corset apart and freed me. He took one nipple in his mouth and sucked me gently, then moved to the other, giving it the same attention.

He kissed down between my breasts to my stomach. I put my hands between my hips, over my stomach. "Don't look at my scar," I begged. It had faded some, but to me it was still red and ugly. I didn't like him looking at it.

Chris gently removed my hands and kissed along the red line. "I love you, Tori. Scar and all." He kissed down my legs and unbuckled my shoes. "This is how I love you. Totally naked for me."

He crawled back up my body and made love to me. It was soft and gentle. I loved him so much, I felt like my heart was going to explode. The plug in me, made the sex even better. I could feel every long, hard inch of him.

I writhed on the bed, as he made me come yet again. I couldn't imagine sharing this with anyone else. I was always so wet and ready for him. He made my toes curl and my back arch with every thrust.

His hand traveled to my neck and wrapped around it. I closed my eyes and bent my head back. He squeezed tightly as his mouth traveled to my tits. He worshipped my body, and I got lightheaded as his hand tightened around my neck. It was another high. Another form of control he had over me. "I'm gonna come, again," I whispered. His hand loosened around my neck, as I fell over the edge, and he did too. We came together, and I could feel him leaking out from between our bodies. He had finally marked me as his. And I would always be just that… his. There was no question that we belonged together.

When we both came down, I was exhausted. Our night together had exceeded all my expectations. "You wanna take a bath together," he asked.

"Ummm. That sounds nice," I answered sleepily.

"I'll go get the tub ready." He kissed me. "Turn over a sec." I did, and he pulled the plug from me. Chris smirked at me as he walked away. He went to the bathroom, and I heard the tub running.

God, I loved this man! He was everything I ever wanted. He returned to me, lifted me up like a child and cradled me to his chest as I wrapped my arms around his neck. I was all too happy to let him carry me. He set me on my feet outside the large tub and waited for me to get in.

I dipped a toe in. The water was warm and welcoming. I stepped in completely and settled into the middle of the tub. Chris stepped in behind me and pulled me to his chest. I leaned back against him and sighed. "This is perfect."

Chris wrapped his arms around my stomach and rested his head into the crook of my neck. "It is perfect. I can't wait to lay in bed with you and when we wake up, I'm going to make love to you again."

We went to bed that night wrapped around each other. I was warm and content. Chris was my own personal heating blanket. My naked body molded to his as I drifted off to sleep.

I woke to soft kisses running along the side of my face and down my neck. My lips curled into a smile. "Good morning." I stretched out and his mouth went right to my tits. He rubbed and sucked and nipped at me.

He released my nipple with a pop of his mouth. "Good morning, beautiful. I know it's early, but I haven't had breakfast yet and I'm starved."

I giggled as he kissed down my stomach and between my legs. My laughter stopped and was replaced with a moan the moment he pulled my clit into his mouth. "Oh, god…" I writhed on the bed. He pulled one of my legs over his shoulder and then the other. His hands came under my ass and lifted me to his mouth. He feasted and feasted, until I could take no more. I fisted his hair and pushed his face into me as I shattered. He released me, and I sunk down into the mattress panting.

Chris quickly flipped me over and pulled me to my knees. He ran his hand along my back and pushed my chest to the sheets. "God, you're perfect like this. When I marry you, I'm gonna do this to you every morning before work."

"I can't wait," I gasped out.

He ran his fingers through my drenched pussy and pushed them inside. "You're all mine, baby. Say it, Tori. Tell me you're mine."

"I'm yours. You'll be the only one to fuck me. Ever."

"Damn right, I will be!" He replaced his fingers with his dick. His hands gripped my hips as he thrust into me faster and faster. I pushed back into him just as hard. I was sure I would have bruises on my hips, but I didn't give a shit. All I cared about was the pleasure he was bringing me.

He slowed and wrapped his arms around my stomach. Keeping himself inside me, he pulled me up so that my back was against his chest. His one hand caressed my breasts, and the other went to my clit. I wrapped my arms around the back of his head and tilted my head to lean on his shoulder. He kissed my neck as I sank down onto him. I found my rhythm and fucked him as he rubbed me in all the right places. I loved this angle. He felt so good inside of me. It was intimate and sensual.

The thing about Chris was, I never knew what to expect. He could be controlling and dominant one minute, and then gentle and tender the next.

"I'm gonna come, baby," he whispered in my ear.

"Me too," I whispered back.

"Come with me, Tor. Squeeze my dick with your pussy. I want my cum deep inside you."

His dirty words pushed me over the edge, and I came hard. I could feel myself pulsing around him. He grabbed my hips and pushed up into me. I felt him tense as he came. I pushed my hips down into him as hard as I could and clenched around him. "Fuck, baby, I can't get enough of you."

"I don't want you to ever get enough of me. I want you to always want me," I confessed.

Chris ran his hands through my hair. "I'll always want you, Tori. You're my girl."

We laid down on the bed and held each other. Chris pulled the sheet up to cover us and I snuggled into him. "You're starting work on Monday, right?" I asked.

"Yeah," he answered. "They're paying me good money, so I can't really complain. Plus, it will help me get a job when I graduate college. If I work at General Motors every summer, I'm basically guaranteed a job. We'll need that security if we want to get married right away."

"Will you be able to get time off to go up north with me?" I asked.

"We'll be able to do weekends for sure and I think I'll be able to squeeze a week in for us," he answered. "Is Mike gonna be cool with you taking time off?"

I was going to be working for Mike at his repair shop. I would be doing secretarial stuff—answering phones and making appointments. "Yeah. He's cool with whatever I want. I'm kind of spoiled in that regard." I tapped my fingers on Chris's chest. "I wish I knew what I wanted to do for a career. I'm jealous that you already have a plan. I feel like I should already have a plan too."

Chris kissed my head. "You'll figure it out, babe. Quit stressing. You have time." He kept telling me that, but I didn't feel that way. I needed to have a direction. I really wanted to pursue photography, but there weren't many jobs I could do with it. I would never let Chris carry the financial burden of supporting us. I needed to get serious and soon.

Chris ran his fingers along my forehead, smoothing out the wrinkles. "You're doing it again," he stated. I stared at him like I didn't know what he was talking about. "You're stressing. I think I'm going to have to fuck you again. That way you won't be able think."

Homecoming night flashed in my mind. I had ruined it that night, but I wanted to make up for it now. "Shower sex?" I questioned.

He got a sexy smile, that showed off his dimples. "You read my mind. Give me a few to refuel, and then we'll go get all wet together."

"What time are we meeting Kyla and Tyler for breakfast?" I asked. I knew he had told me, but honestly, I think I had sex brain. I could barely remember my own name, let alone what time we were having breakfast.

"Not until ten-thirty. We have time," Chris tapped me on the nose.

I looked over at the clock on the nightstand. It was only seven-thirty. "I guess we do have time." I closed my eyes. I was so tired from last night and waking up early this morning. "Can you set an alarm for an hour?" I asked. "I just need a little more sleep."

"Sure, baby," Chris kissed my forehead, and I was out like a light.

I woke to the sound of water running in the bathroom. "You didn't start without me, did you?" I shouted so he could hear me over the running water.

I heard the water turn off. Chris leaned against door, wearing only his boxer briefs. "Nope. I was just brushing my teeth. You didn't think I would miss out on fucking you in the shower, did you?"

"Just checking." I smiled at him. I pushed my messy hair out of my face. I was sure I looked like a wreck, but I didn't even care. All I knew was I felt thoroughly fucked. Yet, I was still ready for one more round with this gorgeous man. "Do you know how much I love waking up with you?"

He came over and sat on the edge of the bed and rubbed my back. "I think I have an idea. Because if you love me, half as much as I love you..." He faded off and kissed me. "Come on. Let's go shower."

He held out his hand for me. I took it and he led me to the bathroom. He turned on the shower, while I looked in the mirror. There were purple bruises on my hips, my hair was a mess, and my makeup was smudged under my eyes. "Ugh! You must really love me, because this is downright scary," I said, trying to tame my hair.

He smirked at me in the mirror. "You know why I love you looking like that?" he asked.

"Hmmm?"

Chris wrapped his arms around my waist and set his head on my shoulder as I looked at him in the mirror. "Because I did that to you."

"Yes, you did." I kissed him on the cheek. "Let me brush my teeth and I'll join you in a minute."

Chris released me and stepped into the steamy shower. I quickly brushed my teeth and wiped my face. I opened the shower door to find him stroking himself. The sight of it, got me wet. I felt the throbbing between my legs as I watched him.

"You just gonna watch me or are you coming in?" he asked.

I stepped into the shower and placed my hands over his. We rubbed his cock together and then I went to my knees. I took him in my mouth. I slowly sucked him up and down, using my lips and tongue to please him. Chris's hands went to the back of my head as he pumped into my mouth. "God Tori, your mouth is amazing. But I want to come in your pussy, not your mouth."

The words he said turned me on. I was so filled with need I could barely stand it. I released my mouth, and he pulled me to my feet.

He flipped me around and pushed me against the wall. "First you're gonna come for me." My hands, breasts and cheek were pressed against the cold tile. "Spread your legs," he demanded. I obeyed and was rewarded with his fingers pushing into me. "Fuck, Tor, you're drenched. I love the way your body responds to me." He pulled his fingers out and started rubbing my clit.

Chris leaned in close to my ear. "Do you like when I talk dirty to you, baby?" I nodded my head against the tile. "You love when I finger fuck you, when I eat your pussy, when I stick my dick inside of you?"

"Yes," I murmured. I couldn't think. All I could do was feel. "Please," I begged. Chris increased his pace on my clit and the waves of pleasure racked my body, from my head down to my toes. My legs felt weak, as I leaned against the wall. "I don't think I can stand."

"You don't have to." Chris flipped me around, so my back was against the wall. He put his hands under my ass and picked me up in one fluid motion. "Wrap your legs around me." I did, and he lowered me onto his hard cock. My arms wrapped around his neck, and he pushed me against the wall. His muscular arms lifted me up and down on his dick. I squeezed him tighter with my legs. My clit rubbed along is hard abs. Fuck this was good! I felt myself building towards another orgasm. "Chris...fuck me harder. I'm gonna come again. Harder, Chris!" He lifted me up and slammed me down on his dick. The water poured over us, making his abs so slippery as I rubbed up against them. Just a little bit more and I would be there.

Chris threw his head back and roared as I came around him. His sped up the pace and then stilled as he poured everything into me. I looked down on him, as he held me against the wall. He was breathing hard. I kissed his lips, as I unwrapped my legs from around him. He gently set me on the floor and leaned against the wall with one hand above my head. "That was fucking amazing," he panted.

"I'm sad," I confessed. I stuck out my bottom lip and pouted like a child.

Chris's eyes popped open. "What? Why?"

"Because I don't want this to end. And now we have to go back to reality."

He cupped my face. "I know. But the reality is that we have our whole lives to do this, and I plan on doing it forever." He kissed me passionately and wrapped me in his arms. I don't know how I got so lucky, to have this man so madly in love with me. How we were going to wait four more years to get married was beyond me.

The next day, Kyla and I were meeting the guys at the beach. I suggested we get there early so we could catch some rays. That was my excuse, but the truth was I wanted to get the dirt on their first night together.

I picked Kyla up and waited patiently for her to say something. Anything about losing her V card. She had a lot to say about prom, but I didn't care about that. I wanted to know about their night after the dance. We got to the beach, and I parked my beetle. I thought she would be dying to tell me something, but so far nothing.

We found the perfect spot on the beach and laid out our towels. Kyla and I plopped down. I turned my head and stared at her from behind my sunglasses.

"What?" she asked innocently.

"Did you chicken out?" I accused.

She got an embarrassed smile on her face and her neck started to turn red. "No."

I slapped her on the shoulder. "You bitch! You're holding out on me. Start spilling."

Kyla threw her hands up over her face. "What do you want to know?"

"Aaah… everything!" I could tell I was going to have to prod to get her to say anything. "Come on. I've told you all kinds of shit. There's nothing you can tell me, that I haven't already done."

"I can't!" she practically yelled. "It's too embarrassing."

I was getting frustrated. "It's not embarrassing. It's sex. Want me to tell you everything I let Chris do to me last night? All those toys we bought…"

"No! I'm still processing sex with no toys. I don't think I could handle it," she said hiding her face.

I pulled her hands away. "Okay. Let's try this. I'll ask you questions and then you can fill in the details."

Kyla huffed. "Fine." She got a little smile on her face. I knew she wanted to tell. "Ask away."

"Did you give him a blow job?" I asked.

"Yes." I motioned with my hand for her to continue. "And he was really big." She winced. "I accidently nicked him with my teeth, but he was really patient with me. He didn't make me feel bad about it. And… I want to do it again… and again." She smirked.

Finally, I had gotten her talking. "Did he..." I didn't want to embarrass her too much, "you know… in your mouth?"

Kyla shook her head. "He said it was about me, not him. He was more interested in making me feel good." She closed her eyes, as if remembering. "And boy, did he make me feel good. Now I know why you like sex so much."

"Did he go down on you? Make you come with his tongue?" I pressed.

She smiled over at me and nodded her head. "And it was soooo good."

I clapped my hands excitedly. "I'm so happy for you. How many times did you guys do it?"

She started to count on her fingers and then gave up. "It was more like one long marathon, but I would say at least four."

"And how do you feel today?"

"Sore, but unbelievably happy."

I heard Tyler's car pull up, and the doors slam shut. "Guys are here," I said. "Put your sunglasses on. We can't let them know we were talking about this. It'll be our secret."

We laid back on our towels and tried our best to look innocent. Epic fail! They knew immediately what we were up to, probably because they were doing the same.

Monday, I started work at Mike's repair shop. I dressed in a cute pair of capris and a sleeveless blouse. I was going to be working in the reception area, dealing with the customers.

I walked in and went right to Mike's office. I gave a little knock and peeked my head inside. "Morning," I said.

Mike put down the paperwork in his hand. "Hey, sweetie. Come on in. Ready for your first day?"

I sighed as I sat in the seat across from his desk. "Yes. Thank you for giving me this job. I don't know much about all this stuff," I waved my hand around, "but I promise to work hard and learn."

"I know you will, honey. I'm not worried. You'll be fine," he assured me. "Come on. I'll show you around."

I stood and followed him to the reception area. "This is where you'll spend most of your time." Mike had done a nice job making it look inviting and comfortable. Most people dropped their cars off, but some decided to wait. It had comfy chairs, a couple of TVs, lots of magazines sitting out, and a nice coffee station.

He walked over to one of the desks where an attractive woman with long blond hair pulled up into a ponytail sat. "This is Courtney. She'll help you learn the ropes."

Courtney stood and thrusted her hand forward. "Hi, Tori. It's nice to finally meet you. Mike talks about you all the time." She gave me a warm smile and I instantly liked her.

I shook her hand, "Nice to meet you. You'll have to be patient with me. I don't know much about this stuff."

She waved me off. "Oh, it's easy. You'll be a pro in no time."

Mike placed his hand on my back. "I'll show you the rest of the place."

I followed him around as he explained everything to me. The actual shop was a lot cleaner than I expected. In all the years Mike owned this place, I had only been here a handful of times, usually to get a tune-up on my beetle. I was impressed with everything I saw.

No wonder Mike was able to support us so well. This business was obviously successful. My mom worked a few part-time jobs over the years, but we primarily relied on Mike's income. I wondered if my mom would work more now that I was going away to college. She'd always been around when I was growing up. I never worried about an absentee mother. She'd already been hinting around at how much she was going to miss me. I was going to miss her too.

After my tour, I headed back up front to find Courtney. She spent the morning showing me everything I would need to know.

"So, how long have you worked here?" I asked her.

Courtney pursed her lips and looked at the ceiling. "Like six years."

"Wow! That's long time. How old are you?"

"I'm twenty-five," she answered. "I started when I was nineteen. My dad knows Mike and he got me this job. I didn't go to college, so this was perfect for me. And Mike's a great boss. He pays me well too. It's better than waitressing."

"Mike's a great guy," I confirmed. "Are you ready for lunch? I'm gonna run over to Jimmy John's. Do you want something?"

"That would be awesome." She gave me her order and then I went to find Mike.

I peeked in his office. "Do you want something from Jimmy John's? I'm gonna run over there if it's all right."

Mike smiled at me. "It's fine. Can you get me a Turkey Tom?" he asked. Then he reached in his pocket to grab his wallet. "It's on me," he said.

I waved my hand at him. "I'm getting lunch for both Courtney and me. I got it."

"Nonsense. I'll buy you girls lunch." Mike pulled some money from his wallet and slid it across his desk. "My treat."

I picked up the money and waved it at him. "This wasn't part of the deal."

He smiled at me. "I'm just glad you're here, sweetheart."

My first day at the shop was great. Courtney showed me everything I needed to know. She was super sweet, and I could see us being more than co-workers. We could be friends.

I texted Chris when I left the shop to see when he would be finished for the day.

Tori: How was your day?
Chris: Not done yet. Call you later.
Tori: K. Luv U.

I drove home from Mike's shop feeling kind of shitty. Would this be our life? I would work some crappy-ass part-time job, while Chris worked long days and came home exhausted. This wasn't the 1960's. Yeah, I learned some cooking from his mom, but I was in no way ready to be a homemaker. I wanted to work. To earn decent money and contribute to our financial security.

I got home and pulled out my laptop. I pulled up Western Michigan's website and started looking at the programs they offered. I had to figure something out. I clicked on the journalism link. After working on yearbook for the last four years, I wanted to do something in communications. Writing, designing, photographing... but I just couldn't figure out what I would do with it. How could I take something I loved and make it into a career?

I felt like everyone else already knew who they were and what they were doing. Chris was going to be an engineer. Kyla was going into graphic design. And Tyler... he was probably going to end up playing pro football. Me? I didn't have a clue. I felt like a loser. Chris deserved better. I never wanted him to feel like he had to take care of me.

Chapter 11
Chris

I shut off my computer and looked at my watch. Fuck! It was already seven. Almost everyone was gone, except for Amanda. She was working here for the summer too. Since we were low on the totem pole, we always got stuck staying late and finishing up last minute details.

I'd only been back here for three weeks, and already was feeling stressed. I didn't mind the work, but the hours were killing me. I shouldn't have cared because more hours meant more money, but I missed my girl. By the time I got home, I was wiped out and had to be back by seven the next morning.

I watched as Amanda shut down her computer and grabbed her purse. She walked toward me, and stopped at my cubicle, leaning on the half-wall. "You wanna grab something to eat?" she asked.

I shook my head. "Nah. I just want to go home and crash." I grabbed my bag, and we walked out together. "These hours are killing me," I said, trying to make small talk.

"I know what you mean," she answered. "But it's all working toward something better, right? A lot of people would kill to intern for the Big Three. Especially people like us, who don't have that much experience." She smiled and shrugged her shoulders.

"True," I said.

"Maybe, we can go out one night after work. Grab something to eat," she suggested.

"Maybe," I said as I clicked the lock on my truck. "See ya tomorrow." I opened my truck and jumped inside. I was so damn tired I could barely keep my eyes open. I was trying to work and see Tori every night. Bottom line was, I needed more sleep.

My phone buzzed in the cup holder. I picked it up and smiled. Tori's face flashed across the screen. "Hi, baby," I answered.

"Hey," she said. "Are you still at work?"

"I'm just leaving. What's up?"

"Nothing. I was just checking on you. You've been working so many hours. I worry about you."

"I'm fine," I lied. "What do you want to do tonight?" I honestly didn't want to do anything. I was exhausted.

"Well, I tried your mom's lasagna recipe. I made dinner for my mom and Mike. I thought I would bring you some and we could just watch a movie or something. Are you up for it?" she asked.

And this was why I loved her. She knew I was tired. And although she probably wanted to go out, she was happy staying in. "That sounds perfect. I should be home in about twenty minutes."

I woke to a cold empty bed. I looked over to where I thought Tori would be and she was gone. After eating her lasagna, which rivaled my mom's, we came up to my room to watch a movie. I think I lasted about fifteen minutes before I fell asleep. Damn! Tori deserved better than for me to fall asleep on her all the time. Sometimes she would spend the night, but I guess tonight she decided to head home.

I reached over to grab my phone and a piece of paper fell to the floor. I turned on the lamp and picked it up. Her neat, girly writing stared back at me. *I have to work early and didn't want to wake you. Hope you have a great day. Love you! xoxo*

God, how long had it been since we'd had sex? I hadn't had my dick buried inside her since prom. How had I gone three weeks without touching her? Thinking about it now, had my dick awake and ready. I picked up my phone and texted her.

>*Chris: R U up?*
>*Chris: Tor? Wake up, baby!*
>*Tori: It's 2:30. What's wrong?*
>*Chris: I'm horny!*
>*Tori: I'm sorry. I'm sleepy.*
>*Chris: Really horny! Skype me?*
>*Tori: Give me a minute.*

I pulled out my laptop and set it on my legs while I sat up in bed. Tori's call came through and I answered quickly. She was sitting against the headboard, wearing a pink tank top with no bra. I could see her hard nipples poking through the material. She took her hand and pushed her long hair out of her face. "What's wrong?" she asked.

"I miss you," I answered. "Do you realize we haven't had sex since prom?"

Tori smiled at me. "I know. You've been working a lot. It's okay," she assured me.

"No. No, it's not. I need you. How come you left tonight?" I asked.

Tori let out a little huff. "I have to be at the shop at six. I didn't want to wake you up. Besides, you were dead to the world."

"I'm horny, baby. I wanna have sex right now," I told her.

"Chris, it's too late. I'm not coming back over. Maybe tomorrow," she answered.

"No. Now," I demanded. "Show me your tits. I can see your nipples through your shirt and it's making me hard."

"You wanna have Skype sex?" she questioned.

I nodded my head. "Strip."

"You're nuts, you know that?" Tori reached for the hem of her tank and pulled it over her head. Her dark nipples stared back at me through the screen. "Better?"

I nodded again. "Rub them for me. Pinch your nipples."

Tori rolled her eyes. "This is silly, Chris. Really? What are you getting out of this?"

I pushed my laptop to the side and pulled my shorts off. I set the computer back on my legs, so my dick was in full view of the camera. I fisted my cock and Tori's eyes went wide. "This is what I'm getting out of it. I'm horny and I'd rather jack off to you than some porno." I wasn't shy about the fact that I had watched porn. But why resort to that when I could have the real thing right in front of me.

Tori's eyes hooded with lust. "Well, then..." She massaged her tits, pinching her nipples between two fingers and rolling them into hard peaks.

I stroked myself as I watched her. "Fuck yeah, baby. That's sexy as hell. Go get your vibrator. I want to watch you fuck yourself with it. I want to watch you make yourself come."

Tori disappeared from the screen. When she came back into view, I watched her wiggle her shorts down her hips. She placed her laptop on the bed and sat in front of it. Then she laid back against the pillow and spread her legs.

"Is this what you want?" she said in a raspy voice.

"Yes," I groaned. "Rub it over your clit and make yourself come." I continued stroking myself as I watched her turn on the vibrator and run it through her folds. She closed her eyes and leaned her head back. The vibrator disappeared as it sank deep inside her and my dick got harder. At this point, I was going to come before her.

Her movements became more frantic as she rubbed herself up and down with the vibrator. Her other hand rubbed and pinched her nipples. "I'm gonna come," she whispered.

"Let go, baby. I wanna watch you." I rubbed myself harder and I felt my balls tighten. Her body tensed and then shook with her orgasm. It was sexy as fuck! I gave myself another hard jerk and cum shot out all over my stomach. I let out a breath of relief. "That was fucking hot, Tor. I love you."

I fell back asleep thinking about only one thing. I needed to get back inside her. And soon!

On Sunday, I decided to surprise Tori. I showed up at her house on my brother's Ninja. I walked to the door holding her helmet in my hand. When she answered, I held it up. "Wanna go for a ride?"

Tori bounced on her toes and clapped her hands. "Yes! Yes! Yes!"

I kissed her on the cheek. "Throw your bathing suit on under your clothes. I thought we could go out to Port Huron."

Tori quickly went upstairs to change and returned wearing jeans and her Converse. She grabbed her leather jacket from the hall closet, and we were out the door. I strapped the backpack with our towels on her back and she hopped onto the bike. "This was a good surprise," she beamed. "Will you teach me how to drive this?"

I wasn't sure if that was a good idea. Tori sensed my apprehension. "Please," she begged with big doe eyes.

I was having a hard time resisting her. "We'll see," I said, kissing her on the nose.

"Thank you," she smiled.

"I didn't say yes. I said we'll see." I plopped the helmet on her head and lowered the visor. I straddled the bike in front of her, while she tightened the strap under her chin. I started the bike and turned over my shoulder. "Ready?"

Tori nodded her head, put her feet up on the pegs, and wrapped her arms around me. I clicked on my playlist and music streamed into our helmets. I eased out of the subdivision and towards I-94. We headed down the expressway and Tori rested her head against my back, her arms securely around my waist. I rubbed my hand over hers and enjoyed the quiet ride toward Lake Huron.

It didn't bother me that we couldn't talk, I just enjoyed the time with her. I liked the way she held onto me and trusted me with her safety. We passed the Blue Water Bridge that crossed over to Canada and continued to the public access on Lake Huron. This beach was way better than the ones along Lake St. Clair. It was a little further away, but well worth the drive.

I parked the bike, and we headed toward the beach. It was crowded, but we managed to find an open spot that didn't have a million kids surrounding it. I took the backpack from Tori, pulled out our towels and laid them on the sand.

I sat on one of the towels as Tori undid her jeans and shimmied them down her legs, toeing off her shoes. Then she pulled her T-shirt off, revealing the black bikini beneath it. I stared up at her, taking in all her curves.

"What's wrong? You wore your bathing suit, didn't you?" she asked.

"Nothing is wrong. I'm just admiring the view."

"You're not tired of it?" she teased.

"Never." I reached up and grabbed her around the waist, pulling her down on top of me. "I could never get tired of looking at you."

Tori placed her hands on my shoulders and pushed her nose against mine, "That's good, because you're stuck with me. Now strip, mister."

"Always so bossy," I laughed. I pulled my shirt up over my head and untied my boots, then undid my jeans. Tori reached up and grabbed them at the thighs, tugging them down. I grabbed my bathing suit underneath, so it didn't come off too. "You're trouble, you know that?"

Tori shrugged her shoulders. "I think it's one of the things you like about me."

I sat down next to her. "You're wrong. It's one of the things I love about you."

"Speaking of trouble, do you think we could Jet Ski?" Tori pointed to the rental building up the beach.

Tori loved adventure as much as I did. "I think that could be arranged." I reached down for her hand, and we walked over to the rentals.

"I want to get two of them." She smiled up at me.

"You don't trust me?" I asked. I knew that wasn't the case, but I wanted to see her reaction.

Tori crossed her arms over her chest. "I trust you, but you never let me drive. I know how to drive them." She waved her arm over to the watercrafts.

"That's because I like your arms wrapped around me. But if you don't want that, then we can get two."

Tori scowled at me. "You know that's not the reason. You're trying to make me feel bad, but it won't work." She stepped up to the counter and rented two. I couldn't help but be amused by her determination.

I took a set of keys from her and grabbed us lifejackets. We walked down to the dock to our waiting Jet Skis. "Pick which one you want," I told her. "When I beat you racing, I don't want to hear that I got the faster one. I want to beat you fair and square."

"I won't need an excuse, because you'll be eating my spray all across the lake," she bragged.

Her confidence was cute. I had no intention of letting her beat me. "We'll see."

"Yeah, we will." Tori took her lifejacket from me and strapped it on. She took my outstretched hand and climbed onto her watercraft, and I climbed onto the one next to her. We started our machines and idled out to deeper water. When we were a safe distance from the shore, she held up her finger. "Give me a minute," she said seriously.

"What's wrong?" I asked.

She gave me a sly smile. "Nothing." She cranked the steering sharp to the left and gunned the engine. Tori spun in a tight circle, shooting spray up all around her, drenching me in the process. When she finally stopped, she looked smug. "Oh! Did I get you wet?"

I wiped the water off my face. "Cute, Russo. You ready to race?" All she had done was make me more determined to beat her and wipe that smug smile from her face.

"I'm ready. Where to?"

I pointed to a spot far off in the lake. "To that buoy. If you beat me, I'll teach you how to drive the bike. If not, you stay on the back."

Tori nodded her head. "Challenge accepted. We wait until that boat passes, and then you're on."

I didn't think she realized how big of a wake that boat was going to make but, I agreed. I just hoped she didn't fly off the damn thing. I watched the boat pass in the distance "Ready. Set. Go!"

We both gunned our engines and set off across the lake. We were flying. I snuck a peek at Tori, and she was keeping right next to me, the wind blowing her long hair behind her. She looked determined, but happy. We were approaching the wake from the boat, and I slowed to accommodate the wave. Tori soared past me, and I immediately regretted my decision to race her. If she got hurt, I would never forgive myself.

I was still going fast, but not as fast as her. She hit the wake hard, and the Jet Ski soared high into the air. My heart caught in my throat as I watched her. Tori stood at the height of it and landed hard back into water, only to take the next wave just as fast. She never slowed once and sailed across the water to the buoy.

I took the wakes at a slower speed, then raced to catch her. By the time I got to the buoy, she was sitting there bobbing in the water with a look of satisfaction. "What took you so long?" she asked, as I sidled up next to her.

"Are you crazy? You scared the crap out of me." I asked harshly.

She scowled at me. "Don't get pissy because I'm better at this than you."

"I'm not being pissy," I insisted.

"You are. And a sore loser," she pointed out.

Okay, maybe I was. I had greatly underestimated her ability. "Fine. You out-rode me. I'm impressed. Where'd you learn how to ride like that?"

"Mike. He and I have been doing this since I was ten," she said with a smile.

"You should have told me that before," I insisted. I felt like she tricked me into making the bet.

"You didn't ask. Just because you assumed you'd be better than me, that's not my fault." Her smile never faltered. She was really amused with the situation and the fact that she had beat me.

"I didn't assume that," I defended.

"You did, and now you have to teach me how to drive the bike." She wasn't about to let that go.

"I will, but you can't be fucking reckless." I sure hoped she wouldn't drive the bike the way she drove the Jet Ski.

"I won't. I promise." She was all giddy now. "Come on, no more racing. Let's just have fun."

Tori and I spent the next hour speeding across the lake together. I loved seeing her happy. Her being happy, made me happy. I quickly let go of the fact that she beat me and just enjoyed our time together.

We turned in the keys to the rental office and went back to our towels on the beach. We laid in the sun holding hands and talking softly. Since her surgery, I never took one moment I had with her for granted. If it had been cancer, she and I wouldn't be lying on the sand together. I cherished every moment we had because you never knew when those moments might end.

All my days at the Tech Center started to blur together. I had learned a lot about CAD in high school and last summer, but this year they threw me into Unigraphics, and I was picking it up quickly. I was good at what I did. It just made sense to me. The work was easy, and the pay was good.

"You ready for lunch?" Amanda asked.

I looked up from what I was doing, and Amanda was leaning over the half-wall that surrounded my cubicle. The tops of her tits were hanging out. I looked back at my screen.

"I'm leaving early today," I answered. Amanda was pretty. She had strawberry blond hair that almost reached her waist. She'd been super friendly with me since we started. At first, I thought it was just because we were both new. Now, I was starting to think it was something else.

"You still have to eat, right? I made extra for lunch. I thought we could eat together," she coaxed.

I looked at the picture of Tori and me on my desk. Amanda had to know I had a girlfriend. Maybe I was reading too much into her friendliness. It was only lunch, right? I didn't want to hurt her feelings.

"Yeah. Sure. Why not?" I answered.

Amanda pulled a chair up to my desk and pulled out the sandwiches she made, along with some potato salad. "I hope you like turkey," she said.

"Yeah, turkey is great," I answered lamely. "Soooo… what's this about, Amanda?"

She shrugged her shoulders. "Nothing. We both eat by ourselves. I just thought it would be nice to have lunch together," she said nonchalantly.

Seemed innocent enough. "Thanks. It was nice of you to think about me," I said as I took a bite of my sandwich. My phone buzzed, and I expected it to be Tori, but Tyler's name flashed across the screen. That was weird. He should have been working. I picked it up, "Hey. What's up man?"

Ty seemed stressed. "Can you pick me up at Kyla's house? It's kind of an emergency."

"Sure, man. What's up? Is everything okay?" I asked.

"No. Everything is fucked up. I went to see Kyla at the marina and some drunk guy had his hands all over her. Fucking grabbing her and groping her. I fucking freaked out and punched him in the face. Kyla's shook up and I'm taking her home."

I started packing up my things. "I can be there in a half hour."

"That's perfect. Thanks man. I appreciate it."

He hung up and I finished packing up my shit for the day. "I'm sorry," I told Amanda. "I gotta go. Thanks for lunch." I grabbed my sandwich and headed out the door.

That night I was at Tori's. Mike and Elena had gone up to the Lake House for the Fourth of July weekend, so we had the house to ourselves. We were out on the back patio drinking beer, courtesy of my brother. I liked the fact that Tori would drink beer. She didn't need the fruity shit that a lot of girls drank. "You should have seen him," I said. "I've never seen Ty so pissed off. I thought he was totally going to lose it."

"I've tried to call Kyla, but it keeps going straight to voicemail. I'm just glad Tyler was there for her." Tori pulled a bag of weed out of her pocket and tossed it to me.

"Where'd you get this?" I questioned. I always got us our weed. I didn't want Tori to deal with that shit.

"Courtney. Her boyfriend deals. I don't know if it's any good."

I raised my eyebrow at her. "You know Mike would have a fit if he knew about this."

"He's not going to find out." Tori rolled her eyes. "It's not like she's dealing in the front office. It came up in conversation and I asked her for it. She's cool."

I ran out to my truck and pulled some papers from the glovebox. I sat back down at the table and rolled us a joint. I handed it to Tori along with a lighter. She took a hit, closed her eyes, and handed it over to me. "Are we okay?" she asked.

I took a hit and handed it back. "Yeah. Why do you ask?"

I patted my lap, and she came over and sat down. Tori wrapped her arms around my neck. "We've both been busy. I feel like we barely see each other. I just don't want to be one of those girls who's the last to know."

I cupped her face in my hands. "I love you, Tori. That's not going to change."

"Still?" she asked.

"Always."

Tori looked up at me, like she was nervous.

"What?" I asked.

"Nothing," she said shaking her head. I knew she was lying. She was afraid to tell me something and I didn't like it. That wasn't my girl. She wasn't afraid of shit.

"What's going on?"

"Don't be mad, okay?" she said. Anything that started with "don't be mad" couldn't be good. I tried to run all the scenarios through my head of what she could have done. I came up empty.

"Unless you tell me you cheated, I'm not going to be mad?" I finally said.

Tori pulled back in shock. "I'd never cheat on you. Why would you say that?"

I ran my hand through my hair. "Cuz I can't figure out what you think I'd be mad about. I haven't been giving you the attention you deserve lately. I feel bad about it."

Tori wrapped her arms around my neck. "I love you. I'm not going anywhere." She placed a soft kiss on my lips. My mouth opened to hers and our tongues tangled together in a slow dance. My dick got hard as she pressed into me. Then she pulled back, leaving me wanting more. "Weed is not the only thing I got from Courtney."

I scrunched my face up in confusion. Tori reached into her pocket and pulled out a small baggie containing two pills. I snatched it out of her hand and inspected it. "What is this?"

"X," she answered.

I'd wanted to try Ecstasy before but didn't think Tor would be up for it. I'd heard it could dramatically increase the pleasure from sex.

"Are you pissed?" she asked nervously.

I shook my head. "I'm not pissed. Just surprised. You really want to try this? I don't know what it's going to do to us," I answered honestly.

Tori shrugged her shoulders. "I guess I figured that we might do it eventually. I mean, this shit is going to be around at parties next year. I thought we should try it in a more controlled environment. We have the house to ourselves for the weekend. I trust you. I feel safe with you. I know you wouldn't let anything bad happen to me."

I pulled out my phone. "Let me call Jim. I bet he's done this before." I didn't want to go into this blind. Yeah, we could just take the pills and see what happened, but I knew I'd feel better knowing what to expect. I quickly called him, hoping he'd pick up.

"Hey, little bro. What's up?" I heard music and a girl giggling in the background. He and his friend got an apartment together and they were always having parties.

"Are you having sex?" I questioned.

"Not yet." He laughed. "But the night is young, and we're having a party. You and Tori want to come over? You guys can stay the night," he offered.

"Thanks for the offer, but Tori's parents are gone for the weekend. We're hanging here. But I got a question."

"What's up?"

"You ever do Ecstasy? Tori got some pills…"

"Tori did?" he interrupted. "God, how in the fuck did you get that girl anyway? She's like perfect."

I laughed. "Yeah, she is perfect." I smiled as I looked at her. Then I got back to my reason for calling. "So, have you ever done it?"

"Yeah. You're gonna love it. Everything is so much more…intense. But only take a half a pill each. Too much of that shit makes your dick limp and that just sucks."

That was important information. I was glad I called him. "Thanks, bro."

I was about to hang up when Jim spoke again. "Chris, this isn't like weed. It's not something you can do every day. Take that other pill and save it for a few months from now. It'll fuck you up if you do it too much and you'll both feel like shit."

"Okay. Thanks again. Have fun tonight."

"I'd tell you the same, but I'm pretty sure that won't be a problem."

I hung up the phone, "He said to only take a half." I didn't tell her the whole pill might make it hard for me to get it up. I'd never had that problem with Tori, but I wasn't taking any chances. I took one pill from the baggie and broke it in half. "Are you sure about this?"

Tori nodded her head. "I'm sure." She stuck out her tongue and I placed the pill in her mouth, then popped the other half myself. "How long does it take for this to kick in," she asked.

"I have no idea," I said truthfully.

We sat in silence, waiting to feel something. After fifteen minutes, we both finished off our beers.

Tori placed her bottle on the table. "Maybe we have to be aroused for it to work." She shrugged her shoulders. "Wanna go upstairs and fool around?" Tor licked her bottom lip and then bit it. She knew that drove me crazy. All I could think of when she did that was her soft lips wrapped around my hard cock. She stood up and wiggled her luscious ass at me.

I reached out and grabbed it. She squealed as she ran for the slider, and I was right behind her. I caught her, picked her up, and spun her around. I pressed my lips to hers. "I love that you're not afraid to try things with me. I love that we do this crazy shit together. I love knowing that whatever we do, we're in it together."

"I can't imagine my life without you. Promise that no matter what happens tonight, that you'll stay. I don't want to be alone."

"I'm not going anywhere. I promise." I locked the door behind me and turned on the outside lights. If we didn't come back down, I wanted to make sure everything was locked up tight for the night. I checked the front door, then reached for her hand and led her up the stairs.

Tori grabbed her phone from her back pocket. "I made us a playlist," she said. "All songs that that make me horny." She pressed play and Saving Abel's "Addicted" started to play.

I stalked toward her. "I don't need music to make me want to fuck you, Tor. All I need is you." I pushed her up against the closed door. "Do you feel anything yet?" She shook her head. "Me neither, but I can't wait." I grasped her arms and held them above her head in one hand. "I need you now."

She looked up at me and begged, "Please."

I pulled her shirt up over her head and ripped her shorts down her legs. She stepped out of them and kicked them to the side. I loved seeing her in just her bra and panties. "You are so fucking sexy, babe. Do you know what you do to me?" I pressed my erection into her stomach, so she could feel how hard I was.

Her hands went to the button on my shorts, as I pulled my shirt over my head. "I need you inside me, Chris," Tori gasped.

I kicked out of my shorts. "Patience, baby. You'll get what you need. I promise. And you know," I licked her from her neck down to the top of her breasts, "that I never break my promises." She shuddered beneath my tongue.

"My skin is tingling, Chris. Touch me." I knew what she meant because I could feel it too. The Ecstasy was kicking in and we started to roll. She ran her nails down my back and it felt so good. I didn't want to fuck her anymore. I wanted to make love to her.

I undid the clasp on her bra and slid it off her shoulders, tossing it to the floor. I clamped down on one of her nipples and her head fell back as she let out a moan. My hand gripped the back of her thighs, and I carried her to the bed. I gently laid her back on the bed and pulled off her panties.

She pulled her legs up on the edge of the bed and I disappeared between her thighs. All I wanted to do was please her. I ran my thumb over her clit as my tongue delved deep inside her. I looked up at her and she was rubbing her tits. So fucking sexy! I moved my mouth to her clit and sucked her hard. Her legs wrapped around my head and her heels pushed me in deeper. Tori's back arched off the bed and she shook as she came. "Oh, my God. It's so intense!" she exclaimed.

I stripped my boxer briefs off and crawled over the top of her. I slowly slid inside her and my dick felt every soft little part of her. Her pussy was so tight. So wet. "You feel amazing, Tor." I slid in and out slowly, savoring every second. My senses were definitely in overdrive. I sucked her tits as I continued to make love to her. She whimpered and moaned.

"I can feel everything, Chris. You feel so good." I couldn't get close enough to her. My love for her was overflowing. I pushed her legs to her chest and pushed in deeper. I needed to be as deep as possible. So deep that you couldn't tell where she ended and I began. I wanted to be one with her. I wanted to watch myself disappear inside her. I wasn't coming anytime soon, but that was okay, because it felt so amazing. So intense. I could last all night with her.

We made love well into the early morning. Every position provided a new sensation. This was the most intimate, sexually pleasing night we ever shared. We kissed like we did when we started dating. We hadn't made out like that in forever and I realized I missed it. I needed to cherish this woman. Make her feel beautiful and loved because that's what she was. She was beautiful, and I loved her with all my heart.

Chapter 12
Tori

After my amazing weekend with Chris—our marathon on Friday night, Cole's Fourth of July party Saturday, and a Sunday of just hanging out together—I walked into Mike's shop with a smile on my face. I threw my purse in the bottom drawer of my desk and looked over at Courtney. "Thank you. It was amazing."

She got a big smile on her face. "I know, right?"

It was the perfect way to rekindle our relationship. I felt like we were losing our connection, but that feeling was gone now. I had poured my heart out to Courtney, and she suggested the Ecstasy. I didn't regret it one bit. "It's different now. We used to spend so much time together and now we're both working. It was just what we needed."

"That's life, sweetie. It's okay to spice it up once in a while. All relationships need an occasional kick-start."

I felt guilty talking to Courtney about this stuff. It felt like I was betraying Kyla, but her relationship with Tyler was in a totally different place. I didn't think she would understand. Hell, I was having a hard time understanding. Chris and I had always had an active sex life. The physical connection we shared was electric. It wasn't that I would ever look outside the relationship, but I didn't want to fall into the comfort zone either. I needed sex. He needed sex. It was an important part of our lives. It wasn't just physical. It was the closeness we shared when we were pleasing each other.

I didn't know how Kyla and Tyler were going to survive going to different colleges. I couldn't do it. But I knew Kyla, and she would do everything in her power to make sure they made it. She encouraged Ty every chance she got, and I admired her for it, but I also knew that Chris and I would need to be there for her. It was going to be hard, and she would need our support.

I was looking forward to our upcoming trip to the Lake House. The four of us were going to spend the week together and I knew it would be the last time we would all be together for a while. We were going the end of July, because Ty had to report to Michigan State for football training the beginning of August. Ty was like a brother to Chris, and I knew it would be difficult for him. Deep down, I think Chris wished he was going too. And he would be if his knee hadn't given out on him. It was a combination of a problem he ignored and our accident. The guilt weighed heavily on me. I caused that accident. But my guilt didn't just stem from the accident. It came from the fact that I was happy Chris couldn't play football for State. It was selfish, and I knew it.

I would never let Chris know how I felt. I planned on being there when Ty left, because it was going to hit him hard. Although Chris assured me that us being together was more important, he also harbored a certain amount of jealousy. I couldn't blame him. His dream was ripped away before it even started. He just wanted a chance to prove he was good enough. Prove it to his friends, his coach, his dad… to himself.

On the upside, Chris received a full-ride scholarship to Western. All the studying we did paid off. He blew away my score on the ACT. I wasn't as smart or motivated as Chris, but I still managed to get a partial scholarship, so that was something.

A few weeks later, I was filing some paperwork when Mike approached me. He looked over the paper in his hand with confusion. "Tori, can I ask you a question about this work order?"

I smiled up at him. "Sure. What's up?" I hadn't made too many mistakes, so I wasn't worried.

"It says here, and I quote, 'Mouse in the Engine'. What the hell does that mean?" he asked, scratching his head.

I shrugged my shoulders. "I'm not sure. That's what the lady told me, so I wrote it down. I suspect there's some kind of squeaking sound, but I'm not the mechanic." I cocked my head at him. "Aren't you supposed to be the expert?"

He laughed. "Yes, but I need to know what the problem is to be able to fix it."

"Mike, seriously!" I threw my hands up in the air. "That's what she said. Why don't you drive it around the block? If it's squeaking, you should be able to hear it. Who knows? Maybe there's an actual mouse in there."

Mike gave me a *Really?* look, then shook his head. "Let's try to be a little more specific in the future, all right?"

I huffed and placed my hands on my hips. "I'll do my best."

"That's all I ask, sweetie. You've been doing a great job. I didn't mean to make you feel as if you weren't." Mike gave me a warm hug and kissed my forehead. "I'm happy you're here."

I squeezed him back. "Me too."

Fun fact... when Mike popped the hood there was a dead mouse laying on top of the air filter. It wasn't what was making the squeaking sound, but it was gratifying none the less.

After lunch, Courtney left for the day. She wasn't feeling well, and the office was slow, so Mike sent her home.

A shadow swept over my computer screen, and I turned to find the culprit. Danny, one of the mechanics, was leaning over my desk shamelessly checking out my cleavage.

"Can I help you?" I asked.

He flashed me a dimpled smile and his blue eyes shone. "We're out of coffee."

I narrowed my eyes at him. "And?"

"And Courtney always makes our coffee," he said nonchalantly.

What the hell? These guys couldn't make their own coffee? "Do I look like Courtney to you?"

He gave me a seductive look up and down. "Definitely not. You're a lot sassier."

I laughed at his forwardness. "You have no idea."

Danny brushed his long blond hair out of his eyes. "I'd like to find out," he said with a wink.

I pushed back from my desk and stood up. "Not gonna happen," I answered, crossing my arms over my chest. I waved my fingers at him in dismissal. "Now, why don't you run along and learn how to use the coffee maker? I'm sure even you can figure it out."

He let out a low laugh and started to walk away. He turned and walked backwards pointing his finger at me. "I'm not giving up on you. You won't be able to resist this forever."

"Keep dreaming, darling," I shot back. Danny had been hitting on me for weeks. It was all innocent flirting, but underneath it was a hint of inappropriateness. I knew it was wrong. I should have ended the charade we were playing, but the attention he showed me was flattering. It was a dangerous game. A fine line I was riding. I would never step over that line, but I also knew I was having a hard time taking a step away from it.

What the hell was wrong with me?

Our trip to the lake house was in a couple of days. I didn't want to wait until the last minute to start packing, so I started pulling clothes from my drawers and laying them out on the floor in my room. I reached for the shopping bag in my closet and pulled out the new bikini I bought. It was purple and black with just a hint of pink running through it. I bought it with Chris in mind. He was going to love this on me. My mom's beach cover-up would look great with it.

I found her in the kitchen, making a batch of brownies. My mom wasn't much of a cook, but she was trying to make brownies for Mike's birthday. It was sweet. "Mom?"

She turned to me, and I covered my mouth to hide my giggle. "Yes?" She blew at the strands of hair that fell in her eyes and had a big streak of chocolate smeared across her right cheek. "What's so funny?" she asked.

I used my thumb to wipe the batter from her face. "You got a little something on your cheek." I laughed as I licked the chocolate from my thumb.

"I'm terrible at this." She shook her head. "Maybe I should ask Trina for some lessons. It seems to be working wonders with you."

I hugged her around the waist. "You're perfect just the way you are." I pulled back and helped her finish up the brownies. I popped them in the oven and set the timer. "I was wondering if I could borrow your pink and purple beach cover-up?" I asked as I ran my finger across the bottom of the bowl, scooping up some of the leftover goodness.

My mom swatted at my hand and washed the bowl from the brownie batter. "Sure. It should be in the bottom right-hand drawer of my dresser."

"Thanks, Mom," I kissed her on the cheek and bound up the stairs. I pulled out the bottom drawer and shuffled through the clothes. It wasn't there. I opened the next drawer looking for that cover-up.

Buried in the bottom of the drawer was a flat box. I don't know why, but it intrigued me. There had to be something precious inside if it was hidden in there. I slowly pulled the box out and carefully lifted the top.

I shouldn't have.

I really shouldn't have.

Staring back at me were pictures of my mom. She was young. About my age. And she was beautiful. Her long dark hair cascaded over her shoulders. Her eyes sparkled, and she looked happy. Really happy.

The man who had his arms wrapped around her waist was stunning. He had amber eyes and dark hair. He looked at her as if she held the moon. You could see the love between them. Tears pricked at my eyes.

"Did you find it?" my mom asked from the hallway. She stepped into the bedroom and froze.

I held up the picture in my hand. "Is this him? Is this my dad?" My voice trembled, as I watched my mom. She didn't have to say anything. The answer was written all over her face.

"Tori..."

"It is, isn't it? Why would you hide this from me?" I asked.

"It was complicated," she sighed. She entered the room and sat next to me on the floor, taking the picture from my hand. Her eyes welled with tears as she gazed at her past.

"Uncomplicate it for me." I sniffed. "Did you love him?"

She ran her fingers over the picture. "More than anything. He was the center of my world."

"What was his name?" We never talked about my dad. It was always taboo. I was taught from a young age that it was something we wouldn't discuss.

She took a deep breath. "Torrenzio Ventimiglia."

My head popped up. "Did you name me after him?"

A smile crossed her lips and she nodded. "I may have lost the love of my life, but I got to keep the best part of him. When I found out I was pregnant, he had already planned on leaving for the Marines. I was brokenhearted. It wouldn't have changed anything to tell him about you." She pushed my hair over my shoulder. "There was never a question in my mind whether or not I was going to keep you. I knew the love we shared couldn't do anything but create a beautiful baby. You're the best thing I've ever done."

The tears ran down my face. "Why didn't you tell him?" I started to get angry, "Maybe he would have wanted me. Maybe he would have stayed!"

My mom shook as the sobs racked her body. "He wouldn't have stayed."

"How do you know?" I yelled.

"I already asked him to stay. For me. He wouldn't. I guess I loved him more than he loved me."

"Maybe he would have stayed for me!" I shouted.

She shook her head. "That would have been the wrong reason for him to stay. I wouldn't use you as a pawn."

"He had a right to know. I have a right to know who my father is."

"We were so young. I was only seventeen. He had just turned eighteen. He wasn't ready to be a dad, any more than I was ready to be a mom. I was scared. When he left, I called him, wrote him letters. He promised he would come back to me. That I just had to be patient. Soon the phone calls stopped coming. His last letter said he was being deployed to Afghanistan. That I should move on. My heart broke and I never heard from him again." Then she looked me in the eyes. "Mike is your dad. He chose you. He didn't have to, but he did. He's the best thing that ever happened to you. To me. Just because he doesn't share your blood, don't think he loves you any less."

"I love Mike too. He's been nothing but good to me, but I want to know where I came from. There's a whole family out there that I'm a part of, and they don't even know I exist."

My mom looked at the ceiling and wiped her eyes. "They know you exist."

I was so confused. "What? Then why...why don't I know them?"

"I ran into his mother when I was seven months pregnant. I asked about Torrenzio. I wanted to know what happened to him. She looked at my bulging belly and called me a whore. Said the baby couldn't possibly be his. Said I wasn't going to use a baby to trap her son."

I looked down at my hands, and let that information sink in. "They didn't want me," I said resolutely.

My mom cupped my face and gave me a hard look. "That's not true. It's me they didn't want. I wasn't good enough for their son. It's their loss, because you are an amazing and beautiful girl and they have truly missed out."

"What if I want to find him someday? Would you be mad? Would Mike?" I wasn't sure if that was what I wanted, but I needed to know how they would feel about it.

"Sweetheart, we'll always support you. We knew this day would eventually come. If that's what you want, then I'll try to help you."

I nodded. "Not today, but maybe someday." I pulled out more of the pictures of my father and the letters he wrote my mother. He did love her. I knew he did. Maybe he could love me too. One day I would find out.

"Can I keep this?" I asked, holding a picture in my hand.

"Of course. I kept all of this because I knew one day it would belong to you. This box is a reminder of the best times of my life. The times that led to you." She smiled softly.

I hugged her tightly. "I love you, Mom. I'm sorry I got so mad. It's just..."

"I know," she said. "You don't have to explain."

I stood up. "I need to see Chris."

She nodded. "He's your Torrenzio. Don't take him for granted and don't let him go. True love like that only comes along once in a lifetime. You hold onto him."

I held onto the picture and went out to my car. Chris should have been home from work soon. I needed him. I needed him to tell me it was okay. That I was wanted.

I parked at the curb in front of his house and stared at the picture. My mom was beautiful. She looked so in love. It was almost like looking in a mirror. We looked so much alike, and my dad... reminded me of Chris. Dark and handsome. Italian through and through.

I bypassed the house and went straight to the backyard. I walked far out onto the property and climbed the ladder to the treehouse. I didn't want to talk to his mom and dad. I needed the solitude.

I sat on the floor and leaned against the wall, staring at the picture. How different would my life have been if my dad... my real dad... was a part of it? Would I have a brother or sister? Would we have ever moved from Ohio to Michigan? Would I have ever met Chris? I always felt like a puzzle that would never be finished, because pieces were lost, and the picture would never be complete. When I found that box, I felt like one piece clicked into place. The picture a little clearer than it was before.

Why didn't my grandparents want me? Would my dad have wanted me if he knew? What if he did know and that's why he cut off contact with my mom? She should have tried harder. If not for herself, then for me. I single tear ran down my cheek.

My phone buzzed with a text.

Chris: Where are you?

Tori: Treehouse

I sat against the wall, processing everything I found out and the questions left answered. I was lost in my own thoughts.

"Tor?" Chris climbed the ladder and his head peeked up through the opening. He saw me slumped against the wall. "Are you okay? Why are you out here by yourself?"

He was still dressed in his work clothes—dress pants, a button-up shirt, and a tie. He loosened his tie and sat next to me. Tears flooded my eyes, and I kept them at bay. I held up the picture for him to see. He pulled me between his legs and wrapped his arms around my waist. "Is that your mom? My god, you look just like her. Who's the guy?"

I swallowed down the lump in my throat. "My dad."

Chris rested his head on my shoulder. "What's his name?"

"Torrenzio."

"You're named after him?"

I nodded my head. "He didn't want me. His family didn't want me. They knew about me, and they didn't want me."

"Baby…"

"I don't know what to think about all of this. It hurts," I confessed. "It really hurts. Why wouldn't they want me?" My voice became urgent as I asked the question that I didn't expect him to have an answer to. "You want me though, right? You're not going to leave me, are you?" A single tear rolled down my face.

"I'll always want you, baby. There's not a thing in this world that I want more." Chris nuzzled into my neck and kissed me. "Tell me what to do. How can I help you?"

"I don't know," I said honestly. "I feel like a missing piece has been found, but at the same time I feel like it just gave me more questions." I ran my fingers over the picture for the hundredth time. "They remind me of us. Promise you'll never leave me, Chris. Promise me."

"I promise. Forever and always, baby." He let out a sigh. "Forever and always."

My insecurities took over and I didn't believe him. Flashbacks of December invaded my mind. Words. Everything was just words. Promises that could be broken. "Are you happy?" I questioned. "Ty's leaving for State soon. Do you wish you were going too? I need to know if you're going to leave me." I was rambling. The thoughts were all jumbled up in my head. It was too much to make sense of. If Torrenzio could leave my mom, then Chris could leave me just as easily.

"Shhh." He held a finger to my lips. "I'm happy. You're my world. I want to be with you. The rest of it doesn't matter. You're all I need."

I felt empty inside. Abandoned. Rejected. Unwanted. "I need to feel something. Anything."

"Tor…"

"Love me, Chris. Just love me," I pleaded.

"I do. More than anything." He ran his hand down the side of my face.

I stood from between his legs and started to pace. "Make love to me like you mean it. Love me like you're my forever. Prove it to me. Fuck me like you love me," I begged. I unbuttoned my shorts and pushed them down my legs. I pulled my shirt over my head and removed my bra. I stood before him and bared everything for him to see. His eyes got wide, but he didn't make a move. "Don't you want me?" I was desperate for him. I begged him. I needed to feel loved. Wanted. I pulled at my hair until my scalp burned, "Please…

Chris quickly took off his tie and unbuttoned his shirt. He shrugged it off and set it next to him. "Tori, come here baby." He reached up from where he sat on the floor and grasped my hand. He pulled me down onto his lap then draped his shirt over my shoulders. He pulled me into his chest and held me there. My safe place, where nothing could hurt me. The tears I'd been holding back, spilled down my cheeks and onto his chest. He cradled my head against his hard muscles and rocked me. "You're okay, baby. I've got you. I'll always have you."

Chapter 13
Chris

I rocked her gently as she sobbed into my chest. I'd never seen her so broken. When Tori got upset, anger always took center stage. She had a sharp tongue and a fierceness about her. But now... now she was broken in my arms. She needed to feel it. To let it in.

Finally, her breathing evened out as she fell asleep. I didn't have the heart to move her, so I kept her there with me. I picked up my phone and called my mom.

She answered right away. "Sweetheart, what's going on? Elena called and she's worried."

"She's okay. Can you let Elena know Tori's going to spend the night here?"

"Of course."

"Mom?"

"Yes?"

"Can you bring some pillows and blankets out here? Don't let dad or Jim come. Just you."

There was silence on the other end of the line. "Okay. Why don't you bring her up to your room?"

I looked down at Tori in my arms. I didn't want to wake her. "She's already asleep. I need a change of clothes too."

"Give me a few minutes."

"Thanks, Mom."

I put down my phone and held Tori. Protecting her. Keeping her safe. She never mentioned her biological dad. I only remembered that one time, years ago, in my truck, when she'd talked about it. I always assumed she accepted Mike as her dad. She'd never led me to believe anything else. Obviously, it ate her up more than she let anyone know.

It was the rejection that killed her.

The feeling of being unwanted.

My heart broke for her.

I felt like a shit for not seeing it sooner. Not knowing how much it affected her. How could I have missed something so important?

It wasn't long before my mom peeked her head up through the opening in the floor. She looked at Tori only cloaked in my dress shirt, with questions written across her face. She could have made a big deal about Tori sitting in my arms practically naked, but she didn't. Instead, my mom came and sat next to me. She ran a hand through Tori's long hair. "What happened?" she whispered.

I picked up the picture from the floor and handed it to my mom, "This."

My mom stared at the picture, "It looks like Tori, but it isn't. Is that Elena?" I nodded my head. "She was so young and beautiful. Who's the boy?"

"Tori's dad."

My mom furrowed her eyes. "What happened to her dad and when did Mike come into the picture?"

"Mike adopted Tori when she was four. Tori never knew her real dad or much about him. He left before Tori was born. Elena kept everything quiet. Tori found this picture today and Elena told her stuff she wasn't ready to deal with." I looked down at my girl and pulled my shirt tighter around her body. "She just broke, mom. I didn't know how to help her. She's afraid I'm going to leave her too. She just stripped down and wanted me to…" I took a deep breath, "but I couldn't. It wasn't what she needed." I let out a low laugh. "The problem is… I don't know what she needs."

My mom ran her hand under my chin. "Yes, you do. You're doing it right now." She gave me a reassuring smile. "Let me bring up those blankets."

She disappeared and came back with blankets and pillows. She laid them out on the floor, then brought a blanket and wrapped it around my girl. I moved her to our makeshift bed and stretched out my sore muscles. "Thanks, Mom, for helping me." I looked at my watch. "It's still early. If she wakes up, I'll bring her up to the house."

My mom kissed me goodnight and left us alone. I changed out of my dress pants and threw on the shorts my mom brought. I laid down on the hard floor next to my girl and pulled her to my chest. I would always protect her, but this was something I had no control over.

Something I couldn't protect her from. I was glad we were leaving for the Lake House in a few days. It might be just what she needed.

She never mentioned her breakdown again. It was as if it never happened.

I woke in the middle of the night alone on the treehouse floor. She was gone. The only reminder of what had happened was the text on my phone. *Thank you for last night. Have a good day at work.* It annoyed me that she left without waking me, but I didn't make a big deal about it. Tori needed to handle things her own way and me bringing it up would only do more harm than good.

Tori became obsessed with using the new camera Mike and Elena bought her for graduation. She took it everywhere we went. It became the distraction she needed. While we were at the Lake House, we'd take long walks in the evening. She'd lay down on the sand to get the perfect angle and capture the sunset over the water. Or she'd climb on top of a huge rock, so that she could get the Sleeping Bear Dunes in the picture.

I knew Tori loved photography, but she had mostly taken pictures for the yearbook because she didn't have a camera of her own. The pictures she was taking now were stunning. She'd always talked about making photography into a career. Maybe she could.

Tori was in the bathroom getting ready for bed when I picked up her camera. I started scrolling through the pictures she took. The colors in the sunsets were vibrant pinks, purples, and oranges.

"What are you doing?" Tori asked as she crawled into bed next to me.

"Just looking. You should think about selling these."

"Those are just for me," she said, taking the camera out of my hands. "Who would want to buy them?"

"Lots of people. I bet if you blew them up and framed them, you could sell them at Frank's store." Frank had known Tori since she was a kid. He owned the biggest souvenir store in the area. I had no doubt he would be willing to hang them in his store.

She waved me off. "You're a big dreamer, you know that? These aren't even that good."

"They are," I insisted.

Tori set the camera on the nightstand. "That's sweet of you," she said leaning over, giving me a kiss. "Maybe, one day."

Our week at the Lake House passed quickly. Too quickly. I already missed all the time I had gotten to spend with my girl, falling asleep with her every night and waking with her every morning. Waking with her was the best. Every morning I sank myself inside her softness, made her promises, and told her how much I loved her.

I was thinking about those mornings when Amanda sidled up next to me. "Daydreaming?"

Her voice broke my trance. "Nah. Remembering."

She shook her head. "Must have been a good memory, because you've got this goofy look on your face."

I let out a laugh. "I've been told it happens." I focused back on my computer screen, "What's up?" Amanda didn't know boundaries and she made me uncomfortable at times. I didn't want to give her the wrong idea.

She set her hand on my shoulder. "I was wondering if you could help me out. The animation on my computer isn't working and I can't figure out what the problem is."

I pushed my chair back. "Sure. I'll take a look."

I went over to her cubicle. I settled into her chair and started fiddling with the drawing on her screen. Amanda hovered over my shoulder. I could feel her warm breath on my neck. She was too damn close. "Here's the problem," I said, clicking into her settings. I made the necessary changes and clicked on the robot on the screen. It came to life, moving up and down.

Amanda kissed me on the cheek. "Thank you. You're my hero, Chris."

"Yeah. No problem." I edged away and went back to my own area.

My dad's voice boomed behind me. "In my office."

Fuck! Now what? My dad rode me harder than anyone else. You'd think being his son would make things easier, but the opposite was true. I stepped into his office, wondering what I did wrong.

"Shut the door," he ordered.

I did and plopped down in the chair across from his desk. My tie felt too tight, and I reached up to loosen it. "What's up?" I asked casually.

"What the hell was that?" He motioned to the area right outside his door.

Confusion clouded my face. "What are you talking about?"

My dad leaned forward, placing his elbows on his desk. "I just watched Amanda kiss you. What the hell is that about? Are you trying to fuck shit up?"

I ran my hands over my face and dug the heels of my hands into my eyes. "It was nothing. She had a problem with her computer. I was just helping." I leaned forward and made the confession to my dad. "I think she's got a crush on me. I'm trying not to encourage her, but she's kind of persistent."

"End it. Now. Make sure she understands. I'm telling you this as your boss and your father. I don't want a replay of the shit that went down with Susie. You've got too much to lose. Am I clear?"

I stood up. "Crystal." I was irritated, but he was right. I turned to walk away but he stopped me.

"How's Tori doing? She had your mom and me worried."

I sat back down. "I seriously don't know. After that night, she pretended like nothing happened. But I know her. She's compartmentalizing. She's too tough for her own good. She buries that shit deep. It'll come back to the surface, but I don't know when."

My dad steepled his fingers under his chin. "Does she want to find him?"

"Not right now, but I think eventually. I don't want to push her if she's not ready." Again, I was lost. I wanted to help her but didn't know how. I didn't want to unbury shit she wasn't ready for.

My dad nodded his understanding. "I've got a friend who's a private investigator. When she's ready, let me know. I'll give him a call."

I was on my way home from work trying to figure out how to handle the Amanda situation. I wouldn't make the same mistake twice. Being complacent hadn't worked out well for me before, I needed to set Amanda straight sooner than later. Tomorrow, I decided. I would do it tomorrow.

My phone buzzed, and Ty's face lit up my screen. "What's up, man?"

"I'm leaving in the morning. I just wanted to see you before I go. You know, without the girls. Can you stop by?"

I let out a frustrated sigh. "Be there in ten."

Jealousy wound inside me and clenched. I'd been trying to keep it at bay, but it kept creeping in. Playing football for Michigan State would have been kickass. Ty and me out on that field together. Spartan Stadium full of fans, cheering us on. It was all just a dream now. Some distant thought about what could have been.

My thoughts veered back to the week Tori and I just spent together—the walks on the beach, the nights by the bonfire, and the mornings of sweet sex. I loved every minute we spent together. If I went to State, we'd only see each once a week, if we were lucky. I couldn't imagine spending that much time apart.

I traded my dream for my girl. I would never regret that decision. A decision that was made for me when we got in that accident. Maybe it was fate. A smile crept across my face because Tori had been it for me since seventh grade. Two years ago, I was lucky enough to make her mine. Fate was an evil bitch, but maybe… just maybe she knew what she was doing.

I pulled up in Ty's driveway and hopped out. He met me in the garage and thrust a beer in my hand. "Thanks, man."

Ty scratched at the back of his head. "I didn't want to leave without talking to you. I don't want this to ruin our friendship. I know you wanted to come to State and now I'm leaving, doing the one thing you wanted."

I waved him off. "I'm over it, man. I'll admit that I was jealous as a motherfucker, but I've got my girl and that's more important to me. I was never going pro anyway."

Ty huffed. "That's the thing. I want to go pro more than anything. It's all I've ever wanted. I've got to take this chance, but leaving Kyla behind is killing me. I never thought I'd find a girl who would make me rethink everything. If I lose her... I don't know what I'll do."

I took a swig of my beer. "If anyone has a chance of making it, it's you two." That was the honest to God truth. "Kyla is about the most loyal person I know. She'll always stand by you. She'll do everything in her power to make this work." I took another swig. "Just keep your dick in your pants. Those girls are relentless and it's going to be tempting as hell."

"Kyla owns both my dick and my balls, so I'm not worried about that." He kicked at the ground, "Just... keep her safe. Please. I couldn't handle it if something happened to her, and I wasn't there to protect her."

I patted him on the back. "We've got this. Kyla's like a sister to me. I won't let anything happen to her. And you know Tori's going to be like a mother hen."

Ty scrubbed a hand over his face. "I know. I know. Thanks, man. Thanks for befriending the cocky kid from Bay City. I owe you. Big time."

"You don't owe me shit." I drained my bottle and set it on the bench in the garage. "Good luck, Ty. We'll see you at your first game."

"You're coming?" he asked incredulously.

I reached out and gave him a bro-hug. "Wouldn't miss it."

At the end of the week, I took my girl out to our private spot. I laid out blankets in the bed of my truck and we gazed at the stars, holding hands and enjoying the silence. Fireflies flickered all around us. But the nagging feeling that something wasn't quite right, hadn't been right for a while now, pricked at me. Although our week up north had been nothing short of amazing, it was there. Just under the surface, waiting to rear its ugly head. Maybe I was paranoid. Maybe my guilt about Amanda kissing me was poking through. Whatever it was, I couldn't leave it alone. So, I picked at it like a scab. Maybe it was wrong, but I had to know where this feeling was coming from. "Tor?"

"Yeah, baby?"

"You know I love you, right?"

"I know."

"I worry about you. You keep everything inside. I hated seeing you break. I felt helpless. You haven't said anything about your biological dad since that night. Do you want to talk about it?" I threw out the lifeline, hoping she was going to grab it.

Tori curled into my side. "I'm sorry I put you in that situation. I'm sorry I made you feel that way." Again, she was hiding shit. Burying it deep. Trying to evade my question. I thought she would be desperate for the lifeline, but she would rather drown on her own than grab what I was offering. I didn't understand it. Not one little bit.

She acted like I couldn't see right through her.

But I saw her. Clear as day.

I pulled her face to mine. "You're missing the point. I'm here for you. Always. This is me and you. I want all of it. The hurt. The fear. The pain. You are never alone. I want to spend my life with you. I want you raw and honest. Vulnerable and exposed. There isn't one thing you could ever tell me to make me love you any less. I don't want you to pretend you're okay when you're not."

Tori pushed away the lifeline with a fierce determination I knew all too well. "I'm not weak," she said with conviction. And there it was. The answer I was searching for.

"No, you're not. You're one of the strongest people I know, but you don't have to always be that way. We're stronger together. Let me in. Let me be there for you."

Tori dropped her head to my chest. "I don't want to burden you with every little thing. They're my issues."

I lifted her head back up. "No. You're wrong. They're our issues. We're a team, baby. When you hurt, I hurt. Don't you know?"

She let out a huff that pissed me off. "Know what?" That wall I tore down so long ago, was going back up. She was rebuilding it brick by brick. Maybe that was the nagging feeling I couldn't let go. Her armor that I hadn't seen in so long... was firmly back in place. And it had everything to do with Torrenzio. I wasn't going to be patient this time. I was going to take a battering ram and demolish that fucking wall.

Holding her face with both hands I told her, "You're everything to me." She tried to look away, but I wouldn't let her. "Damn it, Tori. Look at me! You're everything to me! Do you hear me? Do you understand what I'm saying?"

Tears leaked from her eyes. "Yes." And I was glad the tears came, because maybe that wall wasn't as strong as she thought it was.

"Then what's the problem?" I questioned harshly. I wasn't going to let her hide from me anymore.

Her throat bobbed, and her voice caught. So, I asked again, "What's the problem, Tori?"

"I'm scared." I felt her wall crack. Maybe it wasn't so strong after all.

I searched her eyes and saw it. Her vulnerability was right there. I just had to reach a little further. "Of what?" She swallowed, but no words came from her lips. "Of what, baby?"

"You," she said softly.

That wasn't what I was expecting. I cocked my head to the side in confusion.

"I'm afraid you'll leave me. You terrified me back in December. Practically destroyed me."

I dropped my head back and regret filled my chest, "I thought that was behind us. Tori, that had nothing to do with you. That was all me. I was just pissed that everything felt like it was falling apart."

"No." She shook her head. "No, I don't believe it. There was shit I did that pissed you off. I was too needy. Too clingy. I won't give you a reason again."

"Baby..."

"In a couple of weeks, we're going to college and there's going to be a whole new pool of girls to choose from. Ones who won't be needy or clingy. And that scares the shit out of me."

I held her to my chest and rubbed her back. She let out a soft sob that damn near broke me. I didn't know what to do or say to make her believe me.

With her head resting on my chest, I heard the quiet words she spoke. "You'll leave me, and I'll be all alone. Just like my mom. My dad was everything to her. And he left. Left her alone and heartbroken. I'm just like her."

I rolled Tori to her back and hovered above her, caging her in with my arms. "You're not your mom. And I'm sure as hell not him. We're not destined to repeat their story. We control where this goes. We decide. And your dad... he was a fool. If your mom was anything like you, he was a fool to walk away from the two of you." I pushed her hair out of her face and gently kissed her soft lips. "I may be a lot of things, Tori. I can be reckless, irresponsible, hot-tempered. But one thing I'm not... is stupid. I know exactly what I have. I'm thankful every day that you gave me a chance, and a second, and a third. More than I can count. Because Lord knows I didn't deserve them. But you gave them to me anyway. And I'll never take that for granted because you... you are amazing. The best gift I was ever given. I'm holding on tight to you and I'm never letting you go." She stared up at me with those honey eyes, wide from my confession. "Do you hear me? Do you understand what I'm telling you?"

"Promise me forever," she said.

That might have scared a lot of people. *Forever*. But not me. I never hesitated. "Forever. I'll love you forever. If you're going to build a wall, build it around both of us, because I'm never leaving your side. I promise." I gave her a dimpled smile. "And you know I never break my promises."

Chapter 14
Tori

Age 20
Junior Year of College

And he didn't. Never once did Chris break his promises to me. He remained faithful and true through every transition we made and every challenge we faced. He was always there, right by my side.

I don't know how I got so lucky. Who knew all those years ago, when he was chasing me, that when I stopped running, he would crash right into me. And that it could be soooo good. So pleasing, both emotionally and physically. My soulmate, my lover, and my best friend, all rolled into one delicious package.

We had the push and pull mastered. He pushed, and I pulled. He wanted to get married so bad, but we promised our parents we'd wait until we graduated. We were still so young. He insisted it didn't matter. When you knew, you knew. And we had known for a long time now. But yet, I resisted.

It was a bitter pill between us. But one day... one day I was going to marry that boy. And nothing would stop me. Chris only became more devastatingly handsome over the years. He filled out. His chest broadened, narrowing down to his hips, that led to that perfect V I loved so much. His strong arms provided the security and safety I so desperately desired. He was a long way from the scrawny boy I shared a beer with on the tailgate of a truck. And the best part was he thought I was the best thing that ever happened to him.

That's not to say we didn't ever argue. It was bound to happen with the way we challenged each other, the push and the pull, the sparks that flew between us. But every disagreement, every time he pushed, and I pulled, every fight we'd ever had, ended in kisses and phenomenal make-up sex. Just as he'd promised.

I was waiting for that now. I laid under my covers alone, shivering. Kyla watched me with concern. "Are you sure you're all right?" she asked.

"I'm fine," I assured her. "I just had too much to drink."

Chris and I went to a party just off campus. Yeah, we smoked a lot of pot, but we always kept the drinking under control, especially when we were out at a party. I knew the rules. Don't accept a drink from anyone other than Chris. If one of us didn't make it or open it, I didn't drink it. And don't overdo, keep your senses. We'd gotten separated at the party, he mingled with his friends, and I mingled with mine. I swear I didn't think I had that much to drink, but by the time he found me I was kneeling over the porcelain god.

He took care of me, holding my hair out of my face as I threw up again and again, but that didn't mean he wasn't pissed. I broke our agreement. I knew his anger came from a place of concern. He'd never forgive himself if something were to happen to me. I understood it, but I was just letting loose. Who knew those pink fruity drinks carried that much punch? Before I knew it, my stomach turned, and I was a sweaty mess.

He basically carried me out of the party and into his truck. He brought us home, having to pull over twice so I could throw up. I'd never been this fucked up before. I'd wobbled into our room, supported by Chris. He removed my shoes and jeans, then tucked me into bed. There was no mistaking the anger that rolled off him in waves. He'd left for his own room, two floors above us.

He left me alone to deal with my own stupidity. Guess I ruined his good time tonight. So what, if I overdid? It wasn't like I made a habit of it.

I drifted off to sleep but woke sometime in the middle of the night. My stomach rolled, and I raced to the bathroom, barely making it before my stomach decided to revolt on me. What the hell? This was not normal. Usually if I overdid, I might throw up once and then I'd passed out and sleep it off. Never had it resurfaced like this, over and over again.

I laid my face down on the cool tile. God, that felt good. I ran my hand over my forehead. I was sweating like crazy. I felt disoriented and queasy again. I crawled back to the toilet and hung over it like the pathetic girl I was.

I barely heard Kyla approach. My head rested on the rim of the toilet. "Are you going to be okay?" she questioned.

I barely heard her and tried to nod my response, but everything hurt. My body ached, and my stomach recoiled again. I couldn't believe there was anything left. Kyla pulled my hair back and ran her hand over my back, trying to soothe me. Her hand ran along my head. "Tori, you're burning up."

"I drank too much," I insisted.

"I don't think so. I think you have a fever."

"It's just the alcohol." I laid my head back on the rim of the toilet. Why did something so disgusting feel so good? I couldn't rationalize as chills took over my body. "Can you get me a blanket?" I asked. "I'm freezing."

Kyla rushed from the bathroom and pulled the blanket off my bed. She wrapped it around me and laid me back on the floor. I wanted to die. That's how bad I felt. Death couldn't be as bad as this. "I'm calling Chris," Kyla declared.

"No. He's already mad enough at me. I don't need him to see me like this," I rasped out. The last thing I wanted was the annoyed look I knew he would have. Yeah, I should have known better. *What the hell was in those drinks?* My chest ached, and my breaths were shallow. To breathe was painful.

Kyla sat with me all night. She held my hair every time I threw up. She wrapped her arms around me and held me close, telling me it would be all right. She tried to get me to drink some water, but every time I did, it came back up. I seriously wanted to die.

Sometime around dawn, she broke. I heard Kyla on the phone. I barely made out the words she said. *She's sick. Been up all night. Burning up.* All I heard were bits and pieces. I laid my head back on the floor, drifting in and out of consciousness. I wanted to sleep and never wake up.

I felt his hand sweep along my forehead. "How long has she been like this?"

"All night. She just keeps throwing up. I wanted to call you earlier, but she asked me not to."

"You should have. She's burning up."

A chill swept through my body, sending shivers down my spine. My stomach rolled, and I forced myself to the toilet. I gripped the sides in desperation and hung my head into the basin, as I threw up again. I felt his arms wrap around me and pull me to his chest. I slumped against him. "I'm so sorry." It was desperate plea for forgiveness. I closed my eyes. I wanted the darkness to swallow me up. My whole body hurt.

119

"Shhh… I'm the one who's sorry. I should have never left you last night. I should have known something was wrong."

Kyla handed Chris a washcloth. He ran it over my head and down my face. The cool cloth felt like heaven. "I just need to sleep." I laid back down on the tile and pulled the blanket over myself as I curled up on the floor. "I'll be fine."

"You're going to the clinic, baby. Kyla, get some Motrin."

"I already tried that," Kyla answered. "She throws it right back up." They were talking about me like I wasn't even there. I caught snippets of their conversation. "The clinic doesn't open 'til nine, but there's an urgent care a couple of miles down the road."

"Help me get her dressed then pull my truck up."

Chris lifted me from the floor and carried me to my bed. I barely remembered being dressed and led out to his truck.

A few hours later, I was tucked back into my own bed. Turned out not only did I have the flu, but a respiratory infection as well.

Chris ran his hand through my hair. "I'm so sorry, Tori. You kept telling me you hadn't drank that much, but I didn't believe you. I'm so sorry I doubted you. So sorry I left you alone. So sorry I wasn't there to take care of you." His eyes were glassy. I'd rarely seen my man cry, but I could tell he was on the verge.

I laced my fingers through his. "You're here now. That's what counts."

For three days I fought the fever, the achy muscles, the urge to just sleep. For three days Chris and Kyla fed me, helped me to shower, and made sure I took my meds. They took turns staying with me when they had to go to class. Over the past couple of years, the three of us became our own little family. There was a bond between us, that come hell or highwater, we would always take care of each other.

On day four my fever broke.

"You scared the shit out of me," Kyla confessed. "I've never seen you like that. I didn't know how to help you."

"You were perfect. The way I always imagined my sister would be. Thank you."

Kyla wrapped her pinky finger around mine. "Sisters forever. I'll always be there for you."

"Sisters forever," I confirmed. "Through the good and the bad, we'll always have each other." It was a self-fulfilling prophecy neither of us were ready for.

A week had passed, and Michigan State was playing University of Michigan at Spartan Stadium. Tyler became everything he ever wanted. He was the star quarterback, well on his way to the pros. It was so weird seeing him on TV, not just playing, but doing interviews and really making a name for himself.

The three of us tried to go to as many games as possible, and this was a big one. Tyler always managed to nab us great seats, and to be honest, the four of us being together just felt right. I couldn't imagine a life for Kyla without Tyler. They'd made it this far, no doubt they would go the distance.

Chris and I found our seats while Kyla went down to talk to Ty before the game. I watched Chris, as he took in the stadium we'd been to plenty of times. There was something on his face I couldn't decipher. I reached for his hand and gave it a squeeze. "Do you ever regret it?"

He stared down at our linked hands, then his eyes raked over my body until they reached mine. They were filled with complete love and devotion. "Never. You're worth so much more." He lifted my hand to his lips and kissed it. "I'm not saying I never wonder what it would have been like, but regret? Definitely not. I don't know how Kyla and Tyler do it, but I couldn't. I couldn't stand being away from you."

When the game ended, I promised we'd meet Kyla in the parking lot. She headed down to the locker room where she always met Tyler after the games. Chris fist bumped the guy that had been sitting next to him during the game. "Cool, man. We'll see you there later."

"What was that all about?" I questioned.

"We got invited to a party. Thought maybe we could go hang out later. You know after we grab something to eat with Kyla and Ty. They're going to be making up for lost time and I can't blame them. This will give us something to do."

"Are we going home tonight?"

Chris wrapped his arm around my shoulders. "Figured we could play it by ear. We can always stay at a hotel instead of making that long-ass drive home."

I wrapped my arms around his waist "As long as I'm with you, I don't care where we are."

"I fucking love you, baby." He leaned down and placed a soft kiss on my forehead. "Fucking love you."

After our dinner, Kyla and Ty took off for his dorm to spend the night together. Chris and I sat in his truck deciding what to do. "You want to check out this party?" he asked.

I shrugged my shoulders. "Sure. Why not?"

"Cool." Chris plugged the address he was given into his GPS. Ten minutes later we pulled up in front of a huge house. I would have thought it was the wrong place, but the music pouring out from the inside assured us it wasn't. "Don't leave my side tonight, Tor. We don't know any of these people. I don't want us getting separated."

"I'll stick by your side," I promised.

Chris leaned over and gave me a chaste kiss. "Good. Now let's go have some fun. That guy, Dillon, assured me it would be a good time."

We walked into the party hand in hand. All the furniture had been moved from the front room, which now served as a dance floor. A DJ was set up in the corner and lights flashed, strobing across the room. The music blasted, pounding in my chest.

We pushed through the throng of people and found the bar. Chris snagged us each a beer from the keg. He handed me mine and I took a long drink. We walked through the party taking everything in. This house was huge, with a winding staircase. Couples made their way up and down in easy succession.

We finished our beers and set the cups on a table. Chris pulled me by the hand. "Dance with me?"

I followed him to the dance floor, and we melted in with the dozens of others there. The music thumped as we rocked into each other. I loved dancing with Chris. The way we danced was always like foreplay. He gripped my hips from behind, as I leaned back into his chest, rubbing my ass into him. I leaned my head back and his lips met mine. Our tongues tangled in a slow dance of their own.

After a few more songs, Chris whispered in my ear, "Want another drink?"

I nodded, and he led me back to the keg. Chris filled us two cups, then something caught his eye. He pulled me to the side. Laid out on the counter were small baggies, each containing a single pill. "That X?" Chris asked the guy standing guard.

"You bet. Best around."

Chris gave me a questioning look. "You wanna? We'll take it here, give it time kick in before we head to the hotel."

I bit my lip and nodded. Chris and I had done Ecstasy several times together and it never disappointed. Chris paid the guy and slid the pill from the baggie. He broke it in half, each of us taking it on our tongues.

We grabbed our cups and headed back to the dance floor. Our bodies pressed close together, moving as one. The Ecstasy kicked in faster than we anticipated, and everything was amplified. Lights flashed, and music strummed through my body. We were in our own world. My hands were all over him, and his all over me. We kissed like no one was watching, getting lost in each other. I pulled his head down and whispered, "I want you, baby. I need you."

"Need you too, Tor," Chris whispered in desperation. "I can't wait." He eyed the staircase.

I simply nodded. He pulled me from the dance floor and headed for the stairs. We made our way up the winding steps. We passed through the crowded hall of couples making out until we stumbled upon a room with the door open. We stepped inside and shut it behind us. The only light came from an attached bathroom, where the door was cracked open. I didn't care that we were in a house full of people. We didn't know anyone here anyway. All I knew was that I needed Chris so bad. I needed him to fill the ache inside me. The way only he could. My skin tingled as he ran his hand down the side of my face.

"Love you, Tori." Chris backed me towards the bed. He grabbed the hem of my shirt and slowly lifted it over my head.

"Need you, Chris. Love you so much." My hands ran under his shirt and lifted it away. He pressed his chest to my breasts, and the warmth flowed through me. Our hands were everywhere at once. Rubbing and caressing, taking each other in. Chris released my bra and sucked my hard nipple into his mouth. Fuck it felt good.

He laid me back on the bed and worshipped my tits. Every lick, nip, tug, and pull sent electric currents right to my core. The place between my legs burned with need. This boy knew how to press every one of my buttons.

His hands fumbled with the button and zipper of my jeans. I lifted my hips as he eased them over my ass and down my legs. "You're so beautiful, Tori. I can't get enough of you."

He eased a finger inside of me, then two, and then three. Every nerve in my body came to life, as he pumped them in and out of me. I writhed in the bed as his mouth covered my clit and sparks coursed through me. I was close to falling apart. A few more flicks of his tongue and I shattered. I fell into the abyss and wanted to do it again. "Make love to me, Chris."

Chris undid his jeans and then he was deep inside me. The click of the door barely registered. There was a flash of light and then the room was shrouded in near darkness again. We kept at it. I felt the bed dip next to me. Chris and I both turned our heads to the couple that joined us, seeing them but not caring enough to stop. "Keep going," I said. "I don't wanna stop." Chris continued his slow torture of my body. I was barely aware of the two that shared the same space as us.

Chris's mouth was at my tits again. He sucked and nipped as his hips continued to push into my heat. Soft lips covered mine. I moved with them, our tongues twisting together. A veil of long hair covered my face, as our mouths moved. I felt a hand go down and splay across my stomach, inching towards my sex.

None of it made any sense. But sense, was the last thing on my mind as all my nerve endings lit on fire. I was being touched everywhere at once. The pleasure so great that I didn't care where it was coming from. All I wanted was more. My body felt alive and pulsed beneath the soft touch of the ravenous lips on me. I surrendered to the feeling and let myself go.

Chapter 15
Chris

I woke disoriented. I searched my mind to remember where I was. Tori's head was next to mine on the pillow. The weight on my chest forced me to look down. Blond hair cascaded across it. *What the hell happened last night?* I carefully lifted her off me and rolled out from underneath. The light from the bathroom splayed across the bed. Tori laid on her stomach, with some guy's hand resting on her ass. I quickly threw on my jeans and shirt, then gathered Tori's clothes from the floor. I couldn't find her panties. She'd have to go without. We needed to get out of here. And fast!

I removed the guy's hand from her ass and kissed the side of her face. "Wake up, baby. We need to go."

Tori's eyes fluttered open. She looked at me in confusion. She took in the guy next to her and the girl sprawled on the bed. Both were totally naked. Tori's eyes went wide, as she crawled back off the bed. I handed her the clothes I gathered from the floor. She quickly threw them on and covered her mouth with one hand.

I grabbed her other hand and led her from the room, through the hall, and down the stairs. We made a beeline for the front door and ran to my truck.

Once tucked safely inside, Tori turned to me. "What the fuck did we do?"

I started the truck and pulled away from the curb and headed back to Western. It was barely four o'clock in the morning. The world was silent as we made our escape. I had no answers for her.

"Chris!" She panicked. "What the fuck did we do?"

I ran my hand through my hair as I drove as fast as I could, trying to distance us from the nightmare we'd woken to. "I don't know, Tori," I said honestly. "I don't remember a goddamn thing."

"Fuuuuck!" Her scream filled the cab of the truck. She covered her face with her hands and started to cry. "How could this happen? I don't remember anything."

I grabbed her hand and squeezed. "It's okay, Tor. We're okay."

"The fuck it is! Did I let him…" Her words faded off.

"I don't know, baby."

"Did you…"

"I don't know," I said with more force. It was such a lame answer, but it was the truth. "I don't think we did." I didn't know if that was the truth or what I wanted to believe. I prayed it was the truth. "Come over here." I needed to be as close to Tori as possible.

Tori slid across the seat and wrapped her hands around my arm for security. Her head rested on my shoulder. "How did we let this happen? When we've done Ecstasy before, I've never blacked out. I always remember everything." Tears leaked from the corners of her eyes.

"I think that shit was laced. It kicked in so damn fast. I'm sorry, Tor. This is my fault." I ran my hand through my hair in frustration. "So damn sorry, baby. We should have never gone to that party. What the fuck was I thinking?" *How could I have been that stupid? That careless?*

Tori shook her head against my arm. "No. You're not taking the blame. I could have told you no. I was all in. We did this together."

I kissed the top of her head. "Know what scares me the most?" I asked quietly. "What if I let something happen to you? I was right there. Right fucking there, yet I don't remember anything." I would never forgive myself if something awful happened to Tori and I didn't protect her. That was my fucking job! Take care of her. I failed her tonight.

We rode back to campus in silence. Tori wrapped herself around my arm the whole time, almost as if she was afraid to let go. We went straight to my room, since I had a single, stripped out of our clothes and showered. We washed each other quietly, as if it could wash away our sins. I pulled out a pair of shorts for me and a shirt for Tori. We pulled back the comforter and slipped between the sheets on my bed.

Tori curled into my side, and I held onto her tightly, like my life depended on it. Last night was nothing I ever imagined would happen.

"I remember…" Tori whispered, "I remember her kissing me. And I didn't care. I don't remember anything after that."

"I remember seeing her kiss you and thinking it was probably one of the hottest things I had ever seen. But after that… nothing." I pulled Tori in tighter. I couldn't let go.

"Chris, are we okay? I mean… is this going to change us?"

"We're okay, baby. Nothing changes between us. It was mistake. That's all. Neither of us is to blame. We can't change it. All we can do is move on."

"I can't stop wondering if we," the words got stuck in her throat, "cheated."

"We didn't. There may have been some touching, but I can't and won't believe it went beyond that."

We fell asleep locked in each other's arms. We were afraid to let go.

I looked down at the package in my hands. This was going to destroy Tori. Either way, it was going to be bad. I gave it a lot of thought and made my decision, but it was ultimately hers. I knew how she felt, but this seemed different. My heart caught in my chest. It pounded so hard, I thought it might explode. Anxiety, fear, and hope filled me.

I heard the key turn in the door, and I quickly threw the package under my pillow. Tori walked into my room, throwing her backpack on the floor. She plopped down beside me and pressed her lips to mine. Guilt pressed down on me, but I had to do this. There weren't any choices.

"Hey, baby," she said cheerily. When I didn't return the sentiment, she pulled back. "What's wrong?"

I ran my hand over my face. "We need to talk."

Tori scooted away from me. "That doesn't sound good."

I took a deep breath and spit it out. "You're late."

"Yeah, by like ten minutes. I had to talk to my professor after class about my photography project."

I shook my head. "No, Tori. By a week. You're late."

Tori scrunched up her eyes. She pulled out her phone and clicked open the calendar. "That's not possible. I'm pretty sure…"

I pushed her phone down. "You don't need to check. I'm sure. Ever since you got diagnosed, I've kept track. You've been like clockwork for the last three years."

Tori leaned forward, resting her elbows on her knees. Her head hung in defeat. "I already knew. I was avoiding it."

I rubbed her back gently. "Why?"

127

She looked at me with tears in her eyes. "Because I'm a coward. I kept telling myself, *just give it one more day.* I'm fucking scared, Chris."

I wrapped her in my arms. "You don't have to be scared. I'll be right here with you, but we need to know. If you're not pregnant, then that means the cysts are back. We can't ignore either possibility."

The tears ran freely down her face. "I know."

I reached under my pillow and pulled out the package I hid there. "We find out today." I handed her the pregnancy test. "We'll do it together. I'll be right by your side. You don't have to be scared because I'll always take care of you."

Tori flung her arms around my neck and buried her head in my chest. "Can't we keep pretending?"

I pulled her away from me and framed her face with my hands. "No, baby, we can't. We need to know." I opened the package and pulled out the test and the directions. "It says…"

Tori snatched it from my hand. "I know how it works," she said impatiently. "This isn't my first rodeo." I knew the attitude she was giving me was because she was scared. I didn't take it personally.

Regret filled my chest though. I should have been there the first time she had to take a pregnancy test. I didn't know then, but I did now. I stood up and led her to the bathroom. I leaned forward with my hands on the counter, trying to give her some privacy, as she took the test. This could change everything.

I heard the toilet flush, and Tori thrust the test into my hand. She sank down against the wall outside the bathroom, holding her head in her hands. I sank down next to her and wrapped my arm around her shoulder. Tori leaned into me. We sat in silence, as we waited for the results. The minutes seemed like hours.

Finally, Tori lifted her head. "What does it say?"

I picked up the test and a smile spread across my face. "What?" she asked. I held up the test so she could see the plus sign.

Tori stood up and moved away from me. "How is that good news? What the fuck are you smiling about?"

I stood up and faced her. "Oh, I don't know. It means the cysts aren't back," I shouted, throwing my hands in the air. "Tori, we've been together four and a half years. I can't help it if I'm happy that you're healthy and there's a little piece of me growing inside you. I want this."

Tori narrowed her eyes on me. "Have you forgotten about our little indiscretion? What if it isn't yours? What if that night I did something horrible?"

That thought hadn't even crossed my mind. I approached her as if she were a scared animal. Because right now? That wasn't far from the truth. I rubbed my hands up and down her arms. "You didn't. I'm positive." Okay, so I wasn't positive, but everything told me that what I was saying was true. I wrapped her in my arms. "I want this. I want to have a baby with you. Tell me you want it too," I pleaded.

"Chris, we're still in college. You don't have a job. I don't have a job. How would this work? How would we support ourselves? You know how I feel about this."

I held her by the shoulders and looked down at her. "Yeah, I do. But I also know what the doctor said about you being able to have kids. What if this is our only chance? What if this never happens again and we wasted it? I don't know if I can live with that, Tori."

Her expression softened. "Shit," she said softly.

"I know it wouldn't be easy. We'd have to move back home, and I'd transfer to Oakland, but we could do this. Our parents would help us. I don't think they'd be totally surprised. We've been in love forever. I want this, Tori. I want to have a baby with you." I ran my hand over her stomach. "I love you. That's never going to change. Please tell me you want this. That you want to have my baby."

Tori dropped her head back and stared at the ceiling. "I do. I just don't know if I'm ready, but you're right. What if this is our only chance?"

I smiled down at her. "Is that a yes?"

She nodded. "But this stays between us for now. No one else needs to know."

I did an internal fist pump. I knew this wasn't going to be easy, but we could do it. I couldn't help being totally elated. I picked Tori up and spun her around. "You're having my baby," I said softly. "I couldn't be happier, Tor."

Kyla, Tori, and I headed home for Thanksgiving. I drove while the girls chatted and giggled. I loved seeing them like this. I was glad

Tori had her best friend with her at school. The two of them had always been close, but they seemed to be even closer now. Almost like sisters.

With what we'd found out on Monday after doing the pregnancy test, everything was going to change. Tori and I would have no choice but to move back home. She'd have our baby during the summer. I would end up at Oakland where my brother had gone. I had no idea if Tori would want to finish her degree or stay at home with the baby. It was definitely something we would have to discuss. I didn't want her to give up on her degree. I'm sure our moms would watch the baby, so we could both go to school. There were a ton of details to work out.

One thing was for sure though. I was the happiest I'd ever been. Having Tori was a dream come true, but having a baby with her was on a whole other level. I imagined what she would look like pregnant. Her belly big and round with my baby.

"Ouch!" I rubbed my arm where Tori had smacked it.

"What are you thinking about? You've got this ridiculously goofy look on your face," Tori accused.

I tried to reel it in, especially since Kyla was sitting in the back. "Ummm. Nothing."

She gave me a knowing look. "Yeah, right. I bet it was nothing."

I shrugged my shoulders. "What? Can't a guy just be happy?"

Tori crossed her arms and leaned against the door. "I suppose so." Even though she had agreed, Tori still hadn't totally warmed up to the idea yet. She was scared, and I couldn't blame her. It was scary, for sure, but I knew she would be happy when she was holding that little bundle of love in her arms.

We decided to keep the secret for a while. I wanted to tell everyone. My mom was going to be ecstatic. She loved Tori like a daughter, and she knew this had always been our fate. My dad would be pissed at first, because I hadn't finished my degree yet, but I had no doubt he would warm up to the idea. Eventually.

Tori wanted us to wait until she was at least two months along. She was afraid something might happen, and she didn't want to deal with having to tell everyone if we lost the baby. I wasn't worried. Nothing was going to happen. This baby was meant to be, just like us.

We dropped Kyla at her house and went to Tori's. We were stopping there first and then heading to my house for the night. Tori was helping my mom get things ready for Thanksgiving dinner tomorrow. She'd become quite the cook in her own right. My mom had been teaching her for years, and Tori had been anxious to learn. I never pegged her to be domestic, but she said something about "keeping her man fed and happy". I sure as hell wasn't going to complain. If she wanted to feed me, then so be it.

"This is going to be tough," I said, as I pulled into her driveway.

"What is?" she questioned.

"You know. I'm just so happy. I want to tell everyone, but I know what we agreed to." I cupped her face with my hands. "I love you so much, baby." I touched her tummy. "Both of you."

Tori smiled at me. "We love you too." She pointed at my face and waved it around. "You're really going to have to work on that."

I pulled back. "What?"

"That face," she said. "Everyone is going to know something is going on." Tori huffed out a small breath. "I wish I could be as excited as you. It's just…"

"I know." I caressed the side of her face. "You're scared." She nodded her head. "Me too, baby. Terrified. But it's going to be great. We'll figure it out."

"Okay. As long as you're by my side."

"Always," I promised.

We hopped out of the truck and walked up to the door hand in hand.

"There they are!" Mike greeted us as we walked in.

Tori and I gave hugs to Mike and Elena. Honestly, my family and Tori's family had morphed into one big family. They would be coming to Thanksgiving at my mom's tomorrow. It made everything so much easier for Tori and me because we didn't have to split time between our families. We got to see everyone at once.

Tori shrugged off her coat. I took it from her and hung it with mine on the hook behind the door. "You two need to come home more," Elena said. "We miss you."

Tori gave me a sideways glance. "We'll see what we can do. We wouldn't want you to get sick of us."

Elena waved her daughter off. "Nonsense. That would be impossible."

Tori plopped down on the couch, and I took a seat next to her. "Oh, yeah? What would you think about Chris moving in here for the summer?" I gave Tori a surprised look. I didn't know she was going to drop that bomb. We could have discussed it first, so I was on the same page. I knew what she was doing though. She was testing the waters. She was trying to gage what their reaction would be to us having a baby. My girl was smart. It was probably a good idea to let them get used to one thing before we dropped another on them.

Mike and Elena looked at each other and then shrugged. Mike answered, "I guess that would be all right. You two practically spend all your time together anyways. Before we know it, you two will be married."

I jumped in because, shit, I felt like I should say something. "We promise to be respectful, and I'll help out with whatever needs to be done around here."

Mike laughed. "Oh, I know you will be. Or else I'll kick your ass and you know it."

I laughed back. "You could try, old man, but I assure you it won't be necessary."

The four of us had pizza and salad for lunch, and then Tori and I headed to my house. Before we left, Elena handed us two pies. "You know I can't cook, so this is my contribution. I picked them up this morning from the best bakery in town."

I kissed her on the cheek, "Thanks, Elena. I know my mom will appreciate it."

When we got to my house, Tori went to the kitchen to see my mom and get updated on the plan for dinner. I leaned against the door and watched her put on her apron. She jumped right in to help, taking things from the fridge, and placing them on the counter. When I started dating Tori, I never thought this is what it would turn into.

My dad walked by and clapped me on the shoulder. "She's great. You've done good, son."

I could barely keep that look Tori warned me about off my face. "I'm a lucky guy." I watched her flit around the kitchen, imagining a baby bump under her apron.

While Tori was in the kitchen, I went to my room and opened my laptop. I checked out the Engineering programs at Oakland. Since my brother went there for his degree, I was sure this would work out. It looked like I would still be able to graduate on time if I transferred. Everything was going to fall into place.

Maybe I could pick-up some hours working for my dad, while going to school. A baby was going to be expensive, and I didn't want to depend on anyone to help us financially. We were going to need enough help as it was. I started making mental calculations. My truck was going to paid off in a month, but Tori would need a new car. That beetle wasn't safe for a baby. It was way too small. And eventually, we would need to have a place of our own. Tori was right. We weren't ready. But we'd figure it out.

That night, Tori and I laid in my bed snuggled together.

"I'm exhausted," she declared. "Your mom is a slave driver. You'd think we were feeding fifty people and not eight. There is so much food, we'll be eating leftovers for days."

"That's my mom for you. And eating leftovers is tradition. There can never be enough mashed potatoes and turkey," I reasoned.

Tori laughed. "Sometimes I forget how much you and your brother can eat."

I rubbed her belly. "Don't forget you're eating for two now."

Tori swatted at my hand. "I'm less than a month pregnant. It's like the size of a pea. I don't think I get to use that excuse yet."

I pulled Tori close and nuzzled into her neck. "I'm so happy, baby. You've given me the best birthday slash Christmas present I could ever ask for. Are you happy?"

Tori pulled back and stared into my eyes. "Yes, but I'm scared. Did you know when I was ten, I had a hamster?"

I was a little confused about that random fact, but I played along anyway. "Yeah? What was his name?"

Tori tapped her fingers on my chest. "Her," she corrected. "And her name was Fluff Muffin."

"Fluff Muffin?" I laughed.

"Yes. Fluff Muffin. She was this soft, fluffy teddy bear hamster with long fur. I loved her."

"Yeah? What happened to her?"

Tori's eyes started to water. "I forgot to feed her, and she died," she croaked out. "What if I'm not a good mom and I forget to feed our baby?" The tears leaked down the side of her face.

I crushed Tori to my chest. "Oh, baby. You're going to be a great mom. I'm sure you won't forget to feed her. And if you do, I'll be there to remind you." I rubbed her back softly. "You know you're being irrational, right?" I wasn't sure if it was the pregnancy hormones or what, but regardless, it was kind of cute.

Tori wiped at her eyes. "I know. I know. But seriously, Chris, what if I suck at being a mom?"

"You won't," I said confidently. "You're going to be amazing." I rolled Tori to her back and hovered over her. "I want to marry you."

"I know," she said softly.

"Before the baby comes. I want us to get married this summer."

"Chris…"

"I know we were supposed to wait, but with the baby coming, I don't think anyone would object to us doing it a little early."

She cocked her head to the side as if contemplating what I said. "You don't think it's too much all at one time. We're going to give our parents heart attacks."

"Nah! I think it's perfect." I ran my hand down her face. "I love you, Tori. Will you marry me?"

She nodded her head up and down like a bobblehead. "Yes, Chris. Yes, I'll marry you."

I pressed my lips to hers. "You make me so happy." I deepened the kiss and our tongues twisted together. She was my everything. Everything I always knew I wanted.

Suddenly, Tori pulled back. "Christmas," she stated. I crinkled my eyes at her. "We wait until Christmas to say anything and then we tell them everything. Preferably when everyone is together, so that we only have to do it once."

"Christmas," I agreed. "Now, I wanna make love to my baby mama," I joked.

"Eww! Don't say that! It sounds so… trashy."

I couldn't help but laugh at her reaction. "Okay, okay. How about this?" I tried again, "I want to make love to my future wife and the mother of my child."

Tori's face softened. "Better."

"Now fuck me woman, before I explode."

"There he is! The man I love."

Chapter 16
Tori

We were all sitting around the table for Thanksgiving dinner, and I felt a sense of contentment being surrounded by our family. I couldn't help but think that next year a highchair would be added to the table. The thought made me smile. This baby thing was starting to grow on me.

My mom and Mike were there, as well as Jim and his girlfriend, Rachel. Yes, the ultimate player finally had a serious girlfriend. He and Rachel had been dating for about six months. Chris and I met her a few times before today. She seemed sweet and more to her credit, she tamed the playboy. I knew he loved her, because every time he looked at her, Jim got that same goofy look Chris got. The Capizzio boys weren't very good at hiding their feelings.

"Thank you for inviting us, Trina. Poor Mike never gets homecooked meals like this," my mom said.

"Oh, Elena, it's my pleasure. Consider the invitation open for Christmas, too. We're all going to be related soon enough," Chris's mom stated.

I choked on my water and started to cough. Chris patted me on the back. He leaned down close to my ear. "Are you okay?"

I gave him a forced smile and nodded.

"Not too soon," Chris's dad, barked out. "You two still have a year and half of college to finish." He pointed between Chris and me.

I squeezed Chris's knee under the table, and the joy I felt only a few minutes before started to slip away.

"We're all well aware of your feelings, Dad. If I had my way, Tori and I would already be married." I could hear the frustration in Chris's voice. He wrapped his arm around my shoulder, and I leaned into him.

Feeling brave, I blurted out, "What difference would it make? Our feelings for each other aren't going to change." Chris gave my shoulder a squeeze of encouragement.

"Yeah, what difference would it make?" he pushed.

The table got silent as we looked at our family surrounding us.

Mike spoke up first. "Well for starters, neither one of you has a job. You need to be able to support yourselves."

Sal pointed his fork at Mike. "I knew I liked you, Mike. These kids don't have the first clue what it takes to raise a family and live on their own."

I could see the frustration continuing to build in Chris. "We're not stupid. We know it wouldn't be easy. And we could get jobs." Chris threw his napkin on the table, and I curled into his chest. He wrapped his arms around me in a protective gesture. This was going nowhere good. And fast. If this was the reaction we were getting when talking about getting married, I couldn't imagine what it would be like when we told them I was pregnant.

Trina tried to break the tension. "Honey, we know you two aren't stupid. We just worry is all."

"We only want what's best for the both of you," my mom piped in.

I uncurled myself from Chris's chest and stared at my mom. "And what if what's best for us is each other?"

My mom's face softened. "No one is denying that. We're just asking you to wait. You'll be finished with school before you know it."

I shook my head. They were never going to agree to us getting married this summer. I focused back on my food and shoved mashed potatoes in my mouth to keep from saying anything else.

Chris ran his hand up and down my back, trying to soothe me. No doubt, he was feeling the same way I was.

Jim cleared his throat. "Speaking of getting married. Rachel and I are engaged. We're getting married this summer."

Rachel lifted her hand and wiggled her fingers, showing off her sparkly ring.

The table erupted in rounds of "congratulations" and "that's wonderful".

My heart sank with the news. I stood up and walked around the table. I gave Jim a big hug, "Congratulations, big brother." I embraced Rachel with a fake-ass smile. "I'm so happy for you." I excused myself to the bathroom and locked myself in. I slid down the wall and rested my head back. "This is going to be a disaster," I said to myself. My mind reeled with the reality of our situation.

A soft knock on the door broke me out of my thoughts. "Tor?"

I crawled up on my knees and unlocked the door, then sank back down. Chris came in and shut the door behind him. "What are we gonna do?" I asked quietly, as he sat down next to me. I rested my head on his shoulder.

"Whatever is best for us. Fuck them."

"I love you, Chris." I knew he would do everything he could to follow through on every promise he'd ever made me.

"I love you, too, Tori."

We came back to the table, and everyone stopped talking as we took our seats. All eyes were on us. We sat without saying a word and focused on our meal. I didn't want to ruin Thanksgiving.

The conversation returned to the details of Jim and Rachel's wedding. I pushed the jealous feelings down and tried to smile and act interested. I did a good job of faking it too.

Chris, not so much. It didn't take long for him to crack.

"Jim, I'm totally happy for you and Rachel. And I wish you nothing but happiness, but this is bullshit." Chris pushed away from the table, threw his napkin down again, and stood up. "You two have known each other for six months and everyone is ecstatic that you're getting married. Which they should be. But Tori and I want to get married after four and a half years and everyone acts like were stupid and ridiculous. It's fucking bullshit, and you all know it!"

"Chris..." I grabbed his hand.

"No, Tori! I'm done tiptoeing around this. I would have married you two years ago. We've done everything to try to make everyone else happy. When do we get to be happy?"

"Christopher..." Sal interrupted in a harsh tone.

"Whatever, Dad. I don't want to talk about it anymore. I need some air." Chris stormed through the house and out through the front door. I flinched when it slammed behind him.

I looked at all the shocked faced around the table. "I'm sorry," I said. "We really are happy for you two. Chris and I have just been waiting a long time to get married. This was... unexpected." I pushed out of my chair. "If you'll excuse me, I'm going to go check on him."

I grabbed both our coats and went out on the front porch. It was freezing outside. I looked around and finally found Chris leaning against his truck. I handed him his jacket and he slipped it on. "You okay?" I asked.

"Yeah. I just got fucking pissed." He pulled me into his arms. "It's frustrating. Why can't they be happy for us and supportive? I don't want to spend anymore nights away from you. I know we spend the night together a lot, but even one night apart is too much for me. I want all of you, every day and every night. Is that too much to ask?"

"Well… maybe they'll change their minds when they find out about the baby. But I definitely think we should wait until Christmas. Maybe, they'll all cool down by then. For now… it's just you and me, baby," I smiled up at him.

"You mean, me, you and a baby." He kissed the top of my head.

"I guess I do." I gave him a little tug. "You gonna come back inside? Or stay out here and freeze your balls off?"

Chris took my hand and put it between his legs, "You could always keep them warm for me."

"Yeah?" I started to rub him through his jeans. "Right here? Right now?" I gave him a little squeeze.

He grabbed my hand. "Hey. Be nice to our future children."

I pulled him toward the house. "Come on, Romeo. I heard your mom made crow pie for dessert."

He groaned. "I hate crow pie. Do I really have to eat it?"

"Yes. Yes, you do," I laughed.

The rest of the weekend passed uneventfully with no more talk of marriage. Chris and I decided to drop it for now, because soon there would be a whole lot of stuff to talk about with our parents.

Before we knew it, it was time to go back to school. Chris and I picked up Kyla on the way. "How was your holiday?" I asked her.

"It was good. It was nice to be able to see Tyler for more than one day. But," she sighed, "he had to go back early. Practice calls." Kyla rolled her eyes. "Ignore me. I'm being a total bitch right now. I knew this was what I signed up for, but I'll be glad when football season is over."

I leaned over the seat. "Just because you knew it would be this way, doesn't make it easy. I get it. You miss him."

Kyla closed her eyes and leaned back against the seat. "I do. I really do."

Chris looked at her through the rearview mirror. "Hold tight, baby girl. Once the season is over, it'll get easier. It always does."

"I know. I know. Just a few more weeks, then Christmas vacation will be here, and I'll have him until next August."

I felt bad for Kyla. She wouldn't trade Tyler for anything, but it had to be tough. Kyla never talked about it, but we all saw how the girls flocked to him at the games. It couldn't be easy to watch. What had to be even harder, was living an hour and a half apart. Ty and Kyla had one of the most trusting relationships I'd ever seen. But it had to be that way, or they'd never make it.

We'd been back to school for almost two weeks. Chris and I had practically locked ourselves away in his room, making plans and figuring out the best way to tell our parents about the little peanut growing inside me. Despite still being scared, I was excited. Maybe it didn't fit into our initial timeline, but life doesn't always go as planned. What was there to be upset about? I was finally going to marry Chris and have his baby. The doctor had said it might be difficult to get pregnant and it turned out not to be hard at all. The antibiotics I took for my respiratory infection must have interfered with my birth control. Sometimes fate had a plan all her own.

I was feeling hopeful and had finally made peace with our unplanned future when I knocked on my professor's door. This was our last meeting before I turned in my photography project. I'd finally settled on a major. I took Chris's advice and chose something I loved. I majored in photography with a minor in journalism. Surely, I could find something to do with that. At the very least I could work for a studio taking pictures of families and graduates. Maybe work for a local paper. It was a place to start anyway.

I knocked on my professor's open door and gave her a little wave. "Am I early?"

"You're right on time. Come on in, Tori." She looked at me over her glasses, with a soft smile. "I've been looking over what you've turned in so far and I'm really impressed. This is good."

I sat in the chair opposite her desk. "Thank you. I have a question about my collage though. Something feels off about the layout."

She stared at the collage, turning it sideways and then back again. "I think you need to add a few more candid shots to balance it out. You've really captured your theme though."

I smiled at her compliment. I titled my collage, "Love is Everywhere". My relationship with Chris was my inspiration, but not the subject of my work. Some of the photos were staged and others a result of me being in the right place at the right time.

"What about adding...?" I froze. I felt the wetness seeping out from between my legs.

No, no, no! This isn't happening!

I panicked.

My professor gave me a quizzical stare at my evident change in demeanor.

"I'm... I'm going to have to reschedule." I quickly stood and backed out of her office. "I'm sorry. I... I have... have to go," I stammered.

"Tori? Are you all right?" she questioned. "You look white as a ghost."

"I'm sorry," I apologized again. "I need to go. I'll call to reschedule."

I sped through the hall and down the stairs. I looked in my purse. "Shit! Shit! Shit!" I didn't have anything on me. I didn't think I'd need it. I took off my flannel shirt and tied it around my waist.

Pushing through the doors, I took off into the cold towards the dorms. I made it there in record time, bypassed my room, and went right up to Chris's. Fumbling with the key, I finally got the door open and raced to the bathroom. Thankfully, Chris wasn't back from class yet. I prayed that I was wrong. That this was a false alarm.

I tore my pants down my legs and just as I had feared, my underwear was covered in blood. Lots and lots of blood. It seeped through to my jeans, which were now soaked. My heart sank. Just when I started to get happy and excited, it was ripped away from me. Life was a cruel fucking joke.

My walls started to go up again. The walls that protected my heart from the hurt. The walls Chris worked so hard to knock down. The bricks were snapping into place one at a time. I didn't know if I would be able to build them high enough to protect me this time, but I was going to fucking try.

There wasn't much to do but clean myself up. I went into auto-pilot mode. Doing what had to be done without thinking about it. I jumped in the shower and watched the evidence of my failed pregnancy wash down the drain. *Snap! A brick fell into place.* Feeling empty, I dried off, then reached under the bathroom cabinet where I kept some of my girly stuff. *Snap! Another brick.* I found a pair of Chris's sweatpants and threw them on along with a pair of his boxer briefs. It wasn't ideal, but I didn't give a fuck. *Snap!* I put my underwear and pants in a garbage bag. *Snap!* I tossed the garbage bag in the corner of the bathroom and laid down on Chris's bed.

Damn it! As hard as I was trying to build that fucking wall, it seemed the bricks kept falling out of place. My heart felt exposed and raw. Nothing could protect me from the hurt I was feeling.

I pulled the covers up over my head. That's when the first tear fell. Fuck Fate! I hated her! She was an evil bitch! I let the tears fall fast and hard. I didn't even bother trying to wipe them away. Chris was going to be devastated. That's what hurt me the most.

A half hour later, Chris came in. "Hey. You're here. I brought us dinner. I figured you'd be late since you had that meeting for your project. How'd it go?" His happiness was evident. He'd been on cloud nine for the last two weeks.

I kept my head buried in the blankets. "I had to reschedule. Something came up."

He sat on the edge of the bed and pulled the blanket from my head. I knew he could see the sadness in my eyes. I probably had tear streaks running down my face. "With her or you?" he asked cautiously.

I swallowed hard and closed my eyes. "Me," I choked out.

Chris pulled me onto his lap. "What happened?"

My eyes welled up again. "I…" A deep breath released from my chest, and I looked him in the eyes. I needed to just say it. There was no way around this. "I started my period. We lost the baby."

Chris leaned back, and he shook his head in denial. "Are you sure? Maybe it's just spotting. That happens sometimes, right?" The hope in his voice was crushing.

I dropped my head. "No, Chris. I was standing there in my professor's office when it happened. Full blown gushing. Not a little blood. A lot. And it hasn't stopped. I'm so sorry."

He lifted my chin. His eyes were full of tears, and one fell down his cheek. "Hey…"

"I'm so damn sorry, Chris. I don't know what I did wrong. I'm sorry I disappointed you." Now we were both crying. I didn't realize this was going to hurt so much. I'd never seen him like this. He'd always been my rock.

"Don't you dare apologize!" He wrapped his arms around me and buried his head in my hair. His voice hitched. "Don't you dare. Do you hear me? This isn't your fault."

I nodded into his chest. "What do we do now?"

"I don't know," he admitted. "I never thought this would happen. How do you feel?"

I pulled away from him and sat cross-legged on the bed. I wiped my eyes and steeled myself, grasping for the bricks I needed. "Oh, you know me." I stared up at the ceiling and tried to pull it together. I tried to build that wall. "It's probably for the best. We weren't ready…"

"Don't!" Chris snapped, standing from the bed. His eyes bored into me. "Don't make this into nothing, Tori! Don't pretend it doesn't matter! Don't you dare build that wall!"

I wasn't going to sit there and take his shit. I stood and faced him. I threw my arms out to the sides. "What do you want from me? You want me to admit that I'm crushed? That I fell in love with our baby? That I wanted it so bad? That I feel empty? That I feel like a failure? Is that what you want?" I shouted.

"Yes," he hissed.

"So, you want me to fall apart?" I yelled at him.

He pointed at me with an accusatory finger. "I want you to admit that you feel something!"

I pointed my finger at my own chest. "I fucking feel everything! But if you think I'm going to let it destroy me, then you don't know me at all!" I was done with this bullshit. I'd had more than enough for the day. I grabbed my backpack and headed toward the door. I felt my heart harden a little more.

Chris's voice stopped me. "Excuse the fuck out of me, if I expected you to care!"

I looked at him over my shoulder. "Maybe that's the problem," I said softly. "I cared too damned much."

I walked out the door and toward the stairs. He didn't follow me. Maybe this was it. It could have been a speed bump or the end of the road. I wasn't sure. My heart hardened with every step I took.

I walked into the cold, dark night and stared up at the stars. Snowflakes fell in a light flurry around my head. I kept walking. I didn't know where I was going. I just let my feet lead the way.

I wanted to get trashed. I wanted to drink until I couldn't feel the pain. My twenty-first birthday was still a few weeks away, so buying alcohol was out of the question. I could get high, but Chris had all our pot. I wasn't going back there. Not tonight.

My feet kept walking and I ended up in front of a party store a few blocks away. As luck would have it, a guy from my journalism class was standing out front smoking a cigarette. I approached him, like we were friends. We weren't. "Hey, Joel."

He turned toward me, with a big-ass smile on his face. "Hey, Tori. How goes it?"

I kicked at an invisible rock. "Been better. Can you do me a favor?"

His smile grew wider. "For you? Anything."

Bingo! This guy was putty in my hands. I should have felt guilty about the way I was going to use him, but I couldn't bring myself to care. "Can you buy me a pint of Absolute?"

He cocked his head at me. "Sure. Celebrating something?"

"Not exactly," I said honestly. "I need an escape. Do you mind?"

He looked at me with something like pity. Of course, he had no idea what I'd been through, but he agreed anyway. He took the money from my hand. "Wait here," he said.

Joel disappeared into the store and came back a few minutes later. "Here you go," he said, holding out the bag.

"Thanks." I placed it into my backpack. "I owe you."

"You look like you could use a friend," he said. I don't know if he was actually concerned or thought he could get into my pants. Either way, it didn't matter.

"I'd prefer to be alone," I insisted. "It's kind of a one-person party tonight." I tapped on my backpack to drive home my point.

"That's cool," he said. "If you change your mind, let me know." He reached into his backpack and scribbled his number on a piece of paper.

I took the paper and winked at him. "I will." I made my way into the store and left him standing outside.

I walked to the counter. "I'll take a pack of Newports," I told the clerk. I grabbed a lighter and placed it on the counter. I had never smoked before, but something about this felt right. Another escape. He rang up my stuff and I paid him. Before I left, I crumbled up the number Joel gave me and handed it to the clerk. "Can you throw this away for me?"

I exited the store with no destination in mind. All I knew was that I wanted to be alone. I headed back toward campus and found myself under my favorite tree. It was the place I always went to think. I didn't want to think tonight. I wanted to get fucked up.

I sat down on the grass, the sweatpants I was wearing not fending off the cold very well. I leaned against the tree and rifled through my backpack. I pulled out the bottle and twisted off the top. Holding the bottle to my lips, I took a long swig. Then I opened the pack of cigarettes and lit my first one. The menthol was soothing, but it tasted like shit. Of all the stuff Chris and I had tried, I couldn't believe smoking wasn't one of them. "We're so fucked up," I said to myself.

I continued my pity party, smoking the godawful cigarettes and drinking straight from the bottle. It provided me precisely what I was looking for. An escape. My own little world where nothing could hurt me.

Chapter 17
Chris

I found her exactly where I thought I would. She was leaning against that tree, bottle in one hand and a cigarette in the other. I approached her slowly. She was that scared animal again. I knew it. The slightest wrong move would cause her to run. Cuz my girl was a runner. When things got tough, it was always her first instinct.

She didn't see me. She was too lost in her own world as I crept up on her. "I know you care," I said softly. "Too damn much."

She looked up at me with sad eyes. She was hurting, and I hurt her more. But damn it, I was hurting too. I hated when she did this. Escaped into her own little world. "We're fucked up," she said.

I sat down beside her. "Yeah, but we're fucked up together."

Tori leaned her head on my shoulder. "I do care."

I wrapped my arm around her. "I know."

She took another swig from the bottle and passed it to me. "Why? Why did this happen to us?"

Taking a drink, I let out a sigh. "I don't know." I let her continue to smoke that damn cigarette, even though I hated it.

She held the cigarette out and looked at it. "This tastes like shit."

I laughed. "Then why are you smoking it?"

She shrugged her shoulders. "Seemed like the thing to do. You know, pity party and all." Then she took another hit.

"Whatever makes you happy," I said.

She kissed me on the cheek. "You make me happy."

"You got room in there for both of us?" I asked. Tori looked at me with confusion. "Inside that wall," I clarified. "I know you're building it. I just want to be on the inside, not the outside."

"Might get a little cramped. There's not much room in there for anything but me," she answered with a chuckle.

"That's okay. I like being close to you."

"Yeah?"

"Yeah." I kissed her on the forehead. "Let's go home." I pulled Tori to her feet, and she stumbled a little. "How much did you drink?" I asked.

"Not that much. I took small sips."

I held up the bottle and inspected it. "A lot of small sips."

Tori shrugged her shoulders. "Meh."

I wrapped her in my arms and walked her back to the dorms. As we passed a garbage can, Tori threw the pack of cigarettes into it. "Those were so gross," she said.

I laughed at her, squeezing her tighter. "Let's go to bed," I said.

"I gotta stop in my room and grab some stuff," she insisted.

We made our way up to Tori's room. Kyla was sitting on her bed studying. "Where have you two been? I haven't seen either of you much this week."

Tori searched through her drawers and threw a few things in a small bag. "Just had a lot going on, that's all. I'm gonna spend the night in Chris's room. I'll see you in the morning?"

Kyla nodded. If she noticed something was off, she didn't say anything. "Have fun you two," she said with a smirk. Little did she know that "fun" was the furthest things from our minds tonight.

Back in my room, Tori crawled under the covers of my bed, and I slid in behind her, pulling her in close. "I'm sorry I got pissed and left earlier," she whispered.

I kissed the top of her head. "Don't worry about it. I shouldn't have accused you of not caring. I know you care."

"I didn't want to because it hurt too much. I didn't realize how much I wanted our baby, until it was gone. It was easier to pretend that it didn't matter. But it does. I'm sorry if I made you think otherwise," she apologized.

"You think I don't know you by now? I know you feel everything. I know you always try to hide the way you feel. I know you don't want others to see you as weak, and you hold everything in. I knew you we're building that wall around yourself the minute you told me about losing the baby. I know you, Tori. Better than anyone."

"You always could see right through all my bullshit. Sometimes it scares me because I can't hide anything from you," she admitted.

"Doesn't keep you from trying though. I want to be inside that wall with you, Tor. That way I can keep you safe with me. You'd think after all this time, you'd understand."

"Understand what?" she asked.

"That it's you and me against the world. We share everything. Not just the good, but the bad too. And if you're scared or sad or pissed off…I'm here. I want to be the one you run to, not away from."

"I don't know why I run. You catch me anyway."

"I'll always catch you, whether you're running or falling. Always," I promised. "Now… I want to talk about the baby." She started to protest, but I put my finger over her lips. "We need to. I need to. I can't keep everything inside like you. I need this."

"Okay," she agreed reluctantly. "I only have one stipulation." I nodded for her to continue. "I want to keep this between us. I don't want anyone else to know. It's too personal."

"Agreed. It'll be our secret." I'd always been more forth coming with my feelings, from the first time I told her I loved her until now. "I'm sad. Devastated, actually. I wanted this so bad with you. I already had this perfect family planned in my mind. A little girl with dark hair and honey eyes. You're going to make the best mom ever one day." I ran my hand over her stomach. "I know now why you wanted to wait to tell everyone. You're smart that way. I'm so much more impulsive than you."

"I wanted this too. Don't think that I didn't. I didn't realize how much, until it was taken away from us. I knew losing the baby was going to crush you, and that killed me as much as anything." She leaned her head back and placed a gentle kiss on my lips. "Now I don't have a birthday gift for you."

"Tor, you're my gift. Every day."

"I guess Christmas won't be crazy, since we won't be dropping any bombs on our parents."

"I still want to marry you," I told her.

"I know."

"This summer. Losing the baby doesn't change that."

"You still want to fight with everybody?"

"I don't care about anyone but you." I left it at that. We'd already had enough stress today without talking about a wedding. I just wanted to snuggle up to her tonight. I eased out of the bed and stripped my jeans off. Then, I pulled my sweats off her. I hadn't given a second thought as to why she was wearing them. I looked at her legs and laughed. "Why are you wearing my underwear?"

She pouted her lip. "Mine got ruined, so I improvised."

"That just looks so wrong, but it's kind of sexy," I admitted. I crawled back in bed and twined our legs together. "I love you, Tori. You and me. Forever."

Tori and I made it through Christmas. We kept our secret. I didn't think we could get any closer, but the loss we shared made our bond impenetrable. There was nothing that could break us apart.

And it made us even more desperate for each other. Our sex life was totally out of control. I wasn't complaining. We'd added to the collection of toys she bought for prom. I loved making love to my girl, but the down and dirty kinky sex we had... fucking phenomenal.

We ended our Christmas vacation by flying out to Pasadena. That fucker, Tyler, had managed to get Michigan State to the Rose Bowl. Un-fucking-believable. I was so proud of my best friend. Not only had they gotten there, but they won. Again, un-fucking-believable.

We headed to Michigan State for a celebration party. Kyla, Tori, and I drove through a goddamn snowstorm to get there, but I wouldn't have missed it for the anything. Kyla went to find Tyler, while Tor and I hit the bar.

We'd only been there ten minutes before all hell broke loose. Kyla ran down the stairs and out the door crying. Tori ran after Kyla. I stood in the doorway and watched the two of them running down the sidewalk. Tyler bumped me out of the way, shirtless, and screamed after Kyla. His eyes were glassy, and he was totally out of it. He never even saw me before he stormed back up the stairs.

I stood there in total confusion. *What the hell was going on?* This was supposed to be a great night, and... well, I didn't know what happened. My phone buzzed in my pocket, and I immediately picked up Tori's call. "Can you get the truck and come get us? We're just down the street."

"Be right there," I answered. I didn't even ask questions because I was sure I was going to get an earful soon.

I pulled up and Kyla was in tears. "What the fuck is going on? Why is she crying?"

Tori jumped in the back with Kyla and shook her head. "Just drive. There's a hotel a few miles up. We're staying there for the night."

Alrighty! I drove to the hotel and checked us in. When we got to the room, Kyla went straight to the bathroom and Tori explained the debacle that occurred. Kyla walked in on Tyler screwing some other chick.

I was fucking pissed! I could have understood—not approved of—but understood if Ty cheated on Kyla while away at school. But to do it when he knew she was coming to see him? Fucking unacceptable! I couldn't imagine cheating on Tori and I thought Tyler felt the same way about Kyla.

I stormed out of the hotel and back to that fucking party. I was going to get some answers. I pulled up in front of the house and called Tyler. He answered on the first ring. "You still at that party?" I asked.

"Yeah, I'm getting ready to leave," he answered in a clipped tone.

"Meet me out front. We need to talk," I barked at him and hung up on his ass.

A few minutes later he stumbled out of the house and climbed into the cab of my truck. He was fucking wasted out of his mind. I suspected alcohol, but he could have been fucked up on something else too. I'd never seen him this far gone. He was always the guy who had a few drinks and cut himself off. But not tonight.

"You wanna explain to me why Kyla's sitting in a hotel room with Tori, crying her eyes out?" I didn't even try to keep it a secret that I was pissed. Kyla was like a little sister to me, and I felt protective of her.

He ran his hands through his hair. "I fucked up! That's why!"

I rolled my eyes. "Obviously! Care to explain?"

"Dude, I don't even know! Arrrgh!" I waited for more of an explanation than that. I tapped my fingers on the steering wheel impatiently. "I don't know. I was waiting for you guys to get here. I started doing shots. I got drunk. I thought I saw Kyla, so I went up behind her and took her upstairs to one of the rooms. It was dark. One minute I'm inside what I think is my girl, the next she's standing in the doorway. That's when I realized it wasn't Kyla, but some chick I don't even know named Madison." He knew he had fucked up and he looked miserable.

"That's fucked up!" I told him flatly.

He glared at me. "You don't think I know that!" he screamed at me. The guy had balls tonight. I'd give him that.

"How, after being with Kyla for three years, did you not know?" I asked the obvious question.

"I was drunk! I still am, but this has sobered me up pretty fast. I'm telling you this chick looked just like Kyla from behind. I never looked at her face until it was too late!"

No way that would ever happen to me. I knew every curve of Tori's body. "I don't even know what to say. I believe that you didn't mean for this to happen, but it did. Now what?" I actually felt bad for him. He'd dug a hole so deep for himself that his chances of getting out were slim to none.

"Take me to see her. I have to talk to her," he pleaded.

"No way, man! You're still drunk and nothing good can come of that. I'm taking you back to your dorm. Sleep it off. Then come see her in the morning," I suggested. Even though I was pissed, he was still my friend. The four of us had been friends for a long time and I didn't want to see it end. Not like this.

"You're right. I know you're right. But not seeing her is killing me. I need to get her back. This is going to destroy us."

"I'm not gonna lie, it might. But just wait 'til the morning." I took him to the dorms and then headed back to the hotel.

Tyler must've had a magic dick, because somehow, he convinced Kyla to give him a second chance. Two days later she was back at Western, and it was officially over. I guess his dick wasn't that magic after all. I couldn't blame Kyla for not taking him back, but it still bummed me out.

Kyla was miserable. She barely left her room except for classes. Tori's mother hen instinct came out, and she spent a ton of time with Kyla, trying to get her out of the funk she was in.

Tori sauntered into my room and plopped down on the bed. "I'm exhausted!"

I set my calculus book aside and rubbed her back. "You seem so stressed out lately. What's going on? You wanna talk about it?" I asked. Tori had been acting strange. I knew she was keeping something from me, I just didn't know what it was. I saw her internal struggle. She wanted to tell me, but she wouldn't. I wasn't going to push her. She'd tell me when she was ready.

It couldn't have been about us because we were closer than we'd ever been. "It's this thing with Kyla and Tyler. I wish they would fix things. She really needs him. She's so goddamn stubborn and independent," Tori stated.

That made me laugh. "You mean just like her best friend?"

Tori glared at me. "We're not talking about me right now."

"Just saying." I pulled Tori into my side. "I talked to Tyler today."

"Yeah? What'd he say?" she asked.

"He's just as miserable as Kyla. But he insists that Kyla wanted space and that he's going to give it to her. He's leaving the ball in her court, so to speak."

"Ugh!" Tori exclaimed. "They're both stubborn jackasses!"

The weeks went by, and my girl was getting more and more depressed. I could see the weight pressing down on her. Sometimes I would see her get lost in her own thoughts and tears would fill her eyes. She'd push it all down and pretend like everything was all right. But I knew better. She was going to crack soon. Since she wouldn't talk to me, all I could do was be prepared to catch her when she fell.

Then, one day she barged into my room and her smile was back. "Think I can crash in your room for the weekend?"

"Is that even a real question?" I asked.

Tori pressed her lips to mine. I ran my tongue along her bottom lip and pushed into her mouth. Our tongues tangled together, and she straddled me. "Didn't know if you were sick of me yet?" she teased.

I laid down, bringing her with me. I cradled her face with my hands. "Never."

"Good, because Tyler and Kyla are finally getting their shit together. He's coming here tonight, and I want to give them time alone."

"No shit! Who cracked first? Him or her?" I asked.

"She did. I've been telling her for weeks to call him. They really need to talk. We both know they belong together," Tori said. She seemed relieved. Although I would be happy to see Kyla and Tyler back together, I couldn't understand why Tor was so invested in their relationship. I mean, people break up. It happens.

"When's he getting here?" I hadn't seen my best friend in weeks, and I missed that fucker.

"I'm not sure. Tonight sometime."

"Let's go get your stuff," I suggested. "I'm going to keep you in bed the entire weekend."

"I like the sound of that," Tori kissed me long and hard. Whatever had been bothering her, seemed to have disappeared.

We went down to Tori and Kyla's room to get her things. "Kyla, I hope you're decent. Chris is here," Tori called out.

I waited in the doorway for the all-clear. Although the three of us were like family, I never wanted to make Kyla uncomfortable. I tried to respect her privacy. "Chris, get in here! Now!" Tori's voice was panicked as she called for me.

I rushed inside and what I saw made my stomach turn. Kyla was splayed out on the bathroom floor. Blood was smeared all over the white tile and down her legs. It looked like a goddamn murder scene. Tori had Kyla's head cradled in her hands. "What the fuck? Where is all that blood coming from?"

Tori looked up at me with a mixture of fear and guilt. "She's miscarrying. We need to get her to the hospital."

What. The. Fuck? "She's pregnant?"

Tori got impatient. "Yes, I need you to help me pick her up."

I shook myself out of my stupor. "Screw that!" I tossed my keys to Tori. "Go get my truck and pull it up front. I got her."

Tori rushed out of the room. I grabbed a blanket and scooped Kyla up in my arms. I could tell she was close to passing out. Her eyes were dilated, and her breathing was shallow. "Don't you pass out on me, baby girl. You gotta stay with me. You hear me?" She nodded her head weakly and then went limp in my arms.

I rushed her down the stairs and out to my waiting truck. I slipped Kyla into the back seat. Tori jumped into the back with her. I hopped into the driver's seat and started off towards the nearest hospital. I was in shock, but I was pissed too. Tori obviously knew about this, and she kept it from me. I glared at her in the rearview mirror. "How long, Tori? How long have you known about this?"

Tori wouldn't meet my eyes. "A while."

"How long is a while?" I persisted.

Tori's eyes filled with tears as she met my gaze in the mirror. "Since the party. She's fourteen weeks pregnant."

"Jesus Christ, Tori! How could you not tell me?" I yelled at her.

The tears were streaming down her face. "I couldn't! I promised her! She made me promise not to tell! I didn't have a choice!"

"Fuck that! You had a choice! Does Tyler even know about this?" I questioned.

Tori shook her head. "No. She was going to tell him tonight."

"Fuuuck!"

We pulled up to the emergency entrance and I carried Kyla inside. Tori explained to the nurse what happened. They whisked Kyla away and we were left alone. Tori ambled over to one of the hard, plastic chairs in the waiting room and sat down. She looked lost.

I sat down next to her. "I'm pissed at you," I said quietly.

"I know, but I can't fight with you right now." She looked over to the doors they had taken Kyla through. "I'm worried about her. There was so much blood. What if we hadn't found her?"

I wanted to wrap her in my arms and tell Tori that everything would be okay, but I was still mad. Tyler was going to flip the fuck out. "I have to call Tyler. Damn both of you girls for making me be the one to do this. This isn't fair."

I stood up and walked out the doors into the cold night air. I pulled out my phone and stared at it before finally making the call. He answered, sounding happier than I had heard him in weeks. "Hey, Chris. Long time, no talk. What's up, man?"

I closed my eyes. How could I tell him this? "Tyler, you need to come out here right now."

"I'm already on my way. Kyla called yesterday. We're going to try and fix this shit between us. I should be at the dorms in a little over an hour. What's going on?"

I took a deep breath, "Don't go to the dorms. You need to come to the hospital."

There was a long pause, "What the fuck is going on? Is Kyla okay?"

I had no choice but to tell him the truth, even though I knew it was going to tear him apart. "Honestly, I don't know. She scared the fuck out of us. Tori and I came back to her room, and Kyla was laying on the bathroom floor. There was fucking blood everywhere." *Just spit it out,* I told myself. "Tori thinks she's having a miscarriage."

The silence on the line was deafening. "A... miscarriage? She's... pregnant?"

"Apparently. I didn't know. And from the tone of your voice, I'm assuming you didn't either."

"Is it... is it mine?" he asked tentatively.

"Yeah fucker... I'm pretty sure it's yours. She hasn't been with anyone else. She barely leaves her room except to go to class. Just... just get here. She passed out on me when I carried her out to my truck. She didn't look good, and nobody has told us anything yet."

I gave him the name of the hospital and ended the call. *Is it mine?* Jesus Christ! I couldn't even believe he would ask something like that. After everything that girl had stood next to him through, and his first instinct was to question if the baby was his. He was my friend, but that... it was a dick move.

It was late when Tori finally got to see Kyla. She was going to be okay, but she lost the baby. Tori and I left the hospital in silence. I was still mad at her. She knew it and I saw the regret in her eyes. The sadness that had taken over. No doubt I would forgive her. It would take some time, but how could I not?

154

Chapter 18
Tori

We got back to the dorms and went straight to my room. Chris had barely said three words to me. I couldn't stand the tension between us. It was my fault. It was all my fault.

I should have told him, but I couldn't break my promise to Kyla. When she told me the night of the party that she was pregnant, everything in me broke.

Chris sat down on my bed, while I went to the bathroom. He watched me as I grabbed the bleach cleaner from under the sink and began to wash away the evidence of what happened. I was on my hands and knees wiping away the blood when I couldn't take the silence anymore. "I wanted to tell you," I whispered.

"Why didn't you?" he asked.

I met his eyes. "I made her a promise. I couldn't tell you until she told Tyler. I begged her to tell him, but she wouldn't. Not after he cheated."

"Why couldn't you tell me? Didn't you trust me?"

"You know I trust you, but I couldn't put that burden on you. How could I ask you to keep this from Tyler? And how would he feel if you knew before he did? Can you imagine if Tyler had known I was pregnant before you did? How would that make you feel?"

Chris hung his head. "I get it. I don't like it, but I get it."

I wrung the washcloth out in the sink and watched the blood circle the drain. The memories of my own failed pregnancy flooded my mind. "I saw her baby," I said softly.

Chris's head snapped up to meet my eyes. "I took her to the doctors, and I saw it on the ultrasound. Twice. I heard the baby's heartbeat. And all I could think was… it should have been me. That should have been our baby I was looking at on the screen. It should have been us." I sat down on the floor in the bathroom and looked at Chris through the open door. "I was so jealous and sad. I was mad at her for not sharing it with Ty. But she was afraid Ty would reject both her and the baby. That it didn't fit into his plan for playing pro ball. All I could think was that she didn't deserve to have a baby if she wouldn't tell him. And now look what happened? I'm such a shitty friend."

"You're not. You helped her when she needed you most. You kept your promise to her, even though it hurt you. You've been the best friend she could ask for."

I threw the cloth down on the floor. "But at what cost? Now, no one is happy. Tyler's pissed and hurt. Kyla's heartbroken. And us? I don't even know what we are."

"We're us. I'm still hurt that you didn't tell me, but that doesn't mean I don't love you. It wasn't fair I found out this way. And Tyler? I can't imagine what he's going through."

"I know," I said. "I'm sorry. I felt so torn. I wanted to tell you, I just couldn't break Kyla's confidence. She was so alone and scared, but she loved that baby. She wanted it more than anything. I tried to be her strength and her shoulder to cry on. It wasn't easy to keep this from you for the last two months."

"Does she know what happened to us?" he asked.

I shook my head. "I wouldn't betray you like that."

"Is this why you've been so depressed lately?"

I nodded, and a tear fell down my cheek. "I couldn't stop thinking about what we could have had. She had the cutest little baby bump. I felt like it was being thrown in my face day after day. I couldn't escape it."

Chris rose from the bed and entered the bathroom. He kneeled before me and took my hands in his. "That was a lot to carry around by yourself. We'll have our chance." He pulled me up to my feet. "Kyla's gonna need you tomorrow. We should get some sleep."

"Please don't be mad at her. She made a mistake. An awful mistake, by keeping her pregnancy a secret. This is going to destroy her. She's going to be alone. Even if Ty forgives her, he lives an hour and a half from here. I don't want to feel like I have to choose between the two of you."

"I would never make you choose."

A blood curdling scream woke me from a dead sleep. It was the third time this week. I pulled back the covers and rushed to Kyla's side, shaking her out of her nightmare. She was sweating, and tears were running down her face. "Kyla, wake up, sweetie! It's just a dream!"

Her eyes popped open. Her breathing came in short, ragged breaths. Her eyes darted around the room as she got her bearings. "I'm sorry," she gasped. "I didn't mean to wake you again."

Kyla had been home from the hospital for over a week. She'd called me, the morning after her miscarriage, crying. She needed me to pick her up from the hospital. Tyler left her in the middle of the night. No goodbye. No note. No nothing. She hadn't heard from him since. Losing Tyler and the baby all in one night more than destroyed her. She barely attended classes. She wasn't eating. And she sure as fuck wasn't sleeping. Lately, neither was I. Her nightmares were getting worse.

"It's okay. Wanna talk about it?" I pulled back her covers and crawled in bed next to her.

Kyla covered her face with her hands. "I don't know what to do. I call, and he doesn't answer. I text, and he doesn't respond. I didn't get pregnant on purpose. I'm not the one who cheated, yet I'm the one being punished. I know I should have told him earlier, but would it have made a difference? He never wanted a baby to begin with." Her silent tears turned into full out sobs.

I wrapped my arms around her and held her close. "It's his loss. You're the best thing that ever happened to him. If he can't see that, then he's blind."

"Do you think there's someone else? Do you think he's with Madison?" she asked.

"I don't know, but I doubt it. He wouldn't have come here to work things out if he was with her."

"Then it's just me. He hates me. And he left me all alone to deal with this. Why can't I hate him back? Why do I have to love him so much?" she cried.

"I'm sorry it hurts, but I'll be here for you and so will Chris," I assured her.

"Chris has barely said two words to me. He hates me too."

I pushed her hair off her face. "He doesn't hate you. He's still in shock from finding you on the bathroom floor. He's pissed at me too, don't take it personally. Maybe you should talk to him. It might help."

"I will."

"In the meantime, you need to talk to the doctor about getting something to help you sleep. You can't go on like this."

"I will," she said again.

"Now try to go back to sleep. I'll be right here," I promised her. "I won't let anything happen to you."

"Thank you for being my friend," Kyla said softly as she wrapped her pinky finger around mine.

"Always." We both closed our eyes and drifted off to sleep.

Chapter 19
Chris

I was finishing up a project for my Detailing and Design class. Mötley Crüe played through my speaker, helping me get lost in the monotony of the mouse clicking. The project was fucking easy since I'd been doing this type of shit for the past several summers. I could practically do it with my eyes closed.

A soft knock sounded at my door. I thought it was nothing, until I heard it again. *Who the hell could that be?* Tori always barged in and most of the guys I hung out with wouldn't have been so gentle. I got up from my desk and opened the door a crack.

On the other side of the door stood Kyla. She looked like shit. Her hair was stringy, piled on top of her head. She didn't have any makeup on, and she had dark circles under her red, puffy eyes. The over-sized sweats she wore did nothing for her.

"Can we talk?" she asked timidly.

I nodded my head and opened the door wider. She maneuvered under my arm and into the room. She sat down on the edge of the loveseat shoved against the wall. I sat down in the desk chair across from her and crossed my arms over my chest. "You look like hell," I said.

"Thanks," she said, forcing a weak smile. "I feel like I'm in hell."

"What do you want to talk about?" I felt sorry for her. She looked miserable, but she hurt me, and I couldn't let that go.

"I'm sorry I lied to you. I'm sorry I made Tori keep it a secret from you. That wasn't fair to her, and it wasn't fair to you."

I steeled my eyes on her. "Yeah. Kind of sucked finding out the way I did. Do you know how scared I was when I saw you covered in blood laying on the bathroom floor?"

"I'm sorry," she said again. "I didn't want you to tell Tyler. You're his best friend."

I pointed at my chest. "I thought I was your friend too. You could have told me." I clenched my teeth. "Do you have any idea how much stress you put on Tori?"

Kyla dropped her head. "I know."

"I don't think you really do, but that's not your fault." I almost told her about our own failed pregnancy, but I couldn't do that without hurting Tori. "Why didn't you tell Tyler? He deserved to know."

Kyla threw her hands in the air. "How? How could I tell him? I didn't want to tell him during football season. I didn't want him to be distracted. I thought I was doing the right thing by waiting. I was going to tell him after the party, but then I walked in on him with his dick buried in some other girl." I cringed. "I tried to tell him even after that. And do you know what he told me?"

I shook my head.

"He told me that having a baby would a be a disaster. A fucking disaster! His words. He didn't want it. All he cared about was his damn football career. Having a baby would have put a major kink in his plans. And then that stupid bitch, Madison, showed up when we were out to dinner. Told him how amazing he was in bed. I knew after that; I couldn't tell him." She looked at me sadly. "I could barely fucking breathe, let alone tell him I was pregnant."

I guess I didn't really know the details of their situation. And honestly, the more Kyla talked, the more pissed I was at Tyler. He made it impossible for her.

"I'm here because I'm sorry I didn't tell you when I should have. I'm here because I caused a problem between you and Tori. It wasn't her fault. I made her keep the secret. It would kill me for this to come between the two of you. I know you're Tyler's best friend and I'm just Tori's sidekick. I came as part of a package deal. I understand that. Please don't take this out on Tori. I'll step aside. As for Tyler, I know where your loyalties lie. I'll always love him, but he doesn't love me." Kyla stood from the loveseat and headed toward the door. "Make things right with Tori. That's all I ask."

"Stop!" I insisted. Kyla looked at me over her shoulder with tears in her eyes. "You'd give up your friendship with Tori, for me?"

"I'd do anything for you two. I just want you and Tori to be happy. You two were meant to be."

The coldness around my heart started to melt. How could I stay mad at this girl who would give up her best friend for me? She was selfless. And I saw, and not for the first time, how much she cared about everyone else.

"What about you?" I asked.

"I've already lost everything. At least this will make someone else happy."

She continued walking toward the door and reached for the knob. I jumped out of the chair and pushed my hand against the door, effectively keeping her from leaving. She looked up at me, the sadness evident on her pretty face.

"I'm your friend, too. I hate this. You're like my little sister. We're family, and family doesn't bail on each other when things are tough."

"What about Ty?" she asked. "He's like your brother."

"Do I have to choose? Can't I be friends with both of you?"

"I don't know. Can you? Because I could really use a friend right now."

I reached down to her small frame and gathered her in my arms. She wrapped me in hers, as well. "I love you, Kyla. I forgive you. Do you forgive me for being a stubborn jackass?"

"There's nothing to forgive. And for the record, I love you too."

I didn't think it would be that easy to forgive Kyla, but once I heard it from her point of view, what else could I do? I couldn't take Kyla from Tori. It would kill her. The situation sucked all the way around. But I couldn't abandon Kyla. She had lost so much, I wouldn't take my friendship from her too.

That didn't mean that I wasn't friends with Tyler. Balancing the two would be difficult, but it was worth every internal struggle I had. I didn't know who was right and who was wrong, but it didn't really matter.

After Kyla left, I called my girl. We were struggling. The tension between us grew to be unbearable, and I couldn't stand it. I'd been so cold with her, and she was walking on eggshells with me. She was trying to give me the space I needed to come to terms with everything that happened.

I didn't want space.

I wanted her.

In my bed.

Underneath me.

She picked up on the second ring. "Tor? I need to see you. Now. We need to talk," I demanded.

She sounded unsure, "Umm. Okay. I'll be right up."

"Hurry," I ordered and hung up. She was probably wondering what the hell was going on. Good. I wanted her wondering.

A few minutes later, Tori knocked on my door, which in itself was weird since she usually let herself in. It was another sign of how messed up things had gotten between us. I opened the door and moved aside so she could enter.

Tori walked in with a pissed off look. There was the girl I loved. She turned on her heel and gave me a hard look. "You think you can just order me around after acting like an ass for over a week? Better fucking think again! I know I messed up, but for Christ's sake get over it." She threw her hands in the air. "We're fighting over something that doesn't even really have anything to do with us. Okay, I lied. Technically it wasn't a lie though. It was an omission of information. I can't take it back, so I don't know what the fuck you want me to do about it now!"

I loved the fiery side of my girl. I couldn't help but smirk at her.

"What the hell are you smiling about? Do you think this is funny? Because I sure as hell don't!"

"You done?" I asked calmly.

Tori glared at me. "Not even close." Then she started on another tirade. "You know what you are?"

I stalked towards her and pushed her against the wall. "No. What am I?" I demanded.

"You're... you're..."

I grabbed her arms and held them over her head in one hand. My other hand snaked up under her shirt and rubbed over her tit. "I'm what?"

I could tell she trying to hang onto the anger, but her body betrayed her when I rolled her nipple between my fingers, and she bowed into my body that was pressed up against her. My dick was so fucking hard, and I pushed it into her stomach, so she could feel me. I leaned down next to her ear and whispered, "I'm what?"

"Frustrating," she gasped. "You think you can just decide you're horny and everything is fine? That I'll do anything you want? Because you need it?"

I lowered my hand from her tit and ran it down between her legs. I rubbed her jeans-covered pussy and she let out a moan. "You won't? I must be losing my touch." I crashed my lips against hers and pushed my tongue inside. The kiss turned frantic and feverish. I dropped her hands

162

and lifted her. Tori's legs wrapped around my waist and her hands went to my hair, as we drowned in the kiss.

I carried her to the bed and laid over the top of her. "I missed you," I said breathlessly.

"I missed you, too."

We didn't waste time on words when our bodies could say everything that needed to be said. I ripped my shirt up over my head, then quickly stripped out of my jeans. Tori lifted off her shirt and I got to work on her pants. I ripped her pants and panties down in one smooth motion, only to be stopped by her boots. I quickly unlaced and removed them, so I could get her pants all the way off. "Bra. Off! I want all of you."

Tori removed her bra and threw it to the side. She was laid out on my bed in all her naked glory. She was pure perfection. "God, you're beautiful. It's been too long."

She got an evil little grin on her face. "You gonna stare at me or are you gonna fuck me?"

Game on. "I'm not gonna be gentle," I warned.

"I won't break," she assured me.

Tori opened her legs and I settled between them. I ran my fingers over her pussy. She was so wet and ready for me. I thrust in with one quick motion. Her head dropped back, and she let out a loud gasp. I thrust in again. "No." Thrust. "More." Thrust. "Secrets."

"No more secrets," she rasped.

I pushed in again. Harder this time. "Promise?"

"I promise. Fuck me harder! I missed you so much."

I pulled one of her legs up around my waist and thrust in and out of her fast and hard. My balls slapped against her ass, the sound of it filling the room.

Tori reached between her legs and furiously rubbed her clit, searching for her release. Usually, I took care of that for her, but tonight I was too damned impatient. Her body shuddered and she clenched my dick. I watched her face as she came. It was one of my favorite things to look at. A few more thrusts and I followed her over the edge.

I released her legs and laid over the top of her, caging her in with my arms. "No more fighting," I said breathlessly. "I can't stand it," I admitted.

"Me neither. I hate when we fight. I always feel like half of me is missing."

"Stay with me tonight. I hate sleeping alone."

"Fine." She rolled her eyes. "But I'm only staying because I haven't gotten my fill of you yet. I'm using you for sex."

"Oh! You think we're having sex again?"

She winked at me. "I'll make it worth your while. Trust me."

I talked to Tyler a few times since "the incident", which I was calling the whole Tyler screwing someone else, Kyla getting pregnant, Kyla losing the baby, and Tyler walking out on her, situation. It was one big fucked up mess, is what it was. So, calling it "the incident" was a much-needed euphemism.

Despite it all, I missed my friend. I hadn't seen him in over a month. I headed over to State on Friday afternoon to reconnect. He needed to know that just because he and Kyla weren't together anymore, didn't mean that our friendship was over.

We went to the gym together and talked about everything but the mess they made. Kyla had been trying to talk to him, and he hadn't made any effort to talk to her. If anything, he avoided her like the plague. It seemed crazy that after over three years, he could walk away so easily.

That night we went to the bar with some of the guys from his football team. I got to know most of them over the past few years and they were cool with me. We walked into the club and headed straight for the bar.

"What do you want? First round is on me," I offered.

"I'll take a Jack and Coke," he told the bartender. "Bud Light," I added. In all the years Tyler and I hung out, he was never much of a drinker. I guess things had changed.

The pretty girl behind the bar placed our drinks in front of us and I paid her. "Hitting the hard stuff tonight, huh?" I questioned.

"Beer's not quite cutting it lately," he replied. He took a long sip of his drink and eyed me like there was a question on the tip of his tongue.

"What? If you wanna know, just ask."

Tyler huffed, "I shouldn't care, but how's my girl?"

I nearly choked on my beer. "Your girl?"

"Hey, don't give me any shit. What she did was wrong. We may not be together, but that doesn't mean I don't care. I'll always love her, I just can't be in love with her," he said, downing the rest of his drink. He signaled to the bartender for another.

"Yeah, I get it. The whole situation was fucked up." I was alluding to his cheating too, but he didn't get that part.

"Damn right it was. Who does that?" He grabbed his second drink off the bar. "So? How is she?"

I didn't know how much to divulge. Kyla was a fucking mess. I settled with, "She's not doing as well as you, but she's coping." It wasn't a lie, but it sure as hell wasn't the truth either.

"Give her time. Soon she'll forget all about me. It wasn't that hard while she was pregnant, so this should be a piece of cake." Ouch! Someone was jaded.

I brushed off his comment. "Yeah. I'm sure with time, she'll move on too."

Ty placed his empty glass on the bar. "Now, if you'll excuse me, I see a hot, little brunette calling my name." He sauntered onto the dance floor and cozied up to a tall girl with dark hair and bright blue eyes.

I shook my head. I couldn't understand how he moved on so easily. If Tori and I were to break up, I would be devastated. Ty's roommate, Cody, sidled up next to me. He followed my gaze over to Tyler and the brunette.

I shook my head. "He says he's fine, but I'm not so sure. What do you think?" I asked Cody.

"It's all a front. He's miserable without Kyla. I know shit went sideways, but fuck, I don't know how he can walk away from her. If I had a girl like that... I'd do everything in my power to make it work. He had it all, and he's just walking away. Fuck! I'm half tempted to call her and ask her out myself," Cody laughed at the ridiculousness of his statement. "But I have a feeling, no matter how much he fucks around with other chicks, he wouldn't be cool with Kyla being with someone else."

I drained my beer. "That's kind of fucked up." I motioned to the bartender for another.

"Fucked up or not, it's the truth. He's still got it bad for her."

I grabbed my beer and downed half in one gulp. Trying to be neutral was harder than I thought it would be. I watched as Tyler grabbed the brunette by the ass and whispered in her ear. She threw her head back and laughed. "He better be careful what he wishes for, because, eventually, Kyla will move on. He's got some blame to accept, but right now I don't think he sees any of it."

"True that, my friend." Cody held up his bottle to mine and we clinked them together.

Tyler approached me with his arm wrapped around the brunette. "We're gonna get out of here. Are you cool catching a ride with Cody?" he asked.

I forced a fake smile. "Yeah, I'm cool. See ya back at the dorm?"

He winked at me. "Don't wait up. I'll see you in the morning."

"Yeah. I'll see ya before I leave." I patted him on the back. My stomach turned, but I didn't want him to know I thought this was messed up on so many levels. I needed to accept his relationship with Kyla was over. It was a harsh realization after all the years we'd spent together as a foursome.

Ty didn't roll in until nine in the morning. He walked in looking disheveled and thoroughly fucked. He grunted his greeting and headed straight for the shower. I looked over at Cody, who watched the same scene as me. "How many?" I asked.

"I've lost count," Cody answered. Tyler was clearly self-medicating. He could do whatever he wanted, but eventually it was all going to catch up to him.

I made it back to Western in the early afternoon and went straight to Tori's room. I sat on Tori's bed and stared at Kyla laying on hers. She had earbuds in and looked dead to the world. She had lost at least fifteen pounds, which was a lot considering how tiny she was to begin with. She looked awful.

Tori sat down next to me. "How was it?"

"Fine," I said. Then I motioned to Kyla. "But this is not. While he's out fucking everything with two legs, she's wasting away." I checked to make sure Kyla wasn't listening, but her ear buds were firmly in place. She didn't even know I was there. "We have to do something."

"I agree. But what?" Tori asked.

"Get tough with her," I said. "Do what you do best. One week. That's all we're giving her. Don't give her any options. You girls can get fucked up. I'll drive."

"I love you, you know that?" Tori wrapped her arms around my neck and kissed me.

"I love you, too," I assured her. "I know I said I wasn't going to get involved, but I can't look at her like this anymore. He's moving on. She needs to also."

I don't know what Tori said to Kyla, but clearly it worked. I showed up to their room a little after seven-thirty. Kyla was showered. Her hair was done and makeup on. She looked better than I had seen her in weeks, albeit a little too thin.

I clapped my hands together. "You ready girls? Let's get you fucked up!"

Tori was all smiles, but Kyla gave me a death glare. "I hate you two, you know that?"

I slung my arm around her shoulder. "No, you don't. You love us. You're going to thank us for this."

"We'll see," she said skeptically.

We got to the bar and found a table. Kyla tried to get out of drinking, but Tori ordered a Captain and diet for her, as well as a round of tequila shots.

When Tori excused herself for the bathroom, Kyla cornered me into telling her about Tyler. I didn't want to tell her, but she needed a harsh dose of reality. "Tori said you saw Tyler last weekend," she said in a low voice.

I pushed back from the table. "Oh no! We're not talking about that!"

"Please! I just want to know if he's okay," she begged. "If he's moved on?"

I let out an exasperated sigh. "I can't believe you're asking me this. Do you really want to know?" This was not a conversation I wanted to have.

She nodded her head. "Yes. I need to know."

"He's happy, Kyla. I wouldn't normally tell you this, but you're right. You need to know. He went home with somebody. He's moved on." Okay, I didn't know if he was actually happy, but the lie flowed easily from my tongue anyway.

Her face fell. "Oh… well, good for him. I guess." The look on her face killed me.

"You need to do the same. He's not coming back," I told her. I felt like shit telling her that, but what else could I say. Tyler obviously wasn't waiting around for her.

Kyla waved me off. "Yeah, I know." She pretended it didn't bother her, but I could see that it clearly did.

Tori came back to the table. "What are you two talking about?" she asked suspiciously.

"Nothing," Kyla replied. Just then the waitress showed up with our drinks and shots. Before she left, Kyla asked, "Can you bring another round of these when you come back?" She nodded and left. Kyla picked up her tequila, "To moving on," she toasted. She threw back the shot and her face contorted in disgust. I seemed to have said something that affected her, because she downed her tequila shot like a pro. "Operation Get Kyla Fucked Up" was in full force.

"Damn girl," I said. I pushed my glass of water towards her. "Need a chaser?"

She took a long drink from my glass to help put the fire out. "Thanks!" She picked up her Captain and diet Coke and downed half of it. After downing the other half of her drink, Kyla pointed to the shots the waitress had just delivered. "Round two?"

I pushed mine toward her. "You can have mine too. I'm driving, remember?"

Tori and Kyla picked up their shots. "To ex-boyfriends fucking other bitches!" Kyla exclaimed. Tori almost choked on her shot when those words came out of Kyla's mouth. She downed her tequila and mine. All I could do was laugh. Soon the girls were off to the dance floor, shaking their asses to the music and having fun. I hadn't seen them dance together in forever, and it seemed right. When the music slowed, Tori returned to the table alone.

"Where's Kyla?" I asked.

Tori motioned to the dance floor. "Dancing. She's a cute girl. I knew it wouldn't take long for someone to scoop her up."

Kyla didn't return to the table until the end of the night. She wasn't drunk, but definitely tipsy. She'd met someone. She insisted she wasn't going to date him, but it was a start. Anything was better than her wasting away in her dorm room.

Kyla was getting better, one little step at a time. At least it seemed she was. Either that or she was one hell of an actress. My bet was on the latter. Tori and I did what we could to break her out of the depression she was in, but I couldn't help but feel it wasn't enough.

The semester ended and the three of us headed home.

I had a plan for this summer. One I hadn't shared with Tori, but I hoped she would be on board. Since my first summer interning, before my senior year of high school, I'd been squirreling away money. I saved enough to put my plan into action, and then some. I'd saved like crazy, and I was going to build my little nest egg even more this summer.

I wanted to take Tori away for the weekend, and not to the Lake House. Somewhere we could break free, with no responsibilities. We'd never been on a real vacation before, and I figured it was about time.

I booked our flight and hotel, without telling her. I talked to Mike about Tori getting time off from working at his shop. He was totally cool with it. I had moved in with Tori for the summer and even though we kept things restrained for the sake of her mom and Mike, I couldn't have been happier. I loved falling asleep with Tori in my arms every night and waking to her in the morning.

The Thursday before the Fourth of July, we'd both come home from work and were sprawled on her bed. "I'm exhausted,' she said.

"I hope you're not too exhausted," I told her. "You need to start packing."

"What are you talking about? Packing for what?" she asked with a yawn.

"Vegas, baby. You and me. Tomorrow morning. We've got an eleven-a.m. flight."

Tori's eyes got huge. "What are you talking about?"

"You and me on a plane headed towards Vegas. I thought we could use a real vacation. I talked to Mike and you're off for the weekend. So, start packing."

"Are you serious?" she asked, clearly in shock.

"As a heart attack. I booked us a room at the Bellagio." I smiled at her. I loved seeing her taken off-guard. Tori was an expert at keeping everything within a plan. I'd just rocked her boat.

Tori covered her mouth with her hand. "We're going on a vacation? A real vacation? Just you and me?"

I pushed her dark hair over her shoulder. "Yeah. You and me. Alone for two nights in Sin City, where we can do whatever we want. Interested?"

"Hell, yeah." Tori jumped up off the bed. "I have so much to do. I need to start packing." She pulled her suitcase out of her closet. "Do you know how to play blackjack, because I really want to do that," she said eagerly.

"I know enough," I told her. I tried to hold back my laughter, but it was hard, because she was so excited.

She raced around the room pulling clothes from her drawers and closet. "Don't forget your bathing suit," I told her. I walked to her closet and pulled out a white sundress. "I love this on you. You should pack it."

"You're right! This does look good on me." She snatched it from my hands and gave me a quick peck. "What about you? Aren't you going to pack?"

"I'm a guy. It'll take me about five minutes. We will need to stop at my mom's in the morning though. I need to grab a couple of things from there."

"Okay," she said. "Should I bring this?" Tori held up the box that held our sex toys.

I wrapped my arms around her waist. "Abso-fucking-lutely! I plan on taking advantage of our time alone."

"I can't believe we're in Vegas," Tori exclaimed. She wrapped herself around my arm, as we walked down the strip, checking everything out.

I pulled her tightly into my side. "What do you want to do while we're here?" I asked.

She looked up at me with those honey-colored eyes. "Everything!"

I laughed. "We only have two days. Can you be a little more specific?"

Tori got a thoughtful look on her face. "I want to do some gambling. Maybe to go to a club. Oh, I know! I want to get tattoos."

"Yeah?"

She nodded her head. "I want your name on me forever."

"I love that idea. We should do it tomorrow. Right now, we need to head back to our room and get ready for dinner. I made us reservations." Just one more little surprise I had for her.

"Where?" I swear she was like a giddy girl, and it was so damn cute.

I put my finger over her lips. "That's a secret."

She pulled back and crossed her arms, pretending to be mad. But I knew better. "I thought we promised no more secrets." She was going to try to guilt me into telling her.

I held her face between my hands. "You'll like this one. I promise you." There was no way I was giving in. I took her hand in mine. "Now let's get back and get ready for dinner. Maybe a shower first?" I wiggled my eyebrows at her.

"You so don't play fair. You know every one of my weaknesses."

"It's more than fair since you're my only weakness. There isn't a single thing I wouldn't do for you," I told her.

We walked back to our hotel, wrapped in each other's arms. I loved her more than anything.

After showering and a little loving, we walked out of the Bellagio, hand in hand, to get a cab. She looked gorgeous in her white sundress. I wore dark dress pants, with a shirt and tie. "Wherever we're going, must be pretty fancy," she said. "I only ever see you dressed up for work." She was prodding since I still hadn't told her where we were going.

"Quit trying to get me to tell you. You'll find out soon enough." I kissed her on the forehead. The bellman secured us a cab and I opened the door for Tori. She slid into the back seat, and I slipped in next to her. "The Stratosphere," I told the driver.

171

"What's the Stratosphere?" she asked.

"You'll see." We made the short drive to the casino. She still had no idea, and I couldn't be more thrilled.

We walked into the casino, and I headed straight for the bank of elevators. "I thought we were going to eat?" she said, clearly confused.

The gold doors opened, and we stepped inside. "We are," I assured her. I pushed the button for the top floor.

Tori's eyes got huge when she saw that we were going up one hundred-six floors. "We're going all the way to the top?"

I pulled her back against my chest. "Yes. Be patient, my love." Patience wasn't one of Tori's strong suits. I knew this was killing her, but it would be well worth it.

After what seemed like forever, the elevator stopped, and the doors opened to the restaurant. We stepped out and Tori's hand went up in front of her mouth. "Oh my, god! We're eating here?"

"Yes." I pulled her over to the hostess. "Reservation for Capizzio."

The woman nodded and led us to our table by the window. Tori looked out over the lights of Vegas. "This is amazing! Are we moving? Oh my, God! We are, aren't we?"

I pulled her chair out for her to sit. "Yes, baby. We are."

"This is so amazing! Thank you! Thank you for bringing me here," she gushed.

"I'd do anything for you. You're my forever." I meant it. We'd been together for five years, and although there had been some bumps along the road, I didn't regret one single moment we'd spent together.

The food was amazing, but what was more amazing, was seeing my girl so happy. I would never forget this moment with her.

The waiter cleared our plates from the table and poured us another glass of wine. Tori took a small sip. "This was a good secret. I love it. The view is amazing. I'm almost sorry we're finished eating because I could stay up here and look at the lights all night."

I took her hand in mine. "The night's not over. I know I asked you this before, but it wasn't really official." Tori's eyes scrunched up, trying to figure out what I meant.

I got down on one knee and pulled the ring out of my pocket. "Tori Arianna Russo, will you do me the honor of marrying me?"

Tori's eyes went big and teary. She nodded her head quickly. "Yes! Yes! I'll marry you!" She threw her arms around my neck and hugged me tight.

Applause erupted around us as the other diners took in the scene before them. "She said 'Yes'!" I shouted. We were surrounded by hoots and hollers and words of congratulations. I'd say my surprise was a success. I just hoped my next one would be too.

"Tonight. Will you marry me tonight?"

Chapter 20
Tori

"Tonight?" I swallowed back my shock. I looked at the beautiful rock on my finger and the gorgeous man on his knee in front of me. Of course, I wanted it, but… god, there were so many buts.

"Yes. Tonight," Chris said. "I told you I wanted to marry you this summer. Those weren't just words. I can't wait any longer."

I sat back in my chair. "Chris, you know I love you. Would do anything for you. But this… this is crazy. Do you know how pissed our parents will be?"

He held my hand across the table. "I don't care. All I care about is you. I've wanted this since we graduated from high school. I'm done waiting."

"What will we tell them?" I asked. Our parents were going to go ballistic.

"We don't have to tell them a thing. We're already living together for the summer. Instead of going back to the dorms, we'll get an apartment." He had it all planned.

"What about a wedding? I've always imagined us getting married by the water with our friends and family. I want the big white dress. The flowers. A first dance with my husband to some cheesy love song. My parents will be devastated if I deny them that. I'm their only daughter." I wanted to marry Chris more than anything, but there were so many other things to consider.

Chris pushed my hair back over my ear. "You'll get all of that," he assured me. "We'll tell everyone we got engaged and plan a real wedding for next summer. No one will know but us. Please, Tori," he begged. "I want to make you my wife."

We could pull this off. He was right. No one had to know, but keeping the secret would be difficult. We spent all our time together as it was. I'd loved Chris since I was sixteen, nothing was going to change that. I already knew I wanted to spend the rest of my life with him. So what, if we pushed the timetable up a year?

"Yes." I couldn't believe I was agreeing to this craziness.

"Yes?" he repeated.

I nodded my head. "I can't believe we're going to do this. This is insane. You know that?"

"It's us. When have we ever done what we were supposed to? You and I have been breaking rules together for years. Insane is letting everyone else decide what's best for us. We decide. I already know you're what's best for me."

I grabbed his face in my hands with determination. "I love you. Let's do it now! Before reason kicks in and I change my mind."

Chris threw some money on the table, grabbed my hand, and whisked me away to the elevator, "You're not changing your mind." We made the long trip down in the elevator, while Chris kissed me the whole time. "You're not going to regret this," he said between kisses. "I promise you. And I…"

"Always keep your promises," I finished for him. "I know. Where are we going?"

"You'll see. I've got it all planned out." The doors opened, and we raced out of the casino into the warm, sultry night.

I stopped on the sidewalk, jerking him back. I stood there and looked up at the stars as people bustled around us. Chris put his hands on my hips. "What's wrong?"

I focused on my future husband. "Nothing. Everything is perfect. I just want to take a minute to remember this moment. Lock it into my brain forever. Did I ever tell you that I used to write your name in my notebook back in high school? Over and over again until the pages were full. And then, just for shits and giggles, I would write Mrs. Tori Capizzio. I wanted to know how it sounded. And I liked it. A lot. After that kiss in the closet, you were it for me. I knew no one would ever kiss me like you did. And I was right. You've always been it for me."

Chris ran his hand down the side of my face. "I asked you out dozens of times and you always told me no. Why?"

"You scared me." I took a deep breath. "You still scare me."

"Baby, there's nothing to be scared of. You and me, we were meant to be."

"I know that. It scares me that I've wrapped my whole world around you. That I love you so much, sometimes it's hard to breathe. You are everything to me and I don't know who I am without you. Promise me, that we'll be together forever. If something were ever to happen to you… I don't know how I would go on."

"I'll do everything in my power to keep that promise. We're going to have kids together, grow old together, and sit on the porch drinking lemonade while our grandchildren run all around us. And if anything were ever to happen, I'll still be with you. Right here." He placed his hand on my heart.

I wiped the tears out of my eyes, "Let's get married."

Chris hailed us a cab and directed the driver to one of the many wedding chapels in Vegas. Of course, he'd done his research.

I squeezed his hand. "Is this why you wanted me to wear this dress tonight?" He answered with a dimpled smile. "We're not getting married by Elvis, or anything else cheesy, are we?"

Chris placed a gentle kiss on my lips. "I think you know me better than that."

The cab pulled up in front of a cute wedding chapel. It looked classy, for Vegas anyway. Chris opened the door and reached for my hand. I began to step out, then stopped. "Wait! I don't have a ring for you," I realized.

Chris reached into his pocket and pulled out a simple silver band. "Ta-da." I should have known he would have thought of everything. "We can get something different later if we want."

I took the ring from his hand and held it up in the light. It was engraved on the inside, *Tori... My Forever Love.* "It's perfect."

Chris pulled me the rest of the way from the cab, and we headed up the cobblestone path. This was it. Soon I would be Mrs. Tori Capizzio. Or would it be Mrs. Christopher Capizzio? Oh, god! I was so unprepared for this.

We stepped from the elevator and quickly made our way to our room. Chris slid the key card into the lock and waited for the green light. The lock clicked, and he pushed the door open. I went to step inside, but Chris grabbed me around the waist. "What are you doing?" I asked.

Chris effortlessly picked me up, one arm under my legs and the other supporting my back. I wrapped my arms around his neck, my shoes dangling from my fingers. "Carrying my wife over the threshold."

He shut the door behind us with his foot, and then carried me to the bed. He tossed me gently into the middle of it and I laughed like a little girl. "I can't believe we're married!" I screamed.

Chris crawled over the top of me and caged me in with his arms. "I know. How does it feel?"

I looked him in the eyes. "Perfect and scary at the same time. How are we going to keep this a secret?"

"Oh, my dear wife," I liked the way that sounded, "we're the masters of keeping secrets."

"Say it again," I said.

"What?"

"Call me your wife again," I insisted.

"You are my wife," he said with a smile.

"And you're my husband."

He nodded in agreement. "And now, your husband wants to make love to his wife. We need to make this whole thing official."

I laughed out loud. "Chris, we've been having sex for five years. I think it's already official."

"That may be true, but I haven't had sex with my wife yet and that needs to be remedied. Immediately." He backed off the bed and stood before me. I propped myself up on my elbows as I watched him remove his tie, unbutton his shirt, and then slide it off his shoulders. He looked perfect. His toned chest and chiseled abs led down to that gorgeous V at his hips that I loved. I sat up and went to work on his belt, the clinking of metal the only sound in the room. Chris brushed my hair off my face as I undid his pants and pushed them down his legs. He stopped only to remove his shoes and then he was pulling my dress up over my head.

I laid back on the bed and waited for my husband. Husband. It sounded so right. I arched my back, so he could undo my bra. He slipped it down my arms and tossed it to the side, then slid my panties down my legs. He stared down at my naked body, with lust and love in his eyes. I wanted him. Needed him. "Make love to me," I whispered.

That was all it took. Chris ran his hands down my arms and laced our fingers together. He slowly brought them over my head and held my wrists together in one hand, as his lips descended upon mine. They pressed gently and then he nipped at my bottom lip. I opened for him, and his tongue pushed into my mouth. Our tongues caressed and twisted in a passionate dance. Chris broke the kiss. "I love you, Tori.

You've made me the happiest man alive tonight. I can't believe we did it. We're finally married. Do you know how good that feels?"

"Yes," I gasped. "I feel like my heart is about to explode, but in a good way. It seemed like it would be forever until this day came. Thank you for planning this. Everything was perfect. You're perfect!"

"I'm far from perfect, but we're perfect for each other." Chris kissed down the side of my face and to my neck. I leaned my head back and absorbed everything that was him. His tongue slid along my collarbone and down between my breasts. "I love your body, baby," he whispered. He cupped my breast with his free hand and swirled his tongue around it.

I opened my legs to my husband, and he slid between them. He pushed into me, and I felt like he was home. I was his home, and he was mine.

Chris made love to me with long, slow, deliberate strokes. My hips moved with his and we found our rhythm. Time stood still when we were connected like this. There was no him. There was no me. There was only us. He reached for my thigh and wrapped it up around his waist, allowing him to push in deeper. I ran my toes along the sculpted muscles of his back, then used my leg to pull him in closer. A few more thrusts and we fell over the edge together. We held on to each other tightly, remembering this moment. Our first time as husband and wife. I couldn't get close enough to this man who owned each and every part of my heart, mind, and soul.

We spent the whole night making love, only stopping when sheer exhaustion took over. We were getting our wedding and honeymoon all in one glorious weekend.

I woke to the sun sneaking through the blinds, a sliver of light piercing my eye. Chris's arm was draped over my body and his head nuzzled into my neck. Even when we slept, we couldn't get close enough to each other. I looked over at my husband and a smile spread across my face. It was hard to believe that last night wasn't a dream. The rings on our fingers confirmed it wasn't and we were indeed married.

I crawled out from under Chris and headed toward the bathroom. Once I brushed my teeth and combed my hair, my stomach growled. I picked up the phone and ordered us breakfast from room service. It wasn't a luxury I would normally indulge in, but hell, it was our honeymoon. I ordered us waffles, scrambled eggs, bacon, toast, and coffee. I so needed my caffeine. There was so much I wanted to do today.

I quickly threw on some clothes and a few minutes later there was a knock on our door. Chris stirred from his sleep, as I rolled the cart inside. "You ordered breakfast?" he questioned.

"Yep. I figured you'd be famished, and we need our energy for all the things I want to do today." I uncovered the food and carried it to the bed.

Chris sat up against the headboard, covering himself with the sheet. "I'm starving. You're already good at this wife thing," he teased.

I poured us each a cup of coffee, then sat cross-legged on the bed and handed him his cup. "We've never had breakfast in bed. I thought it would nice."

"It is," he said taking a sip of his coffee. "What do you want to do today?"

"Pool time, tattoos, casino, walk along the strip, watch the fountains, fuck my husband. Not necessarily in that order," I winked at him.

Chris took a bite a of scrambled eggs and a slice of bacon. "That's a mighty big list, Mrs. Capizzio. Which shall we do first?"

"Well, Mr. Capizzio. I thought I might leave that to you. Although I have some ideas." I flirted.

Chris pushed his food to the side, reached forward and grabbed me, pulling me on top of him. "You do, huh?"

I looked down at him and my hair fell like a curtain around my face. "Yep. Although, if we go with my plan, we may never leave this room and I'm not sure I'm willing to risk that."

"True. It would be so easy to waste the whole day away in this bed. How about this? Pool time for a couple of hours and then we find a tattoo shop." He looked at me skeptically, "Are you sure you want to get a tattoo? It's kind of permanent."

"Like us?" I questioned.

"Like us."

"Will you hold my hand?"

"Of course."

Chris had gotten a couple of tattoos over the last few years, and they were super sexy. He had a cross on his upper left arm and an eagle with its wings spread across his back. I ran my fingers over the cross. "Will it hurt?"

"A little at first, but you're tough. Do you know where you want it?"

I nodded my head. "Right here," I raised my shirt and rubbed the area above my right hip.

Chris licked his lips. "That's going to be sexy as fuck. I can't wait to see it." He lowered his head and kissed my hip.

After finishing our breakfast and some time by the pool, Chris asked about a reputable tattoo shop at the front desk. They directed us to a place called Sinful Souls, which was only a few blocks down from our hotel. As soon as we walked in, my nerves kicked up about ten notches. Although I really wanted this, I was scared too. Chris let me go first. He held my hand and talked to me the whole time. It was a good distraction from the needle going in and out of my hip. I made a note to myself: My next tattoo, if I got one, would be in a place with a little more fat. Like my ass.

We left the tattoo shop marked with our love for each other. Mine was two hearts intertwined. Our names were scripted in the hearts with the word *Forever* underneath. Chris got his tattoo on his chest, right over his heart. My name was scripted there, along with the words *...forever my life ...forever my love*. There was no going back now, not only did we get married, but we had permanently inked our devotion to each other on our bodies. I didn't regret any of it!

After dinner, we took a walk along the strip, stopping in at different casinos. I went to the slots, since I had no experience gambling, and they seemed the easiest.

"Stupid motherfucker! Come on, just another half-inch!" I yelled at the machine. Why couldn't that last seven drop into place. I looked at Chris, who was laughing at me. "Seriously, I think this thing is rigged."

"It's Vegas, baby. Sometimes you win, sometimes you lose. Wanna try again?" he asked.

"A couple more pulls, and I'm done," I answered, pulling the handle of the money sucking machine. Cherry, bar, nothing! "Aren't you gonna try?"

"No. I'm having fun watching you get pissed."

At least I was only playing quarter slots. I saw a machine when we walked in that was a hundred bucks a pull. Who had that kind of money? "I'm not pissed, just frustrated. You'd think after twenty bucks this thing could throw me a bone."

I pulled the handle one more time and turned away from the machine. "Let's try something else…" *Ding, ding, ding, ding!*

"Tor!"

I turned around and watched as the credits started to roll. The machine kept making noises and a light flashed on top as the number went higher and higher. "Oh, shit!"

"Tori, you just won five thousand dollars! Holy fuck, woman!" Chris wrapped his arms around me, and I hugged him tightly.

"What do we do now?" I asked in shock.

"Cash out! We're fucking done!" Lights and bells continued drawing attention to us as gamblers walked by with either looks of jealousy or congratulations on their faces.

After signing the appropriate tax documents, the attendant counted out fifty one-hundred-dollar into my hand. I took the money and put it in my purse, clutching it close to my body.

"We need to get back to the hotel pronto," I whispered to Chris. I certainly didn't want to walk around with five grand in my purse. We never did play blackjack, but at this point I didn't care.

He nodded his agreement, and we headed back toward the hotel. We walked with purpose, pushing through people to our destination. When we got to the Bellagio, Chris stopped, pulling me in front of him. He walked me toward the railing that separated the sidewalk from the water. He wrapped his arms around me from behind and rested his chin on my shoulder. "You wanted to watch the fountains. It should be starting soon." I turned my head and kissed him. Although I wanted to get to our room with our money, I did want to watch the fountains.

Suddenly music flowed from the speakers, as "My Heart Will Go On" started to play and the fountains came to life. The show that played out before us was like a dream. The fountains sprayed in a magically choreographed dance, the lights forming an ethereal glow on the streams of water. In my mind, I saw Kate Winslet floating on a door in the middle of the Atlantic, holding Leonardo DiCaprio's frozen hand, saying "I'll never let go". It was so morbidly romantic, but romantic, nonetheless. I still think he could have fit on the door with her if she had tried a little harder, but what do I know? I would have never let Chris freeze to death in the middle of the ocean, but then again, we'd been together five years, not five days.

When the show ended, we went back to our room. I sat on the bed and pulled the money from my purse. Chris sat down next to me, and I fanned the five grand out in front of him. "Does this cover our trip?"

"It more than covers our trip. I can't fucking believe you won five thousand dollars," he said, shaking his head in disbelief.

"We. *We* won five grand. We're married now. It belongs to both of us. I want to open a joint account when we get home and put this away for our wedding or a house."

He pulled me onto his lap. "I think that's a great idea. I've been saving for years for our future. I can't wait to start our life together." Chris pressed his lips to mine and the money dropped from my hand onto the bed.

I loved kissing him. His hands pulled through my hair as he laid us back on the bed. "What was the last thing on your list of things to do?" he asked smugly.

I tapped my chin with my finger. "Gosh, with all the excitement today, I can't seem to remember. Do you?"

"I fucking remember. Very clearly."

"Refresh my memory," I said as I pushed my hands up under his shirt, digging into his back. Chris reached behind his head and pulled his shirt off. I tugged at the tape holding the bandage on his chest in place, slowly peeled it back, and ran my fingers over the words scripted there. I lifted my head and pressed my lips to his chest.

Chris undid the button on my shorts, pushing them down far enough to expose my hip. He lifted the hem of my shirt, then peeled the tape from my own bandage. "This looks so sexy on you." He kissed over the hearts and then pulled my shorts and panties down my legs, removing my sandals too. He undid his own shorts and kicked them to the side. His erection stood long and hard against his stomach, "Remember now?"

I was dying for him to be inside me, but I enjoyed the little game we were playing. "It's starting to come back to me. Give me more."

Chris moved to my suitcase, brought back "the box" and set it on the edge of the bed.

I propped myself up on my elbows and watched him as he removed the top and began placing items on the bed. The anticipation was killing me. He was in his element when the toys came out. I loved the dominant side of him during sex. His filthy mouth and the way he took control. "Shirt off. All of it. I wanna see your tits and pussy." I quickly sat and ripped it up over my head, then reached between my breasts and released the clip of my bra while licking my lips. He was on me in a heartbeat, pushing the cups back and sliding my bra down my shoulders. He moved his lips to my ear and ran his tongue along the shell of it. "I'm gonna fuck you so hard tonight. You'll never forget. It's not going to be gentle like last night. Do you understand me, Tori?" I nodded my head. "Yes or no? Do you understand?"

I could feel the space between my thighs starting to get wet. I swallowed down my anticipation as his dominant side came out. "Yes. I understand."

"You remember the orgasm I gave you last night? It won't even compare to what I'm going to do to you tonight."

I was all in. I didn't care what he did to me, because I knew it would all lead to one place. Extreme pleasure. "I want you to do everything to me," I answered.

"I plan on it." Chris reached toward the array of toys at the bottom of the bed and grabbed the blindfold. He secured it over my eyes and kissed my lips. "Tell me if it's too much."

"I will." It was always too much, but at the same time never enough. Every time the toys came out, he pushed me a little further. Took me to the edge of my limits and then beyond, until my limits stretched to his desires. Sometimes there was pain, but there was always pleasure. And in the end, he always took care of me. Caressed me. Worshipped me. Loved me.

"On your knees." Chris grabbed me by the shoulders and flipped me over. I quickly got up on all fours. I felt the soft leather of the riding crop feather along my back and down my ass. Then a quick sting as he snapped it against my ass cheek. I flinched and gasped. His hand gently rubbed over the area, soothing the sting. Then he did it again and I arched at the delicious pain. "I love seeing you like this. Tits pushed out. Ass in the air. Totally at my mercy." Another flick of the leather on my ass and a soothing rub. His fingers glided over my arousal and slowly pushed in. "Your pussy is so wet for me."

Even though I was blindfolded, I closed my eyes and arched my back further, letting him know that I loved what he was doing. "More," I gasped. The slight stings of pain never bothered me, only because he would never abuse it. Chris had whipped himself with the riding crop multiple times to try it out before he ever used it on me. I was the one who encouraged him.

Chris wrapped his hand in my hair and pulled my head back. "You'll get yours, but I'm going to get mine first," he said in my ear. I felt the bed dip in front of me. "Open up, baby."

I licked my lips and did as he said. Chris stuck his hard cock in my mouth, and I wrapped my lips around it. I rewarded him with my tongue swirling around the head. He pushed in deeper until he hit the back of my throat. His hands grabbed the sides of my head as he began fucking my mouth.

"I love your mouth on my cock. Take me all the way. I'm gonna come in that pretty mouth of yours." He increased his speed, fucking in and out of my mouth relentlessly. I wrapped one of my hands around the base of his dick and stroked him in time with his thrusts. "Fuck, baby! I'm gonna come. Swallow me!"

I opened my throat and took him deeper. His thrusts became erratic, and I knew he was close. I tightened my grip on his dick, jacking him faster and harder. I felt his dick swell and then hot streams of cum slid down my throat. He pushed my hair over my shoulder and kissed me on the forehead. "You're so fucking amazing."

He laid me back on the bed and shoved a pillow under my hips. He took my hands and lifted them above my head, securing them together with the velvet handcuffs. I wasn't sure if I would like them when I bought them, but the velvet was so soft on my wrists, that even if I pulled, they didn't bite into my skin. "I don't have anything to tie you to, so you'll have to promise to keep your arms above your head."

Usually, if we were at home he'd secure my arms to the top of the bed, but this bed didn't give us that option. "I promise." I would give him anything he wanted.

"Good girl." His lips descended upon mine and were gentle at first but became feverish in a matter of seconds. I wanted to run my hands through his hair, but I promised not to, so I didn't. Our tongues swirled together, and honestly, kissing Chris was my favorite thing. Don't get me wrong, the sex was phenomenal, but when we kissed, it took me back to the days when our kisses were stolen secrets that ended in fireworks. And although they weren't secrets anymore, there were always fireworks.

Chris left me lying there naked on the bed and I wondered what would come next. Not knowing was part of the thrill. "Shit, that's cold!" I exclaimed as he rubbed an ice cube over my nipple. The ice was quickly replaced with his warm mouth, sucking my hardened peak into his mouth. The opposing sensations of cold and warmth were an erotic combination. He did the same to my other nipple, then ran the ice cube down between my breasts and over my stomach.

When he started moving lower, I arched my back in anticipation. Then the ice was gone and replaced by his mouth. He ran his tongue through my folds and to my clit. I gasped at the contact. It was what I wanted more than anything. He sucked my clit into his mouth, while his fingers sank deep inside me. Between his mouth and his fingers, I wasn't going to last long. Then his fingers were gone. My hips bucked off the bed when I felt the cold sensation inside me. He grabbed my hips and moved the ice cube around with his tongue, until it melted. The water dripped out of me, but Chris lapped it up and continued to feast.

I heard the buzz, then felt the vibrator on my clit as he rubbed it up and down just where I needed it. He replaced his tongue with his fingers again and brought his mouth to my nipples. How he was able to hit all my pleasure spots at one time, I wasn't sure. Actually, I didn't care. All I knew was that this orgasm was going to take me to new heights. It started at my center and the tension built in every muscle in my body, from the tips of my fingers to the tips of my toes. I was being wound so tight. "Chris, I can't… it's too much.

"Do you want me to stop?" he growled.

"No! But it's too much. I can't…" I huffed.

"You can, baby. Let go." The vibrations took me higher, wound me tighter.

"I can't! I can't!" And then I did. My body exploded, convulsing out of control. My head thrashed from side to side and my hips came up off the bed. My wrists pulled against the handcuffs, reaching for anything to ground myself. A scream escaped my lips along with a jumbled string of curse words even I couldn't understand.

"So fucking beautiful," I heard him growl.

Before I could comprehend what was happening, Chris's dick was slamming in and out of me. I had barely come down and now the pressure he was putting on my clit had the next orgasm building. I didn't know if I would survive it. It was all too much.

My body breathed in relief when he stopped fucking me, but the reprieve was short lived. He flipped me over and pulled me to the end of the bed. Cool liquid dripped down my ass cheeks and then there was the gentle pressure of the plug, pushing into me. Chris lifted me by the hips, so he could reach his hand underneath me. His fingers went right to my clit, while he thrust into me from behind. His other hand wrapped around my throat and lifted my body up from the mattress. My head fell back when his hand tightened, restricting the blood and oxygen from flowing to my brain. My head grew lighter as he continued to thrust into me. My high got higher and all I could do was feel.

With the plug in place, I felt so full. I could feel him rubbing every part of me from the inside out. My walls clenched him tight. My orgasm building again. He released my throat, and I collapsed back to the bed with another wave of ecstasy. He fucked me to exhaustion. I was having a hard time supporting myself, while my body was being pushed to its limits. The pleasure was so great that my mind was unable to process anything but the feel of Chris's dick inside me and my impending orgasms, as I came again and again.

My body was strung tight as the fireworks went off behind the blindfold. White lights flashed, and my nerve endings were on fire. Every cell in my body was an inferno. "Fuck, Tor, you're squeezing my dick so tight. Fuuuuck!" Chris collapsed on top on my limp body. "That was fucking intense."

I laid there, barely moving. "Are you all right, baby?" he asked with concern. I barely nodded my head. Every bit of life had been drained from my body. Chris removed the blindfold, unlocked the handcuffs, and removed the plug, as my lifeless body laid on the bed. I couldn't move if I wanted to.

I heard the tub running and then I was being carried to the bathroom. My head rested against Chris's chest as my arms hung loosely at my sides. He lifted me into the jacuzzi tub and sat behind me, holding me to his chest. My head rested back on his shoulder, my eyes closed. He used a washcloth to gently wipe down my body. "You're scaring me, baby. Are you sure you're okay?"

"I'm okay," I forced out.

"It was too much, wasn't it? I pushed you too far."

I shook my head weakly. "It was fantastic. Amazing. I love you. I'm just so tired." I felt myself drifting off as I leaned back against him.

I woke cuddled into the space between Chris's arm and chest. I was sore everywhere. A delicious reminder of what Chris had done to me. I lifted my head and rested my chin on his chest. He ran his fingers down the side of my face, "There you are. You scared me last night. You were out. You didn't even wake when I carried you to bed."

"I'm sorry. I didn't mean to scare you."

"Don't be sorry. Did I hurt you?" He picked up my hand and inspected my wrist. It was red from where I had pulled, but it wasn't scraped up. He pulled back my hair and checked my neck. "Fuck. I left bruises on you. I didn't mean to hurt you."

"You didn't," I assured him. "It was just so intense, that it drained me. I'm fine. I loved every minute of it." I reached up and placed a gentle kiss on his lips. "Have I told you how much I love being your wife? This was the best weekend ever."

"It was great, wasn't it?" I nodded. "We have to leave in a few hours to head back home, but at least we have tomorrow off for the holiday. My mom and dad are expecting us for a barbeque. I know they invited your mom and Mike too."

"That sounds good. Should we tell them we're engaged?" I asked.

"I think we should. Then you can wear your ring," he said holding my hand up.

"What about your ring?" I asked, rubbing my fingers over it.

He shrugged. "I guess it'll have to go in a drawer for the next year. Unless you want to tell our parents the truth."

"We can't. Not yet. I want to enjoy this for a while without everyone being pissed at us."

"That's fine. I don't need to wear my ring to know I'm devoted to you. I've been devoted to you for a long time without." He kissed my forehead. "When we get back, we need to start looking for apartments. No way are we moving back to the dorms."

"I agree." I sighed. "What am I going to tell Kyla? I hate leaving her alone, especially with Tyler out of the picture."

"She'll be fine," Chris assured me. "It's not like we're moving away. We'll be close to campus, and she can come over whenever she wants."

"You're right. I know you're right. It's going to be hard to tell her though."

"Are you going to tell her we're married?"

I shrugged. "I don't know. If I tell her, she'll be more understanding as to why we're leaving her. I'm not sure. I want to see how she's doing first."

Chris was always understanding about my relationship with Kyla. He loved her like a sister, but I knew we couldn't protect her forever. Chris and I needed to start our life together. She was going to have to stand on her own two feet. What happened with Tyler and their baby was awful. The grief of losing a baby would never fully go away. Mine hadn't. I was still heartbroken. But she had to find a way to move on from Tyler. It was time. I think she had finally accepted that he wasn't coming back and that was a start.

"Kyla's working a lot," Chris said. "I invited her to the barbeque, but she said she would get a ton of tips at the marina on the holiday. She's going out with some of the girls after. It'll be good for her to get out with someone other than us." Chris tapped his fingers on my back. "Even though I thought Ty was a coward for not coming home this summer, it might just be the best thing for Kyla. At least she doesn't have to worry about running into him."

"I agree. But I have to tell you, I don't think she's doing as well as she wants us to believe. I don't know if Kyla will ever get over Tyler abandoning her the way he did." Even though I could empathize with how Tyler must have felt about losing a baby he knew nothing about, I still thought he could have handled it better. To sneak out on her in the middle of the night was shitty.

"She will. It'll just take time."

Chapter 21
Chris

Being married to the girl of my dreams and not being able to tell anyone sucked monkey balls. I knew Tori was right about keeping it a secret. Our parents would be pissed, and things were going so well right now, it would be stupid to rock the boat. Tori and I had kept so many secrets over the years, I'd lost count. The two of us were like a vault, and only we had the keys.

But this, by far, was the biggest. It was going to be the most difficult secret to keep, because honestly… I didn't want to. I wanted to walk right up to our parents and flaunt the fact that they couldn't stop us from getting married. I wanted to tell everyone. I wanted everyone to know that Tori was more than just my girlfriend or fiancé. She was my wife. I wanted to wear my ring proudly so that everyone knew I belonged to her.

But for now, I would keep the secret. I would keep my wife happy. I would keep my family happy. I would keep the peace.

"So, how was your trip?" Elena asked. We were all sitting around the table on our back deck. My dad barbequed chicken and my mom made so many sides I wondered who would eat all this food. "You two got home so late, I barely got a chance to talk to you."

Tori smiled and started to get animated. It was cute when she was excited. "Chris took me to the top of the Stratosphere. Did you know there's a restaurant up there? It's like a hundred stories up in the air and it spins." She spun her right finger around to demonstrate, keeping her other hand tucked under the table. "You can see the whole city from up there. All the lights. It was beautiful. Sooo romantic." Tori snuggled into my arm.

"That sounds really nice. Sal, how come you've never taken me there?" my mom asked.

My dad rolled his eyes, and I had to bite back my laughter.

"Wait! There's more," Tori gushed. "After dinner, he got down on one knee in front of everyone in the restaurant and proposed. We're engaged!" She held her left hand up, so everyone could see her ring.

My chest tightened at the word "engaged". It was so much more than that.

Elena and my mom stood up and ran around the table to hug us. "Oh, that's wonderful!" my mom exclaimed.

"I can't wait to start planning the wedding!" Elena added.

Everyone started talking at once. Mike and my dad shook my hand and then hugged Tori, giving her kisses. Rachel and Jim offered their congratulations, my brother slapping me on the back.

"That's so romantic. I wish Jim had done something like that." Rachel sighed.

Jim threw his arms out, looking offended. "What? I was romantic."

Rachel scowled at him. "Scaring me half to death while I was in the shower, shoving a ring in my face, and causing me to get shampoo in my eyes was NOT romantic."

"You were naked. It was totally romantic," Jim insisted.

Now, my mom was scowling too. I think he had just painted a picture she didn't want to see.

Rachel shook her head. "Your idea of romantic and mine are very different. It's a good thing you're cute." She reached over and pinched his cheek.

"Whatever! We're getting married. That's all that matters." Jim leaned his elbows on the table and focused on Tori like he had a big secret. "Did he make the face?"

I reached over the table and knocked him in the head. "Fuck off!"

"Language, Christopher!" my mom scolded.

Jim started laughing. "Well, did he?"

Tori folded her hands on the table. "He did." I let out a sigh of aggravation. Why did everyone always have to focus on my face and why did Tori have to tell everyone about it. "But," she continued, "I don't know what you're laughing at, because the face you make when you talk about Rachel is ten times worse."

Now everyone was laughing and confirming what Tori said was true. I stood from the table and pointed at him, "Hah! I'm not the only one."

Jim waved me off. "You guys don't know what you're talking about. There's no way I make that face!"

Rachel giggled. "It's true, Jim. That ridiculously goofy face you make is how I knew you were 'the one'," she air quoted.

Jim shook his head. "You guys all suck."

"Doesn't feel so good to be on receiving end, does it?"

"Oh, who cares?" my mom asked. "That look is how I knew both of my boys were in love. Chris has been doing it forever."

I groaned. "Are we gonna talk about my face or do you want to hear about our trip?"

My dad spoke up. "You guys didn't get married by some Elvis impersonator, did you?" He was teasing, but there was a hint of seriousness in his question. I couldn't help but glare at him.

Tori put her hand on my leg, and I grabbed ahold of it. "Elvis? Really? Is that even a real question?" Her denial wasn't a lie. But we both knew his question wasn't really about Elvis. "Anyway," Tori continued, "I played slots for the first time. And guess what?" She effectively moved the conversation away from us getting married.

"What?" Mike answered.

"I won five thousand dollars!" Tori stood up and did a little dance shaking her ass and snapping her fingers.

"You did?" Elena exclaimed.

I pulled on Tori, so she fell into my lap. "She sure did. Turns out, my girl's lucky. She was just about to give up when the machine started dinging and the light on top started flashing. It was pretty darn cool." I gave Tor a quick kiss.

"What are you going to do with the money?" my mom asked.

I looked at Tori and smiled. "We're saving it for our wedding." Tori nodded in agreement.

"Now that sounds sensible," my dad approved, pointing his beer bottle our way. "When will the wedding be?"

Tori shrugged her shoulders. "We're thinking next June after we graduate."

My mom clapped her hands. "I'm so excited. Both my boys are going to be married. Rachel and Jim in August and Tori and Chris next June. There's so much to do!"

Elena piped in, "We should start looking at places right away before everything gets booked. Do you know where you want to get married?"

Tori looked at me. We had discussed this but hadn't made a firm decision. "I want us to get married by Lake St. Clair. I was thinking the

Grosse Pointe War Memorial on the terrace. But we're open to suggestions."

Mike cringed. "That's kind of expensive, isn't it?"

I saw Tori's shoulders sag. "Probably, but we're only doing this once and we've waited a long time." I saw the disappointment on her face. "If it's too expensive, we'll find something else."

Tori never asked for much. If this is what she really wanted, then I wanted her to have it. I pulled her in close. "You'll have it. I'll find a way to make it work."

She kissed me on the cheek. "Thank you."

After dinner, Jim and I headed over to the bonfire pit and started getting it ready while the girls helped with dinner clean-up. I sat down on the bricks surrounding the pit and took a sip of my beer. All I could think about was the huge secret Tori and I were keeping, and then I wondered if I cheated her out of the wedding of her dreams. The War Memorial was fucking expensive. I knew that without even looking it up. I needed to get a job when we got back to school. I didn't know how I was going to do it but damn it… Tori was going to get the wedding she wanted.

Jim placed a couple of logs in the pit and then sat down next to me. "Congratulations, little bro. I wondered when you were going to pop the question."

"Yeah, well, we've known forever we were getting married. I just made it official." I shrugged.

"Sounds like you did it up right. I'm surprised you didn't just get married while you were there. I mean, it's Vegas," he said nonchalantly.

I lifted my bottle to my lips and glared at him. He stared back at me, analyzing my reaction. We sat like that a while and then his eyes got really big. "You fuckin did, didn't you? You two are married, aren't you?"

I looked toward the house and then back at him. "Keep your voice down for fuck's sake," I whispered.

"When?" he asked, clearly in shock.

"Friday night. It was perfect." I knew I wasn't supposed to be telling anyone, but telling my brother was a relief. "You can't tell anyone."

"No one knows?" I shook my head. "You know Dad's going to flip the fuck out when he finds out?"

"Which is exactly why he's not going to find out. We'll get married next June, and no one will be the wiser."

"You mean you'll get married again. You know Mom would be ecstatic, right? I mean, she'd be hurt that you guys did it without her, but she wouldn't be mad that you're married. She's loved Tori from day one. She'd be thrilled."

"I know. If it wasn't for Dad, we would have been married a while ago. There has never been a question about what we wanted. Between Dad and Mike, they basically forced us to elope."

Jim slung his arm over my shoulder. "I know. I felt like shit at Thanksgiving when everything got so heated. You two deserve this. I'm happy for you."

"Really? You're not going to tell, are you?" I asked. I was second guessing my decision to let him in on the secret.

"Hell no! Did I tell them about the hotel rooms? Did I tell them I caught Tori giving you a blow job in the family room? Did I tell them about the drugs?"

"No. You've been a cool brother," I answered honestly.

He wrapped his arm around my neck, pulling me toward him, and ran his knuckles over my head. "You're cool, too." He released me from his grasp. "I can't believe my baby brother is married."

"It's pretty surreal. It's all I've ever wanted, and now she's my wife."

"How are you going to keep it a secret?" Jim asked, knocking back his beer.

"The same way we've kept everything we've been through a secret. We're masters at this," I said casually. It sounded so easy. I knew this was different though, because it was the one secret I didn't want to keep, but knew we needed to.

"What do you mean 'everything you've been through'?" Jim eyed me suspiciously. "What are you not telling me?"

Fuck! I had just made a huge mistake. I'd said too much. "Nothing," I tried to brush it off.

"It's not nothing. I can tell by the look on your face," Jim prodded.

I dropped my head and shook it. "Tori would kill me if I told you."

"I'm not going to tell anyone. And I won't tell Tori I know. What happened?"

I looked up at the house to make sure no one was coming. "You have to promise to not tell anyone." Jim nodded his head in agreement. "Remember at Thanksgiving when we both got so upset about you and Rachel getting married?"

"How could I forget? I felt like shit."

"It wasn't just about you getting married." I paused because once this came out of my mouth, I couldn't take it back. I looked to Jim, and I already felt guilty because I felt like I was betraying my wife. I swallowed down the lump in my throat. "Tori was pregnant."

"Shit!"

"We lost the baby." My eyes started to water, and I wiped at them. I hadn't really thought about it much since it had happened. I couldn't because it still killed me to think about it.

"I'm so sorry." Jim draped his arm over my shoulder. "Nobody knows?"

"Nobody. We dealt with it on our own. We knew we weren't ready, but we were happy. We were going to tell everyone at Christmas."

"Fuck, bro. That's some heavy stuff. How did Tori deal with it?"

"We were both devastated, but Tori buries that shit deep. She doesn't talk about it. She thinks that if she doesn't acknowledge it, then it didn't happen. But it did. I just hope we get another chance."

"You will," Jim assured me.

"With Tori's condition, we might not." The thought was depressing. As much as it killed me, I wouldn't trade Tori for anything. She never hid this fact from me, and I accepted it. But just because I accepted it, didn't mean I liked it. It bothered me more than I ever let Tori know. She would mistake it for regret, and I would never regret being with her.

"I don't believe that. You two will have kids. You'll have another chance."

"I hope you're right."

Tori and I stayed at my parents' house late into the evening. We all sat around the bonfire bullshitting. Tori told everyone about our great weekend, and we even showed off our tattoos. Around ten, fireworks exploded into the sky all around us. Tori sat on my lap and cuddled into my chest. "I'm so happy," she whispered in my ear. "This is our first Fourth of July as husband and wife."

I kissed the side of her head. "The first of many."

194

After our parents called it a night, Jim, Rachel, Tori, and I sat by the fire drinking and laughing. It was kind of nice that my brother had finally settled down. Tori and Rachel shared ideas about weddings. Jim smirked at me, keeping my secret, and never letting on that he knew.

We finally made it back to Tori's around one in the morning. We quietly tiptoed up to her room and crawled into bed. "I wanna make love to you," I told her.

"Please," she whispered.

And I did. I made love to my wife.

Chapter 22
Tori

I could hear my phone buzzing on the nightstand, but I didn't have the energy to answer it. It was persistent though and I couldn't ignore it. I looked at the screen and the time on my clock. It was after three in the morning. We'd only been asleep a couple of hours. "Kyla, why in the hell are calling me in the middle of the night?" I waited for her to answer, but it was silent. "Kyla?"

Chris stirred next to me. "What the hell is going on? Why is she calling you?" I shushed him with my hand, and he rolled over.

Maybe she butt dialed me. "Kyla?"

Finally, she answered, "Something's happened, Tori. Something bad. Can you come over?"

She didn't sound like herself and now I was worried. "Kyla, what's going on? Are you okay?" Chris sat up and rubbed his eyes, looking at me with questions I couldn't answer.

Her answer came out clipped. "Please, just hurry." Then the line went dead.

I jumped out of bed and threw on the shorts I wore last night. "Get up!" I shouted at Chris. "We need to go!"

"What's going on?" He asked as he threw on some clothes.

"I don't know, but she needs me. Now! She wouldn't call if it wasn't important!" I was yelling, and I didn't even realize it.

We quickly got dressed and rushed out of my bedroom. My mom's door clicked open, and Mike stood there looking disheveled. "What's going on? Where are you going?"

"We're going to Kyla's. Something is wrong. I'll let you know," I answered.

"What?" he asked, sounding irritated.

"I don't know," I said impatiently. "We gotta go!"

Chris grabbed his keys off the dresser and met me in the hall. I ran out to his truck, and we headed over to Kyla's.

"What the hell could be so important?" Chris questioned.

"I don't know," I answered. "But she didn't sound like herself. Something is definitely wrong," I answered anxiously. "Can you drive faster?"

We pulled up a few minutes later and two cop cars were in Kyla's driveway. "What the fuck?" Chris exclaimed.

I barely waited for Chris to park, and I rushed out of the car and up to the house. I pushed open the door. "Kyla, why is there a police car…" I froze when I saw the cops and Kyla sitting on the couch.

She looked at me with vacant eyes. "They're gone."

What the hell was she talking about? I kneeled in front of her. "Who's gone, sweetie?"

Kyla refused to look at me. "My parents. They were killed by a drunk driver."

"Oh, my god!" I hugged her tightly, but she just sat there. Her arms were limp at her sides. She was void of emotion.

"Jesus Christ!" Chris hissed out.

Kyla stared at me with vacant eyes. "What am I going to do? I'm all alone."

I grabbed her by the shoulders. "Kyla, you're not alone. We're your family. We're going to help you." I looked at Chris and then back at Kyla. I could only think of one thing to help her, but it was a long shot. "Do you want us to call Tyler?"

Kyla freaked out at the idea. "No! This isn't his problem. I'm not his problem anymore."

It killed me that she thought she was alone in this. I thought for sure Tyler would be what she needed, but maybe I was wrong. I hugged her again. "Okay, sweetie."

The cops took Chris in the other room, while I stayed with Kyla. I couldn't believe this was happening. I waited for Kyla to show some emotion, but it never came. If I was in shock, I couldn't imagine what was going through her head. "What do you want me to do?" I asked her.

She shook her head. "I don't know. Just be here. Don't leave me, okay?"

I crushed her against me. "I'm not leaving you. I'm staying right here."

Chris came back from the kitchen and motioned to me. I released Kyla and made my way over to him. He swallowed down the lump in his throat. "She has to go identify the bodies."

"Are you fucking kidding me?" I asked incredulously.

Chris shook his head. "I wish I was. They said we can go first thing in the morning."

"I can't leave her," I said. "I have to stay here with her. You can go home if you want…"

"Are you kidding me right now? I'm not leaving. Want me to call Mike?"

I nodded. "Please. This is going to kill my parents. Kyla is like their daughter."

"I know. Should I call Tyler too?"

I thought about it. He needed to know. They might not be together, but this was extenuating circumstances. "Yes, but let's wait until we know more. I don't know what to do. What if he blows her off? She's tried to talk to him, and he just ignores her. I don't want him to come here and make things worse."

"I agree. Let's help her first. We're her family. She's already been through enough."

The cops left, and I sat with Kyla. I didn't really know what to say to her, but she went right into take-control mode. I got a pad of paper like she asked, and we started making a list of everything that needed to be done. She never shed a tear, and that worried me. She was in shock, but her reaction was not what I expected.

At about six in the morning, Kyla went to take a shower. She acted like this was all normal. It was the furthest thing from normal. I sat down at the kitchen table with Chris. "I'm worried about her," I admitted. "She hasn't cried one tear yet."

"I know. It's kind of weirding me out," Chris said. "I can't believe this fucking happened. I thought she was starting to pull it together and now this. What do we do?"

"The only thing we can. Be here for her," I answered. Tears filled my eyes. "I can't believe they're gone. Do you know how much time I've spent here? They were like my second parents." I cried for the first time since walking in the door.

Chris wrapped his arms around me. "I know, baby. Get it all out because Kyla's going to need us to be strong for her."

I wiped at my eyes. "I know." I took a deep breath. "What time do we need to go to the morgue?"

Chris looked at the clock on the microwave. "They open at eight."

I nodded. "I think we should get it over with." I looked at the ring on my finger and removed it. I stared at it and thought about the current situation. "We can't tell her we're married. I can't even tell her we're engaged right now. How can I tell her how happy we are when this just happened?"

Chris took a deep breath. "It sucks, but you're probably right. We'll tell her in a few weeks."

That wasn't what he wanted, but Chris was the best. I moved over to him and sat on his lap. "Thank you for being so understanding."

"You know I care about her too, right? She's your best friend, but she's my friend too. And I could just strangle Ty right now. He should be here for her. He's probably not even home. He's probably out fucking some chick while she's going through hell," Chris said with disgust.

"I know. But he's got his life and she has hers. We can't hold this against him." I couldn't believe I was actually defending the guy. "All I know is that I don't want him here if he's not one hundred percent invested. It would just crush her more."

"Do you think he'll show up for the funeral?" Chris asked.

"I don't know, but it would be shitty if he didn't. I hope she doesn't see it as a sign of them getting back together. She doesn't need false hope." As much as I loved them together, I was still pissed about how he left her at the hospital. He didn't need to come here and fuck her up worse.

Kyla came down the stairs, dressed for the day. Her hair and makeup were done. She didn't look like someone whose whole world had just come crashing down. "What time do we have to go?" she asked.

"We've still got an hour," Chris said. "Do you want to lie down? We'll wake you up."

"I can't sleep," Kyla said. "Thank you for being here. I don't know what I'd do without you two."

"We love you, baby girl. We're not going anywhere," Chris assured her.

Kyla came over and gave Chris a huge hug. "You don't even know what that means to me." Then she looked at me. "Do you think it's too early to call my grandparents?"

I put my hand on her shoulder. "Let's go do this awful thing first. We'll have time when we get home. I'll help you make all the phone calls."

Kyla straightened her shoulders. "You're right. Where's my list of things to do? I'll work on something else."

I couldn't stop her. Kyla was like a tornado, and she still hadn't cried a single tear. I was waiting for the breakdown that I was sure was coming.

Chris and I went to the morgue with Kyla. We stood with her as she stared at her dead parents laid out like they were sleeping. Thankfully, they looked peaceful. I choked back by own tears. Chris held me as I held Kyla. She simply responded, "That's them." No emotion. No tears. No anything. She was scaring the shit out of me.

We went back to Kyla's, and I helped her make all her phone calls and arrangements with the funeral home and church. I sent Chris home to get some rest. I knew he was calling Tyler too and I wondered how that phone call would go. I didn't have the heart to tell Kyla that Chris was calling Tyler. Honestly, I thought he needed to be here, but I wasn't sure what was going to happen. He had the power to help Kyla or totally destroy her. Right now, I wasn't sure which way that was going to go.

The day of the funeral arrived, and I still hadn't seen Tyler. I looked at Chris. "What the hell is wrong with him? Doesn't he understand how important this is?"

Chris rubbed my arms up and down. "I don't know. Maybe he's afraid of getting attached again. He's worked hard to get over her."

"What? Fucking a million other chicks? That's working hard?" I asked sarcastically. "Sounds like torture."

"Tor." Chris looked at me with hardness. "It's not for us to judge. We don't know everything."

"We know enough," I huffed.

I calmed myself down and took my place next to Kyla in the church. I held her hand and waited for her to crack, but it never came. Kyla got up to read the speech she wrote. I watched as her demeanor changed, and she focused on the back of the church. She abandoned her speech and spoke from the heart. I looked to the back of the church and saw Tyler standing there. At least he had the decency to show.

At the gravesite, Tyler stood in the back. Kyla knew he was there, but barely acknowledged him. She placed two red roses on her parents' caskets and kissed them goodbye. After the service, I looked at Kyla. "You don't have to talk to him," I assured her.

"Yes, I do. I need this to be over. I need to set myself free." She walked toward Tyler and spoke to him briefly. Then she walked away.

She had come so far, and I was proud of her.

The day after the funeral, I went to Kyla's to check on her. I let myself in and heard screaming coming from upstairs. I ran up the stairs and into her parents' room. I dodged a shoe that went flying across the room. Kyla sat in the middle of a pile of clothes, screaming and crying. I knew it was only a matter of time until she finally broke. I wrapped my arms around her and rocked her gently. I ran my hands through her hair and soothed her. "I knew this was coming," I said softly.

Kyla cried in my arms. "Everyone keeps leaving me. Tyler, my baby, my parents...why does everyone keep leaving me?"

"I don't know, sweetie. Come on, let's get you out of here." I pulled Kyla to her feet.

She looked around at the mess she had made. "I need to clean this up." Kyla started frantically picking up the clothes from the floor.

I took the clothes from her hand and dropped them back to the floor. "Not today, you don't." I led her from the room and shut the door behind us. That was a job for another day.

"What are you doing here, anyway?" Kyla sniffed as she wiped the tears from her face.

"I came to check on you. It was only a matter of time before you finally broke down." I was relieved to find her in such a state of distress. The front she had been trying to put up wasn't healthy. She needed to let the grief in. Feel it. She had lost so much in the last six months.

I took Kyla down the stairs and to the couch. She sat down and picked up a picture off the coffee table of her and Tyler from prom. "We look so young in this picture. What happened to us?" She asked, without expecting her to answer. She put the picture down and pushed it to the side. "I guess it doesn't really matter."

Kyla laid down on the couch and put her head in my lap. "This is gonna suck, isn't it?"

I played with the ends of her hair. "Yeah. It is. But you'll get through it, just like everything else."

"I'm tired of getting through it. I don't know how much more I can take."

I looked down at her. "How have you been sleeping?"

"Sleep? What's that?" she joked.

I nodded my head at her. "That's what I thought. Where are your pills?"

"They're in my bedroom. On the nightstand," she answered.

I slipped out from under her and walked up the stairs. I found the pills and got her a glass of water. "You need to get some sleep. Take this. Hopefully, you'll sleep through to the morning."

Kyla took the Xanax and grabbed a blanket from the back of the couch. "I love you, girlfriend. See you tomorrow?"

I tucked her in tightly. "Love you, too. I'll come by tomorrow night."

My heart broke for her. How much could one person be expected to take? Life was so fucking unfair. I felt so guilty that I was upset with her during her pregnancy. I would never have wished this upon her. Any of it.

I wished I could have consoled her more about losing her baby. But every time I thought about it, my own sadness surfaced. I needed to do better. I needed to be there for her. Even if it twisted my own heart.

I felt awful for Chris, but my life revolved around Kyla right now. She needed me. Plain and simple. I wouldn't abandon her. Chris went back to work, and I went back to Mike's shop yesterday. I talked to Kyla, but she wanted alone time. I had to respect that. But after the breakdown I witnessed, I couldn't not check on her.

I pulled up to Kyla's house and I swore when I saw Tyler's car in the driveway. It was only eight in the morning. What the hell was going on? I barged into her house to find them kissing on the bottom of the steps. I wasn't sure if this was a good thing or not? I was speechless as Tyler left, giving me a little wave over his shoulder. "Hi Tori. Bye Tori."

"What the hell was that? Are you two back together?" I asked.

Kyla smirked at me and proceeded to tell me about the great night of sex they shared. How they had spent the whole night talking and cleared the air between them. They weren't back together, but damn... she was happy. I was sure Kyla was setting herself up for disappointment, but she was smiling and that was all that mattered for now.

Kyla was like a machine. Every moment she wasn't at work, she was cleaning out the house and getting it ready for renters. After a few weeks, it was almost ready. The work kept her mind busy and off Tyler. For that I was thankful.

It was the first week of August and we only had a month left before returning to school. Chris had found us a great apartment off campus. There was no way we were living in the dorms now that we were married. We were lying in bed and my guilt over the time I'd been spending with Kyla, was eating at me. I had to find a balance. "Chris?"

"Yeah, baby?" he answered sleepily.

"I'm sorry."

Chris rolled over and kissed me gently on the lips, "Why? What'd you do?"

I let out a deep sigh. "This is not the way our marriage should have begun. I've spent so much time helping Kyla, and I feel like I've been ignoring you. I'm sorry it's been this way. I just can't abandon her right now. I hope you understand. I don't want you to think you come second, because you're the most important person in my life. I hope you know how much I love you."

Chris's arm snaked around my stomach. "Honey, I know this is not what we planned, but life had other ideas. I know you didn't plan on Kyla's parents dying three days after we got married. You need to be there for her. I understand."

"Are you sure? I love you so much it hurts. I don't want you to ever doubt that."

"I don't," he assured me. "As a matter of fact, I was thinking... she should move in with us."

"Are you serious?" I asked. That would be awesome, but I certainly didn't want to throw it out there. I felt a certain amount of responsibility towards my best friend, but I couldn't let it interfere with my marriage.

"She needs us," Chris answered. "And our apartment is a two bedroom."

"Do you think that's a good idea? I don't want you to feel like there are three of us in this marriage?"

"Tor, I'm not suggesting she sleep with us. Although a threesome… not with her… could be kinda hot." He smirked at me.

I swatted his chest. "Dream on, big boy. I'm never sharing you."

Chris pulled back, holding his hands up in surrender. "Just sayin'. It could be super hot."

I tapped my chin as if in contemplation. "You know you might have something there. Having two guys at the same time would be kinda hot."

His face changed immediately. "You just killed my boner. That's never happening."

"Not so funny when the tables are turned, is it?" I asked.

"Let's never, and I mean never, talk about that again. And no, I'm not worried about Kyla living with us."

I crawled over the top of him. "You have no idea how happy you've just made me." I rubbed myself along all his hardness that was still there despite my comment.

"Your happiness is my only concern," he assured me. He ran his hands up my sides.

"Let's see if *I* can make *you* happy," I said softly. I pulled my tank slowly over my head and Chris let out a low groan. "I want to make love to my husband."

"I want my wife to ride me." He wrapped his hands in my hair and pulled my lips to his. I opened my mouth to him, and our tongues twisted in a slow dance. I loved the wild, hard sex with Chris, but I also loved the slow, sensual sex too. When we were like this, my heart nearly exploded from the love I felt for him.

Chris slid his fingers in the waist of my panties and slipped them down my hips. I moved them the rest of the way off, as he removed his shorts. I crawled back on top of him and slipped him inside me. I slid down and moaned. "You feel so good, baby." I made slow, sweet love to him, as I rode him up and down.

Chris rubbed my breasts and rolled my nipples. I leaned forward to muffle my sounds into his sculpted chest. The angle allowed me to rub my clit along him and soon I felt my orgasm building.

"You're so close, aren't you?" he asked. I barely nodded my head and Chris pushed his hips up into me. That was all it took for me to fall over the edge. As the waves of pleasure consumed me, Chris continued to thrust up into me. I felt him shudder beneath me as he came. He kissed my lips gently. "I love you, Tor."

"I love you too. Think we could just sleep like this?" I asked as I rested my head on his chest.

Chris ran his hands through my hair. "What if we got stuck together?"

"I could think of worse things." I closed my eyes in pure contentment.

Chris continued to rub his hand through my hair and down my back. "Tor? I have to tell you something and since you're so blissed out right now, it might be the perfect time."

That pulled me out of my comatose state. I lifted my chin and set it on his chest. "I don't like the sound of this. What is it?"

Chris ran his finger down the side of my face. "I've been keeping a secret from you."

My wheels were spinning now. What had he been keeping from me? I couldn't form the words to ask the question, so instead I said, "We promised no more secrets."

His fingers smoothed out the lines on my forehead. "It's not a bad thing," he assured me. "My brother knows."

Knows what? That we almost had an orgy at a frat house? That I got pregnant? That we lost the baby? That we were married? We had so many secrets between us. So many that had the potential to hurt us. "Knows what?" I asked tentatively.

"That we're married," he admitted. "I didn't tell him. He said he was surprised we didn't just get married in Vegas."

"Chris…" I huffed out a breath. Why? Why couldn't he deny it?

As if he could read my mind, he answered, "I couldn't lie to him. Hell, I didn't want to. I couldn't deny how much I was in love with you."

"He's going to tell. He won't be able to keep the secret. What if it slips out?" I asked. My mind flooded with repercussions of this secret leaking to our parents.

"He won't tell. I promise you." Chris pushed my hair out of my face. "And you know what? He was happy for us."

"Really? He wasn't pissed that we eloped?"

"Nope. He loves you like a sister. And he'd never tell, because he knows it's important to us that he keep the secret," he assured me.

Even though I knew Jim wouldn't betray us on purpose, it still bothered me. We were playing with fire, and it was only a matter of time before we got burned. "Chris, this is so much harder than I ever imagined. We're lying to everyone we love. We should have just waited. We shouldn't have gotten married."

Chapter 23
Chris

"I'm sorry. What?" I was sure I didn't hear her correctly.

"We should have waited until June, like we planned. Then we wouldn't have to lie to everyone," she answered.

"So, you regret marrying me?" I couldn't keep the fury out of my voice as I pushed her off me. I wasn't worried about waking Mike and Elena. They had gone to the Lake House earlier in the week.

Tori scooted back on the bed. "That's not what I meant, and you know it."

"Do I? Because you just admitted that you wish we weren't married," I yelled. I grabbed my boxer briefs from the floor and pulled them on.

"That's not what I said. You're putting words in my mouth," Tori defended.

I pulled on my jeans and grabbed my shirt off the chair. "Maybe we shouldn't keep it a secret. Maybe we should just tell everyone. Let the cards fall where they may. Or are you embarrassed to be married to me? Am I your dirty little secret?"

"Are you even listening to yourself?" she questioned. "You're being ridiculous!"

"Am I? Fuck! You didn't even want our baby when you got pregnant. If I hadn't known, you probably would have aborted it without even telling me!" I'd gone too far. I knew it as soon as the words left my mouth. It was one thing to think something. It was something else to voice it out loud.

She scrambled off the bed. Tears poured down her cheeks. "Get the fuck out! Now!"

"Tor." I stepped toward her, and she took a step back. I'd officially moved into asshole territory. "I'm sorry."

"Get. Out. Now! Fucking leave! You make me sick!"

Fuck it! I was out of there.

207

Read the conclusion of Chris and Tori's story in
Eternal Hearts.

Song List on Spotify

Sorry~ Buckcherry
Tangled Up In You~ Staind
Closer~ Nine Inch Nails
Addicted~ Saving Able
My Heart Will Go On~ Celine Dion

Listen and Enjoy!

Acknowledgments

Being a full-time educator, leaves me little time to write during the school year. However, I look forward to coming home every day and writing about true love. I thought this summer I would quickly finish *Secrets of the Heart;* however, it took much longer to tell Chris and Tori's story than I thought. This book took on a life of its own. And to think my original plan was to create one book for Chris and Tori, and now it's three books.

My husband and I joke that right now, I'm making less than ten cents an hour writing. The funny thing is, I couldn't be happier. I enjoy what I'm doing and the creative outlet it provides me. Writing romance novels has been one of the most fulfilling experiences of my life. My dream is to walk into a bookstore and actually see one of my novels on the shelf. One day…

To my husband~ I could have never done this without your love and support. Thank you for putting up with my endless hours of writing, all the take-out dinners, and my hounding of you to read and offer input. I know I've made you crazy, but you were a trooper through it all! Thank you for believing in me!

To Denise, Kristy, and Amy~ You girls are the best beta readers anyone could ask for! You supported my journey and spent endless hours reading and rereading. Your suggestions, critiques, and encouragement helped me in ways you'll never understand. Thank you for listening to my obsession day after day!

To Linda~ Thank you for the endless hours you spent proofreading. After reading the book several times myself, I still missed errors. Your expertise and constructive criticism helped me to make this book so much better. I could never thank you enough for all your help!

To Jill~ You've been a great friend! I was very specific about what I wanted for this cover. I know it was somewhat challenging, yet you came up with something amazing. Thank you for the beautiful cover of *Secrets of the Heart…* I absolutely love it!

To my readers~ Thank you for supporting me in this journey. Please spread the word and leave a quick review on Amazon, if you have enjoyed this book. Without you, writing would still be a dream.

About the Author

Sabrina Wagner lives in Sterling Heights, Michigan. She writes sweet, sassy, sexy romance novels featuring alpha males and the strong women who challenge them.

Sabrina believes that true friends should be treasured, a woman's strength is forged by the fire of affliction, and everyone deserves a happy ending. She enjoys spending time with her family, walking on the beach, cuddling her kittens, and reading great books. Sabrina is a hopeless romantic and knows all too well that life is full of twists and turns, but the bumpy road is what leads to our true destination.

Want to be the first to learn book news, updates and more?
Sign up for my Newsletter.

https://www.subscribepage.com/sabrinawagnernewsletter

Want to know about my new releases and upcoming sales?
Stay connected on:

Facebook~Instagram~Twitter~TikTok
Goodreads~BookBub~Amazon

I'd love to hear from you.
Visit my website to connect with me.

www.sabrinawagnerauthor.com